Deadman's Bust

CORY MARCHESE

ESCARGOT BOOKS ONLINE LTD

Published by

Escargot Books Online Limited
North Yorkshire, England LS21 2JJ Copyright © 2012
Cory Marchese. All rights reserved.

Cory Marchese asserts his moral right to be
identified as the author of this book.

ISBN 978-1-908191-33-5 (Trade Paperback)

Cover photo © Jim Martin 2012

Deadman's Bust

Chapter 1

Humboldt County, California, 1992

I was always told it would start like any other day. Breakfast and coffee. Wash the dishes. Maybe roll a joint. And just as you're lighting that sweet baby up, ten heavily armed cops come charging into every Goddamn opening they can fit their fat asses through. That's how it happens. Other than the usual mind mauling paranoia that pot growers interminably experience, *nobody* ever feels any different the morning they are busted.

I woke with a stuffy nose on the couch in the living room of the old ranch house, which rested unnaturally on the property my older brother, John, and I had bought eight months earlier. In the proper suburban setting, it may have been just fine, but surrounded by the wild hills of Humboldt County, it looked like a misplaced movie set. If you happened upon it on a hike, you might think you were hallucinating. The old couple who'd built it as a place to retire and live out their days, died within six months of each other, leaving the property to their junkie son. We bought it ten years later, when it had become nothing more than a giant rundown shack. For us, it was perfect. We wanted it to look abandoned.

John was cutting fat slices of the beer bread he'd baked the day before, laying them out on a baking pan. He looked up as I walked into the kitchen.

"Morning, Stinky. Seriously, Mike, will you take a shower today?" he implored. We had no hot water. Which basically meant showering was nothing short of barbarism.

"Shut up, man. I will, I will," I said while smelling my armpit, trying to remember how many days it had been.

"Good. I'm gonna jump in the shower as soon as I put these in the oven, so do your deeds if you needs," he smiled. John had a full-face smile that made him look like a gentle old man. Everything squished up from his mouth, his kind eyes appearing to close and his nose stretching out, so that his entire face crinkled. Other than our curly blond hair, he and I didn't look too much alike. He got Dad's face and I got Mom's. At twenty-five years old—four years older than me—he had an air about him that made him seem much older than he was. He looked young enough. Like me (I must admit) he was handsome (thank you); but it became quickly obvious to people that John had lived a lot of life. He had. Fifteen years ago, our Dad was sentenced to fifty years in a Thai prison for conspiring to smuggle a boatload of heroin to Australia. Nine years after that, in 1986, our mom died of breast cancer. John stepped up. Among other things, he took good care of me. So yeah, he had.

"Nah. I'm cool. How's the coffee?"

"Ready to plunge," he practically sang. We were a week or so from harvesting, and because of that, except for the nasty colds we were both dealing with, we were in better than usual spirits. We'd been growing and saving for a long time and this was to be our first big payoff. Yes, we were happy. But we were saving money to bribe Dad out of prison, and we were still far from our goal. Bribing Thai officials took a lot of cash. A fucking dirty filthy shit lot of cash.

We'd certainly created a moneymaker. The old couple had built a three-car garage about fifty yards from the house. That was where we had set up a 60-kilowatt generator, thirty 1,000-watt halide grow lights, a series of intake and exhaust fans, a CO_2 burner, a boom box looping Enya or Mozart, and every other high-tech growing device on the market in 1992. That was also where the feds would find enough plants to get John and me a mandatory minimum sentence of ten years in prison.

I poured two cups of coffee and began digging into a bag of weed, looking for a fine bud to start the day with. As I concentrated,

I asked John if we could at least visit Dad once we'd sold the weed.

"Mike, you know he doesn't want us to do that. He has his reasons. You know. You remember how that affected him, bro. We're going to get him out. We're doing it, Mike." He released his smile, "We're doing it!"

I held up a purplish bud, "I'm going to name this bud Sheri."

He laughed. John was always quick to laugh. I remember almost puking when he had a three-inch fin gash opened up on the top of his head, while he laughed all the way to the hospital.

As I broke up the bud, I continued, "Oh Sheri, beautiful Sheri, we thank you for the joy you will bestow upon our day!"

We ate beer bread toast, finished our coffee, and smoked a joint.

All good.

I went to my bedroom to put on some clean clothes. I heard John stomp to the bathroom yelling, "Alarm! Alarm!" He followed up with an alarm sound, something he always did to announce he was about to take a shit. I chuckled as I dug a clean pair of underwear out from my bag of clothes. I heard an engine and looked out the window. That's when I saw them: three or more white pickups and at least one Blazer speeding down the hill, just at the last cutback before the straight shot to the house. Before I had time to absorb the horror of what was coming, I raced to the bathroom door.

I threw open the door and whisper yelled, "Cops are here! We're being busted, John!"

He reached for the toilet paper and told me to run. I froze, and John leaned over and pushed me, "RUN, MIKE!"

Buck fucking naked, I leapt through the screen door and over the deck rail. The edge of the woods was at least thirty yards from the back of the house, too far to run to without being seen, so I turned back and crawled under the house. When I turned to see if John was behind me, I heard men screaming and doors being kicked open. *We got you, fucka*! *We got you, fucka*! I quickly closed the small door and went for the farthest corner from the opening. I knew I was tearing up my bare knees on the gravel but felt nothing. I lay flat and began to listen. I couldn't really make out what was being said but I could hear how they were saying it. I had never heard more f-bombs uttered in such a short period of time. They were obviously from the East Coast. I assumed they were DEA, but they could have easily passed for mobsters. I'd heard that about the DEA.

After about twenty minutes, I heard them come outside and muscle John into one of the pickups.

"Say goodbye, you stupid fucka," I heard one of them say as the door slammed shut. And then somebody at the garage yelled: "How is it?"

"It's still in the fuckin' pots."

I wondered why they cared about that.

"We shoulda known that fucka wasn't being completely straight. Screw it, at least we got the guy, and we can dry this shit in the mission house. It's just a bonus anyway. Let's load it up."

I scrambled to a vent to try and see something. If these guys weren't true DEA, they sure as hell had a sophisticated operation. The pickups had decals and sirens. They all had the cop thing going—black shirts, guns, jeans, black boots—but I couldn't see any faces. I watched as they loaded all of our plants into the truck beds and covered them with tarps. They did very little speaking while this went on. As they were getting into the cars, I heard one guy ask a third man who, up until then, hadn't said a word, "What do you think?"

I wasn't sure, but I thought I heard him say, "That's definitely him."

Car doors slammed, engines started, and they drove away. I was physically ill at that point. I can't imagine how I would have felt had I known what was really happening.

Chapter 2

I'm not sure how long I stayed under the house that morning. The experience had so blasted my psyche that an entire day could have passed and I wouldn't have known. I had spent years visualizing what being busted would be like, my subconscious endlessly under attack, and suddenly there it was. The nightmare made real.

Above me, a large spider did a little web dance, the kind that periodically turns into a full-on "get the fuck away from my web" freak out. I remained utterly still despite its relatively close proximity and my raging arachnophobia. I felt as if I'd just undergone a cycle of shock therapy and my fear had been instantly erased. A little perspective shoved down my throat and WHAMO ... spiders weren't really that scary anymore. In fact, I felt a strange affinity towards the little monster.

Eventually, I calmed down enough to begin questioning what I'd heard and seen. If those guys were DEA, why were they so annoyed that the weed was not yet cured? Who wasn't being straight with them? Just how much trouble was John in at this point? With that, I realized it was time to get out from under the house and figure out what I needed to do for him. Crawling towards the access door, pain exploded from my skinned knees. I could have crawled over razors earlier and not known it. I reached for my dick and balls and realized they were completely numb. Adrenaline. Crazy shit.

I was greeted by an overcast, rainy afternoon when I emerged. The perfect setting for this sad turn of events, I thought. I tiptoed to the stairs of the deck, looking around cautiously as if someone had stayed behind, and climbed slowly, like a frightened child.

5

In the distance, I noticed the door to the garage had been left open, the faint sound of Enya still playing. *Far and away! Far and away! Far and away!*

"Fuckin A, Enya ... that's where I'm going," I whispered.

I was surprised the cops didn't gleefully blow the radio away. Or at least turn it off. Maybe they liked Enya. I thought about how weird that would be. I made my way along the grey splintering deck boards to the sliding glass door (also left open) and stepped inside. It struck me that the place now seemed like a crime scene, which it never had before. Our beautiful grow scene, rendered a condemned ruin. The few personal items John and I kept in the house were scattered all over the dirt-stained carpet. Goddamn dirty DEA boots. I noticed most of the footprints were of the cowboy boot kind.

"Oh, you gotta be kidding," I whispered to myself. "Fucking cowboy boots ... really?"

They were clearly looking for something. Probably money. Or pot. Again, it struck me that it seemed much more like a robbery than a bust. The chili that John had set out to thaw was splattered across the linoleum. In the dim grey light, it looked like the gory remains of a gunshot victim. I began wiping it up, quickly stopped, and walked down the hall to the bedrooms.

John's room had no door. As I passed by, I could see his sleeping bag, a pile of clothes, and a few copies of *Surfer* magazine. John would've done very well in ancient Sparta. In contrast, my room had an adolescent quality, with a small grade-school desk, a dresser and a mattress with a few posters of surfing superstars and bikini girls on the wall. Both rooms were finished with '70s style "Dad's den" brown paneling, and each had a distinctly different booby light fixture, probably a compromise made between the old couple long ago. The men had emptied all my drawers and exposed my lame hand-me-down porn stash with one flip of the mattress; mostly old *Playboy*s, my relatively tame proclivities laid bare. At one point, I had heard them explode into laughter with "oh yeahs" and "woo hoos." Now I knew what that was all about. The nastiest magazine was missing. Fucking perverts.

I grabbed a new pair of underwear (somehow the pair I'd had in my hand earlier had gone missing), a dirty pair of jeans, and a shirt. I put them on while hopping down the hall. Although I knew there were people I needed to talk to and many things that needed to be done, I stopped at John's door, remembering the day we'd first hiked the property. Another relative of the old couple had kicked the junkie son out, taking control of the property in hopes of making a quick sale to settle a debt, and offered us a ridiculously low price. I remembered following John as he pointed out old patches that could be revived, potential water sources, and other spots begging for a bundle of plants. Being the natural, John was always Mom's star apprentice, and I never resented that. Mom grew only enough weed for us to sustain a simple hippy lifestyle and save a little money for college, but, man, she grew killer, killer weed. In fact, folks from Humboldt to Hawaii knew her bud as "Kellykind" (Kelly Costello, that was my mom's name) and it always got top dollar. She once got over five large for a pound, years before people were paying nearly that much.

I eventually found my boots and coat and stepped back out into the rain. Enya was now singing in Gaelic. I started towards the garage. It was a gabled roof, corrugated aluminum structure with faded green paint barely hanging on in a few places. Since a few of the old cars had become fixtures in front of the place, John and I had the brilliant idea of cutting one in half and letting it stick out of the half open garage door to make the place look completely open and abandoned. We built a false wall behind it and painted it black so that you couldn't tell it was fake until you were practically touching it. We thought we were geniuses; and the next day, we invited friends over for beer and shrooms to celebrate our genius with us. We were so damn proud.

It looked like a bomb had gone off in the grow room. Lights were torn from the hangers, pots were overturned, and plant remains were scattered all over the gravel floor. I walked to the tape player and, resisting the urge to kick it into pieces, pressed stop. All of our work had been destroyed. Our operation lay dead and violated and, angry as I was, I felt that I owed it a bit of gentleness. The cops had been thorough. Leaves and stems were strewn all around but not one bud had been missed. They had torn down the white reflective house wrap along the perimeter; what they thought we might have had stashed there, I had no idea. Fucking dipshits. I picked up a leaf. Examining it, I pondered the nature of my relationship with marijuana, a lifetime of history, and how it was about to change. As far back as I could remember I was involved in the work of pot growing, from seed bath to harvest, like a lot of Humboldt kids, right there with my parents. I looked at one of the rectangular light reflector shields and shook my head. Even though we had over a dozen old school lights—the kind with a tinny round shield—we'd decided to buy all new equipment. Shit. I set the leaf on the folding chair where I'd spent countless hours watching and waiting, then turned and walked away.

I jogged up the driveway to my pickup, a mud-covered Toyota 4WD, just about identical to every other grower's in Humboldt at the time. Not surprised to see both of my doors hanging open, the glove box emptied, and all my stuff thrown in the mud. I gathered what I could, including the registration, which John had insisted on putting in his name, even though I was pissed about it at the time. Even when I resisted, John always looked out for me. I started the engine and pulled onto the dirt driveway.

What I'm calling a driveway was actually a half-mile long, one-lane road that cut back and forth down the southwest side of Wilder Ridge. We had two gates installed to make a total of four that had to be opened to get to our place from the main paved road. We shared them with a whacked out Vietnam vet who went by the name of Sophie. He was calm and friendly, but still I never dared ask about his name. I thought about driving down to his place to inform him in good neighborly fashion, but then remembered he was in Costa Rica. After reaching the gate closest to the house, I realized he'd find out soon enough. It looked as if they'd rammed it with their truck to get through. I could've driven over it, but I couldn't bring myself to do it; more gentleness. I jumped into the rain, dragged the rusted steel gate to the edge of the road, and leaned it against a dead madrone tree. The flesh-colored wood almost entirely exposed, it looked as if it could come to life and crush the gate with one angry grip.

I repeated this with the other gates, except for the one off the main public road; it was left intact. They had used a bolt cutter on the lock and wrapped the chain back around it as they left. This was the one door they actually shut on their way out. I guess they didn't want to advertise what had happened here. That seemed logical enough.

I hopped back in and began the hour-long journey to the coastal town of Shelter Cove, or as we called it, simply, "the Cove." It was a safe haven and, for us, one of the most beautiful places in the world. The population was comprised of fishermen, retirees, builders, and many other law-abiding but tolerant folks who were drawn to its beauty. The Cove was home to Deadman's, the surf spot where John and I had logged thousands of days as kids—our "homebreak" so to speak. We had developed a powerful bond to the place, but what made it most appealing—aside from an occasional sheriff roll-through—it was copless.

My friend Ron lived in the Cove; he had an older redwood fisherman house that looked as though it was half buried in rock and ice plant. He'd fixed it up nicely inside but kept the exterior looking fairly rundown on purpose. I pulled up next to his old Ford pickup and was instantly greeted by his giant dog, Rudy. He was jumping on me in his friendly but annoying way while I tugged on my soaking wet jeans. The rain had drenched my seat.

"Fuckin' assholes," I mumbled.

"Hey, Mike?" Ron had come from inside the garage. He was in his mid-fifties, ponytailed with a backwards baseball cap, gay (though you'd never know it) and healthy. Looked a bit like crocodile Dundee with a walrus mustache. In fact, he had lived in Australia for years and still had remnants of the accent he'd picked up there. He was a successful carpenter and pot grower who managed to lead a seemingly straight life while pulling in pretty decent amounts of cash. Well respected in the growing, surfing, hippie, and even church community, Ron was a true Humboldt success story.

When I looked up at him, his smile instantly disappeared.

"What happened?" he asked, walking towards me. I shook my head.

"Where's John? Mike, where's John?"

"I don't know, we got busted, I couldn't tell-"

"DEA? Were there sheriffs?"

"I don't know, man, I mean ... they had black shirts with DEA written on them and badges and sirens and shit, so yeah, I guess. I was under the house the whole time," I started to explain.

"Wow, I'm sorry, mate, get inside and tell me everything. Jerry and Nerd are in there. Bummer. Damn. I'm so sorry, Mikey."

I stumbled over the threshold and into the foyer. Ron's place was pretty sweet with slate floors, custom woodwork, and medieval furniture. It had become the unofficial meeting place for many local surfers. Jerry and Nerd were sitting at Ron's massive King Arthur-style oak table, drinking beer from pewter mugs and laughing hysterically. Some creepy, instrumental version of "Shine On You Crazy Diamond" drifted between Ron's "bitchin" stereo speakers. At Ron's, one could always count on some form of new age or world music to be fluttering about.

Jerry looked over at me, great tufts of brown hair exploding from under his cap, and asked how we were doing.

"We got busted this morning," I muttered, feeling like I could break down any second. The shock was wearing off and saying it out loud really sent it home.

"You're serious?" At the same moment, Nerd mumbled, "Oh no, no, no."

Then together they asked, "Where's John?"

Everybody loved John.

"They took him," I answered.

Nerd, whom I'd known all my life, but whose real name, like Sophie, I'd never heard, stood up, "How many were there? Were they state? Sheriffs? Did you even see them?"

I told them the story.

Nerd lit a joint and held it out for me to take. I hesitated. It was the first time I'd ever hesitated when offered a hit off a joint and it felt profoundly strange. Just wrong. I shook my head and took it. Nerd leaned back and put his hands behind his head. He had a big reddish blond Afro, probably brown pre-saltwater and sun, and it was hard to tell where his head actually started. I inhaled deeply and exhaled just as fast. I never felt the need to hold smoke in my lungs like some crack-head. Everything began to soften. I took another hit. Softness. Better. Resume.

Ron was pacing like a worried parent.

"You're sure they said that about drying it somewhere?"

"They said the mission house. Yeah."

Jerry, who at thirty-eight years old looked and spoke like he was just out of high school, threw his tattered baseball cap down and said, "Dudes, those guys were fuckin' rip-offs."

"Yeah, but why would they take John?" Ron's voice was trembling slightly.

"And why the big show? Who's ever heard of that? Rip-offs come with guns, say *freeze fuckers!* and steal your shit ... right?" Nerd said.

"Probably DEA," Ron answered. "Just can't figure out why they took John. I wonder if it had anything to do with J.C."

Ron's words got me thinking.

J.C. had a decent size grow room on his property but no one knew whether or not it was still active. A week earlier he'd dropped out of sight and, although he was known to have a mild freebase habit (if there is such a thing), his disappearance had started to worry his friends and mother.

I said, "John told me that J.C. was doin' something big with someone else. You guys know anything about that?"

They shook their heads.

Outside, the rain, accompanied by ferocious winds, had returned in full force and the swell had begun to pick up. Twenty-foot faces closing in at such a rate, that, after years of weathering storms at Ron's, I still felt compelled to run from them. Only a second before the oncoming impact, they'd slam into the reef and instantly crumble. The wind pushed the rain in disorienting directions. We sat in silence for a moment, mesmerized by the storm, drinking and smoking, our senses ambushed by the display.

It looked dangerous out there, but it was a natural danger, different than the shit I'd faced back home. There was nothing natural about that, nothing at all.

"Can I crash here tonight, Ron?" I asked.

"I was just gonna suggest that, Mikey."

I woke up at three in the morning filled with dread. The waves and rain continued their bombardment. As I walked to the bathroom, I glanced down the hall to see if anyone was awake. Nerd was curled up on the couch with his ass sticking up like … I won't even go there. Under other circumstances, I would have laughed uncontrollably; maybe even looked for a camera. As it was, I couldn't even break a smile. My head was pounding.

In the kitchen, I made myself a piece of toast and ate it with milk. Nerd woke up and waved as he passed to the bathroom. When he came out, he told me not to worry, that John would show up and everything would be ok. Nice try, Nerd. He had dread painted all over his fucking face. Back to bed but as far as I know, I never slept. Trying to think things through. Debating. Better to wait before telling Dad. Couldn't imagine how it would affect him. As far as he knew, John and I were living straight arrow lives. If he'd known what we'd actually been doing and what we'd been planning, he'd have gone off his nut a long time ago. Or, I should say, further off his nut than he probably already was.

Chapter 3

JOHN'S STORY

Right in the middle of my morning shit and suddenly Mike is at the bathroom door naked as the day he was born screaming we're being busted. I don't think, man. I just push him and tell him to run. Before I get my pants up, there are four cops doing the "let's all get him!" dry hump dance on me.

"Fuckin A, man, take it easy," I holler. You think I'd know better, yeah?

They yell like a bunch of roid-raging football players as they go to work on me. I get a few in the head but it's the body shots that fuck me up. Feels like a crowbar or something. They finally chill and I open my eyes. Fuck me, no wonder. They're all wearing shitkickers. You kidding me? I can't help but notice their super-tight jeans, too. Cowboy on the bottom, cop on the top. Real practical apparel for a shootout; I'd laugh if I weren't terrified.

The one who seems to be the head boner puts his face close to mine and starts laughing and yelling "We got you, fucka" over and over. Uh huh, yeah, I'd say that's pretty clear, psycho. What's the accent? New York? Maybe Boston. Whatever it is, it's pure asshole.

Mike got away; they didn't even see him. I'm stoked about that. I guess I wasn't thinking. Doing what I always did with my little brother. Looking out for him. Praying he stays out of whatever this is. He doesn't have what-it-takes to deal with this kind of shit. Then again, I might not either.

They cuff me, throw me in the back of a Blazer, and put a hood over my face. The hood freaks me out. I think I know what this is all about. It's J.C.'s Colombian thing. Fuck. Why'd I ever get involved? A bit later, a cop jumps in and starts the engine. Judging by his heaving, I figure he's just finished loading up all our pot. He sounds like a dying animal.

I'm in total blackness, not fully losing it but close. Ask the driver what's going on and he tells me to shut the fuck up. Yep. Ok. Fine. I know what this is. I think of Dad. This is not good. Not good at all. Take a deep breath, Johnny.

Chapter 4

I crawled out of bed after hearing Ron and Nerd talking in quiet voices. An honorable effort not to disturb me, I supposed. I put on Jerry's clothes and shuffled to the kitchen to find them working on coffee and toast.

"Still fucking raining, huh?" I muttered.

"Morning, Mikey," Ron said, desperately trying to sound upbeat.

I passed them and began to rinse a cup in the sink.

As I poured my coffee, I sensed the two of them sharing a look of concern behind me. From the kitchen window I studied the mist covered hills and attempted to clear my head. Without turning around, I asked, "Should I call Randall?"

Jack Randall was a sheriff's deputy and a good friend of Ron's, who vehemently opposed marijuana prohibition and federal intrusion on county jurisdiction. Though he was bound under oath to take part in raids, he despised doing so. This meant that he also despised the Drug Enforcement Agency, Marijuana Eradication Team (his own department's task force), Campaign Against Marijuana Plants (yes, there really is such an organization), and many of the people he worked with. And, I suppose, they hated him back. He was a clean cop, so he asked that, although his position was well known, he never be questioned about his business or told about ours. I sometimes wondered if Ron's friendship with him had anything to do with Ron's longevity in the business, but never inquired.

"Let me do it," Nerd said. "I'll use the pay phone down by Torrio's, keep everybody safe." Already heading for the door, giving neither of us a chance to protest. "I want to check the waves, anyway."

After he drove away, Ron gave me an "everything's going to be OK" speech delivered with the same level of conviction that I got from Nerd, only Ron seasoned his with bits of "Your mom's up there watching out for you, John's got good karma" and various other bullshit. I knew he meant well and humored him throughout, shaking my head in agreement, "I know, I know."

Nerd returned, soaking wet, with exactly the news we thought he'd come back with. No record of any police action of any kind on Wilder Ridge the day before. And, the waves were shitty. At least we had doughnuts. Finally, after eating and drinking coffee, Ron said, "Well, roll a joint, Nerd; let's head up the hill and let Rabbit know what's happening."

Down the street we picked Jerry up and continued on to Wilder Ridge by way of King's Peak Road, a ridiculously dangerous dirt trail that cuts back and forth up the side of a very steep mountain. One wrong move or slip of attention would send us plummeting to certain death as we rode stuffed inside the cab of Ron's truck, silently passing the joint. I took three hits and declined the fourth, feeling as if someone had gently massaged my hangover away.

Rabbit was John's best friend. A hardcore longhaired dirt bike superstar, he had inherited eighty prime pot-growing acres on Wilder Ridge when he was sixteen years old. He loved only three things: weed, girls, and motocross, and he had mastered them all. He had raced a few times but was more into "freestyle," doing tricks and what not. He kept a decent-sized, but low key, indoor grow going in the house on his property, while he lived in a completely hidden luxury trailer. Whether or not his grow was still active, I didn't know. He wouldn't have cared if I did. Rabbit's psychological makeup was of the don't-give-a-fuck kind; more than likely, within the boundaries of his land there were tens of thousands of dollars, many pounds of ganja, and perhaps hundreds of plants, but Rabbit's gates were left wide open at all times. We figured he might be on his track so we took a left at his second gate.

Within seconds, we heard the wicked hum of motocross. We saw two dirt bikes, one chasing the other, hammering through the rain and throwing mud ten feet high like giant digging dogs. One slowed when the driver saw us and just as quickly gunned the engine and aimed for a very steep jump.

"There's Rabbit," Nerd said, smiling.

Nerd, John, and J.C. were all the same age and had known each other since they were young kids. They were all like older brothers to me. Still, in the grey day, I would never have been able to differentiate which rider was Rabbit. Only when he hit the jump, flew at least twenty feet into the air, took his legs and hands off of the bike for a moment, and landed with perfect ease, did I know.

"Who's with him?" I asked.

"Looks like Young," Jerry said, pointing to a yellow Toyota parked next to Rabbit's garage.

Both riders barreled over to the driver's side and Ron rolled down the window. Together they pulled off their helmets, their long black hair blowing in the rain, and shook their heads.

Nerd and I gave Rabbit props for his sick jump while he stared sideways into the rain. He was used to being told how awesome he was.

After a quick briefing, we agreed to meet him back at his trailer for coffee.

His doublewide had wall-to-wall, so we took our shoes off at the door and sat on any random thing we could find while Rabbit and Young parked their bikes and cleaned up in the garage. We'd already burned through a cup of coffee by the time they got to the trailer, Rabbit first, his power hair swinging back and forth in time with his swagger. He was one of those guys who'd had long hair since he was two years old, like Samson, and you couldn't conceive of him functioning without it. Young followed, doing his best impersonation of Rabbit. Poured two cups of coffee and asked if any of us wanted more.

"So, what the fuck, man," Rabbit started in. "This has to be coming from the stuff J.C. was getting into. So they weren't pigs?"

"No, I called the sheriff's office this morning and there was no record of anything," Nerd answered.

"Dirty pigs then?" asked Young.

There were "yeahs," "uh huhs," and "probablys" from everyone.

"What was J.C. up to?" I asked.

"No details, really. Just what John told me, which wasn't much, and that girl Debbie, the one I was pluking for a bit. She was so trout," offered Rabbit.

In Rabbit speak, "pluking" meant fucking and "trout" described something as good or awesome. I guess it had something to do with the tastiness of the fish.

"I talked to her on the phone and she told me J.C. had gotten all spun over her friend from the city, a Colombian chick, and wanted to marry her. She was connected, though, her dad I think, and J.C. had a deal going with him."

"What kind of deal?"

"Don't know. But Mikey, Colombia … probably coke. J.C. and John were hanging out so much lately; didn't he tell you anything? John must've known."

"He told me J.C. was doing something big with someone, nothing else," I replied.

Rabbit took a CD out of its case and slipped it in the player. Nirvana's "Smells Like Teen Spirit" filled the room. Then he turned towards me. "The Colombian chick was Debbie's friend. J.C was talkin' about marrying her. How come you don't know about it?"

"I've been on the mountain," I grumbled. "And John sometimes doesn't tell me much."

"Columbia? Connected? C'mon, you don't think this woman might be full of shit?" Ron said, while nervously pacing.

"No dude, you should've seen this party where we met these girls," Rabbit answered. "There were some serious, serious motherfuckers there. Guns. Gold. Massive amounts of blow."

Ron stopped pacing and flopped down in a beanbag I recognized as Rabbit's Mom's. A bright red fuzzy blob with decades of spills, burns, and who knows what other party scars covering it. I remembered hanging out at Rabbit and his mom's when I was a kid. My mom would take us there every week to watch satellite TV. We'd chill for a couple of hours and get sent to bed, while the moms drank, smoked, and did lines of coke while watching Dallas or Dynasty. We would sneak out and watch from the hall. Yeah ... we wanted to know who shot J.R. Ron rubbed his mustache. "Then ... if we don't find John today, we need to go and talk to this Debbie chick, don't we?"

Rabbit and Young shook our hands, swore their allegiance, and took turns patting my back and telling me it would all be cool and that John would turn up. Rabbit agreed to check a couple of places out and meet us at Ron's later that evening. We climbed into the Ford and Ron started the engine. Standing at the door, the rain soaking his black hair, Rabbit looked like a medieval warrior ready for battle, which in a sense he was; Rabbit, as was well known, was always down.

"Mike!" he yelled.

I rolled down the window.

"Yeah?"

"It's gonna' be ok!"

Chapter 5

If Humboldt County were a city, Whitethorn would be its ghetto. A virtual ghost town, there was no economy left functioning there other than small-time dealers selling coke, weed, and heroin. There were a few small, empty buildings; what used to be a hotel and restaurant, an old post office, and a couple of other places. Our property was a couple of miles south of town and, with little southern exposure, it wasn't exactly stellar pot growing land. Mom and Dad had bought it for a few thousand bucks a few weeks after he returned from 'Nam.

Ron turned onto our road and stopped to lock in the four-wheel drive; with the kind of "driveway" we had, a gate wasn't really necessary, but four-wheel drive was. He continued along, not much faster than walking speed, avoiding the bigger ruts and washouts, mumbling something about the shitty "agromusic you youngsters listen to." Jerry had borrowed a Metallica CD from Rabbit, so after a brief argument and fast vote, James Hetfield was screaming about masters of puppets and sanitariums and death and destruction, and Ron was doing everything he could to ruin every minute of it. The Ford rocked back and forth whenever we drove over one of the many unavoidable boulders, making him cringe and grind his teeth.

"Your dad's security system kicks ass," Nerd joked, his great bushy afro jostling in every direction.

"Hey man, you can hear an engine from pretty far away. I mean you can't come racing down here."

"No, man, I'm serious. Remember when my dad and uncle copied him and tried to turn a perfectly good road into an obstacle course? They thought it was a bitchin' idea till Mom got home in the Volvo."

Like a lot of Humboldt parents, Nerd's dad had convinced him to enroll in community college and stay away from growing. That lasted about a month. Nerd and Jerry pulled off small guerilla grows every summer and spent all their money traveling, fishing, and surfing. Or, more accurately, traveling to places to fish and surf.

I was about to admit I was too young to remember that, when Ron slammed on the brakes and let out an ear-splitting "FUCK." Less than fifty feet away, running towards us with guns drawn, were four men dressed in DEA gear, screaming what really just sounded like "fucka" over and over. The human brain is such a mystery. My first thought was not what it should have been. Instead of "Oh my God, it's them, get away," I thought, "Can these guys say anything without using the word fucker?"

Ron threw the truck in reverse and gunned it; Hetfield blasted from the speakers, *dedicated to, how I'm killing you, Master, Master, Master of puppets is pulling your strings*, and the rest of us screamed like a bunch of little girls. The bullets those psychos started firing were real. They made fast, hammer-on-metal tapping sounds as they hit the truck. By some absolute miracle, Ron got us around the first cutback. Then I got hit. It felt like a red-hot poker in the top of my trapezius muscle, an inch from my neck.

Ron asked if I was all right, then whipped the steering wheel completely around and slammed on the brakes, sending us into an embankment, where we ended up stuck in sort of a reverse wheelie. The cops ran back to their vehicles while Ron struggled to get the truck unstuck. We screamed at him to floor it. *You're falling faster, obey your master* ... I pulled Nerd out of the door and yelled for Jerry to help us push.

"Hurry! Push it up and out! Push!" Ron thundered.

The adrenaline, Ron's yelling, and Metallica created the perfect super human energy concoction, so that Nerd, Jerry, and I practically threw the stuck pickup back onto the road. *Now your life is out of season, I will occupy, I will help you die* ...

"Get in the back! Jump in the bed! GO, GO, GO!" Nerd bellowed as the cops rounded the corner. One cop started firing from the window of the front vehicle, a white Chevy Blazer, and we leapt into the truck bed, landing on our backs. We rolled back and forth, desperately trying to hold on to anything we could. Ron opened it up and the chase was on. I told them to hold on just before we hit the biggest boulder trap on the road, but Jerry flew out anyway. The Ford became airborne and he soared ten feet above the bed and landed a few feet off the road. Terrified for him, I popped up just in time to see him running down the hill like a crazed animal. Within a second, he was out of sight. Jerry was the best athlete among our entire crew and seemed pretty much indestructible. For a few years, his nickname was "Apeman." Those cops had just discovered why. I was holding a tie hole in the wheel well, and my hand had a huge gash in it from the landing, but I managed to stay in the truck.

"You guys jump out when I round this corner," Ron yelled. "There's no way we're gonna outrun them!"

I let go of the wheel well and noticed my hand, along with my shirt, was covered in blood. Since Nerd didn't seem at all keen on the jumping idea, I got on all fours ready to leapfrog right over him if I had to.

"Nerd, they're trying to kill us, man. We gotta go! Next turn! Next turn!" I hollered while grabbing his shirt. *Taste me you will see, more is all you need ...* I tried to visualize my landing, thinking about how quickly Jerry had recovered. Jerry was one of those fearless dudes that made up for any lack of intellectual prowess with sheer physical genius. He'd moved here from San Diego with his tweaker dad late in his teens, so we didn't know him as a kid, but according to his dad, he did his first back flip when he was only six. With a gunshot wound and a ruined hand, I was praying I'd make it without a busted ankle. If I didn't, I'd be dead.

"Get ready, you guys! Don't go to my house! Try to get to Rabbit's!" Ron began to slow down for the turn, a virtual

U-turn-style cutback that would normally be taken at three miles per hour. More shots.

"Fuck! Fuck! Come on, Nerd. We gotta bail!"

Nerd froze.

"Neeeerrrrd!"

A shot hit the back window.

Again, the heavy metal adrenaline combo came into play, and I took flight over Nerd and the road, flying straight into a Manzanita bush, the branches piercing my skin in dozens of places. With the momentum I had going, I rolled right on through it and landed a good twenty feet down the hill. Bolted to my feet, and began running as shots began firing behind me. Within a few seconds, I realized a cop had followed me and was in pursuit, but it took me even less time to lose him. I had seen all four of them clearly when we approached the house, so I knew they were all overweight. I was in good shape and had grown up on this property. As freaked out as I was at that point, I knew I'd get away. A moment later, I heard a barrage of what sounded like machinegun fire further up the hill where Ron and Nerd would have ended up. I stood for one horrified second and turned towards the creek.

I followed it in from the north side, making sure that I stayed covered, until I reached the swimming hole. There, I poured handfuls of water over the bullet hole and swirled my cut hand in the pool. The metal had slashed deep into my palm. I could see meat and tendon. I tore a piece of my shirt off and wrapped it around the hand, tightening a knot with my good hand and teeth. For the first time, it struck me that my brother and friends might actually be dead, and I was overtaken by anger and confusion. I got up, walked to the fallen redwood tree where we used to change into our swimsuits, and fell to my knees. I felt like I'd spent my entire life waiting for the good part to start; and there, staring at the dead redwood, in one pouncing revelatory instant, I realized there would be no such moment. The confusion melted away, leaving only anger.

After a few minutes, I stood up and began the five-hour hike to Ken's place. Ken and his wife, Martha, were old friends of my mom's. Martha had always told my mom that I needed to apply myself more. She taught sixth grade. Ken grew a little weed and was an artist. Their two daughters went to Humboldt State and were perfect. I was a bit reluctant to bring them into this but I really had no choice. I had no lighter, the ground was wet, and I was bleeding. Making camp would have been nearly impossible under the circumstances.

I made my way down to the lower creek and began following it north. I eventually felt pain throughout my body. Even my torn up knees from the day before were on fire. At times, it felt like there was a piece of steel sticking out of my gunshot wound, and I kept reaching up to pull it out and finding nothing there. I stopped to rest and drink from the creek occasionally, but otherwise maintained a fairly consistent pace.

"What the hell were these psychos really after, and why were they willing to kill for it?" I wondered. I shook my head every once in a while in an effort to clear my thinking. Or wake up from the nightmare.

I estimated I had another two hours to go before it started to get dark. With the overcast sky, the night would be pitch black, and finding Ken's would take a hell of a miracle. I knew the only landmark I'd recognize was a small cliff with an old live oak growing out from the top of it. We used to swing from a rope there when Nerd's uncle owned the property above it. It had been sold long ago to someone else, but I knew how to get to Ken's from there.

Ken's daughters, Carrie (two years older than me) and Kay (two years younger), hung out with us there a few times; we were all very young, but I was aware of how different the vibe was when the girls were around. The boys would all become relatively reserved; I was basically silent for the most part, but the rope swing tricks went straight to level ten. Even though I'd known them my entire life, those two girls fascinated me. Even now, the slight chance that Kay might be home gave me a boost of motivation. As if imminent death wasn't enough.

Night fell and seeing became impossible. Struggling to follow the creek and remain dry wasn't happening, and I ended up falling in twice. My lower legs and arms were drenched within a few minutes and I began shaking uncontrollably. Even though I repeatedly told myself to keep moving; I realized that my feet were dragging along the rugged ground and no matter how much I exerted, I could not lift them. The adrenaline had worn off and I felt like I was beginning to die. I lost track of time and tried to recapture the anger I'd felt earlier. I beat myself in the head. Wanted to lie down and sleep. I didn't care anymore. But I kept sliding along and falling, recovering and mumbling, until I came to an impassable cliff. I reached out to touch it, to recognize it, but it was just a cliff. The tree was the only way I'd know. Turning to backtrack, I went down on my hands and knees, crawled to where the land was less steep, and began to climb. Hammering my numb hands into the ground like ice picks, I made my way up the hill and crawled along the grass, slightly encouraged by the fact that I was indeed in a meadow. Something made me stop, and for a split second, I was terrified, my senses distorted, keenly aware of a giant entity directly in front of me. I imagined a massive tortoise from a fairy tale. Gently, I reached out and touched the ancient live oak.

Though I consider myself somewhat of a tree hugger, I'd never actually hugged one until that night. There I was, squeezing and slobbering all over that poor tree, thanking it for being ... it, not yet acknowledging the mile I'd still have to hike if I wanted to live. But I eventually did acknowledge it, and I hiked, and I lived.

Chapter 6

Awake. Searing pain covered every inch of my body. Everything hurt. Even my balls felt like they'd been kicked up into my gut. Groaning, I reached for them and heard two voices, one male and one female, from across the room.

"Don't worry, it's all still there, Mike," the man laughed.

"Ken, stop. Oh, Mike, thank God, how do you feel?" it was Martha, Ken's wife.

She walked over to me and began caressing my hair.

I tried to speak but sounded like I had a mouth full of dirt. My gashed hand and bullet hole had been bandaged and the rest of my body was covered in various Band-Aids, gauze, and bandages. I looked up at Martha, her long grey hair tickling my face, and asked how I got there.

"You got you here, Sweetie. You showed up around 11 p.m., practically dead. We called Tony because you made us promise not to call the cops, but we almost had to take you to the hospital." Tony was a veterinarian. "Yeah, you stormed right on in and started taking off your clothes."

Before I could feel any embarrassment, the previous day flooded my consciousness and I started rambling. In a convoluted, almost entirely incomprehensible way I began telling them what had happened, until Kay, the younger daughter, walked into the room. When she came up to the bed to give me a glass of water, and began stroking my hair, I knew I had to stop babbling.

She asked me how I was feeling and, attempting to be suave, I told her better now that she was there. What a dumbfuck; it was no wonder I rarely got any girly action. But her sitting next to me, encumbering my ability to recognize the dreadfulness of yesterday's story, actually helped me tell it in a slightly less jabbering-idiot fashion. Somehow, the crushing dose of self-consciousness put my racing mind in check.

After some discussion, Ken decided that he would check out the property and then go to Shelter Cove to see if he could find out anything. Before he left, he handed me a bottle of Tylenol 3, the kind laced with Codeine. Martha went to help Ken, and Kay made me soup. I took a sip of water and began to feel the Tylenol. Outside, I heard Ken start Martha's car and drive away. Martha and Kay spoke in quiet voices as the old wood window softly rattled with the wind. I picked up a photo sitting on the bed stand and almost started to cry. The photo, of Ken, Martha, and the girls, their faces radiant with love, locked onto each other in a perfect face-touching-face super-hug, broke my heart. I thought of John and how much I loved him. He kept a photo of himself as a baby at what at first looked like Woodstock, but once you saw the terrified faces of the people, you realized it was somewhere else. It was labeled, *Me and Mom/Altamont Dec 5, 1969*. And then below, *Fucking Typical!* Apparently, a few moms (including mine—she never forgave herself) thought it would be okay to take their babies to the Rolling Stones' free concert at the Altamont Speedway. Four people died that day; one stabbed to death, in what many people felt symbolized the end of the '60s and the last breath of the free-love era. Many of John's friends got to go to Woodstock. He got Altamont. It *was* fucking typical.

That sad photo is the only one of him John kept displayed. He had a few of Dad, mostly from Vietnam, but the one he had blown up and framed was taken after Dad was rescued. In it, Dad looks like he'd lost about sixty of his normally 220-pound frame and he's surrounded by his smiling rescuers. Apparently, John was named after the team leader.

Dad and his friend Carmine Lucchese (who eventually became Dad's partner in crime—he died in prison a few years ago) were on the same Hunter/Killer team in 1969. In the 7th Armored Squadron, 1st air cavalry, they flew Loaches and Cobras. Dad was observing for Carmine during a recon mission just north of the Mekong River near what they thought was the border of Cambodia when they were shot down by small arms fire. It turned out they were *in* Cambodia. They survived for weeks until being rescued by a SEAL team. Since Carmine had fractured his femur in the crash, he was almost entirely helpless and he would have died had Dad abandoned him. My father received a few medals for that, but ended up chucking them away at an anti-war rally.

Still, being a war hero got him no love when he was trying to secure a prisoner transfer a couple of years after he got busted. When I was a young kid, we visited him in Bang Kwang—or as it is also known, "Big Tiger," because it eats people alive—and afterward he and my mom agreed to never to let that happen again. Apparently, it was too painful an experience for everyone. For me, it was pure terror.

I have no idea what my Dad looks like now, but when I daydream about the day John and I get him out, he looks very kind. Sort of like an older version of John.

I finished eating my soup as Ken drove up and slammed the car door shut. I tried to get out of bed but Kay stopped me just as Ken came through the front door and barreled into the bedroom, saying he'd seen Ron's truck sprayed with gunfire. Then he turned around just as fast, said he was headed for the Cove, and split. I fell asleep.

Ken barged back in a little after one o'clock, waving his hands and hollering for me to wake up. Jerry was with him.

"Holy shit, Mike, thank God. I figured you guys were all dead. Dude," he climbed up on the bed and gave me a big hug.

"Where are Ron and Nerd? Do you know, did you find 'em, Ken?"

"No, nobody knows, man."

"Jerry, where'd you go, bro?"

"That was the craziest shit ever. I waited for a few minutes and headed back up to check things out and ended up hitching a ride to Rabbit's."

Of course he did, I thought, and I suddenly felt like a giant pussy.

"What about you, you psycho, I can't believe you fucking walked here in the dark."

"Yeah ... well ... look at me."

I noticed Jerry didn't have a scratch on him and he sounded healthy as a horse. That figured.

"Rabbit's right behind us. He wanted to see you. He's on the war path," Ken said, rolling his eyes. "Did you know that kid is a friggin' firearms collector? Jesus Christ."

Actually I didn't, but it didn't surprise me in the least. I wondered what sort of firearms he was talking about since Rabbit didn't hunt.

"Uh no," I answered. "So did you guys go to the Cove?"

"Yeah, but we didn't find out shit. I don't know what to do now."

"I don't know either," Jerry sighed. "Shit, I'm glad you're OK, Mike. Did you see me fly out of that truck, man? I was like twenty feet in the air!"

"Yeah. That was sick."

"I know," he agreed, looking dreamily beyond me, as if a replay of his fantastic feat was being projected on the wall.

At that moment something moving fast slid to a stop outside as, through the window, we saw Rabbit explode from his truck door and head for the house.

"Martha! Come here ... mmmmmm," hugging Martha. "Oooohh, it's great seein' you."

"You too, Clifford." We all giggled. I always laughed when anyone used Rabbit's real name.

He started down the hall with Martha following, telling him she'd always think of him as clever little Clifford Kazinski who could never keep his mouth shut.

"Where is he, where's Mikey?"

He came in and ruffled my hair, "Mike, Mike, Mike, what a shitstorm, dude."

"I know. I think we should call Sheriff Randall."

"What? Screw that, man. We need to jet to S.F. like now, talk to Debbie, find J.C.'s fine Colombian, and see what's up. Don't get Jack into it, man; he wouldn't want to be there."

Jerry took his cap off and started in about how serious this was, but Rabbit talked over him, "What is he going to do, Jerry? Put out an APB on a bunch of dope growers who may have been kidnapped or killed by dirty DEA? You think he'll give a call to the director and tell him what happened. Yeah, I can hear that, 'Uh, hello. This is Jack Randall with the Humboldt County Sheriff's Department. Yeah, I know you guys know who I am and you hate my fucking guts and would probably love to kill me, but could you do me a favor and figure out which of your agents have gone rogue and started kidnapping, possibly murdering the good dope-growing folks of my fine county? Yeah, could you do that, please? OK great. Thank you. Could you give me a call when you arrest them so I can send down my witnesses or I could just give you their names now?' Hell no, Jerry. Jack's a good dude and this would fuck things up for him big time. His own department doesn't even back him; you know that. Listen, he may have to find out eventually, but right now let's do my thing, yeah? I got an arsenal hidden under my bed-liner, just in case. Mike, you don't look so bad, so up and at 'em. We gotta go, little brother." Rabbit was extremely persuasive.

"Rabbit, you would have made a wonderful attorney," Martha chimed in after I instantly agreed with his plan of action.

And with that, we came up with a plan—where we were going, which motel we'd stay at and so on—and got ready to go. Ken gathered up a ridiculous set of clothes for me and everyone left me alone while I put them on. A pair of size 42 jeans, a Hawaiian shirt, and, since he had no belt that would fit me, a piece of rope.

Rabbit and Jerry cheered when I shuffled into the living room.

"Ken, don't you have a T-shirt for him?" Rabbit hollered.

"That's the smallest shirt I have."

"Whatever," I sighed.

"I think you look cool, Mike," Jerry roared, "like Magnum P.I. meets South Central L.A."

"Are you sure you feel up to this, Mike?" Martha gently asked.

"I'm OK, Martha. Just really stiff."

She brought me my freshly cleaned bloodstained coat and apologized for tossing my shirt and pants. I thanked her and asked about my boots.

"They're at the door, sweetie."

"Let's get going," Rabbit clapped his hands.

We exchanged hugs and said our goodbyes. They stood at the doorway waving as we drove away. Before I could go a big weepy one, Rabbit hit the power button on the stereo, released a boisterous hoot, and did his trademark head bang hair flip. Ozzy Osbourne's ganja cough blared from the speakers as Black Sabbath tore into "Sweet Leaf," an irrefutable Humboldt classic and perfect heavy metal love song.

He reached for the ashtray and pulled out a roach. "We got a long drive, let's smoke."

"Sure, this yours?"

"Uh huh, from Karl's seeds. It's killer, but pretty mellow, you know, perfect driving weed."

"Perfect."

I love you, my sweet leaf, When I first met you, didn't realize ...

Rabbit sang along for a few seconds and told me he never got sick of that song. I agreed.

I started to feel nauseous and asked him to slow down.

"Take a hit off that joint and you'll be hungry enough to eat your own arm in a few minutes."

So I did and I was, and we drove at top speed until we got to Garberville, where we stopped for gas and snacks before getting on Hwy. 101. I stayed in the truck while Rabbit loaded up on various junk food and chatted up a group of college girls bound for Arcata. He pulled back onto the freeway and slammed the gas pedal. Pain shot through my neck as my head flew back with the force. I grunted and touched my bullet hole.

"Hey, shit man!"

"Sorry, I gotta remember how jacked up you are right now. At least you haven't been coughing. How much codeine did Ken give ya?"

"No, man, I need that, OK? That's all mine."

"Well, how much did he give ya?"

"Dude!"

"Alright, alright. What do ya wanna listen to?"

"Something mellow." I opened a bag of Funyuns and thought of John and how much he loved Funyuns. "How 'bout nothing right now."

"Don't get much mellower than that. Hand me the Cheetos."

I leaned my head on the window as I watched the country drift by.

We floated through the grayness in total silence. I looked at Rabbit and was chilled by the deflated look on his face. It was rare to catch Rabbit when he thought no one was looking. I turned back to my window before he noticed and snapped himself back into character. The cliffs rose from the highway like enormous fists, as if Mother Earth was enraged, ready to hurl pieces of herself in defense. Occasionally, we'd pass a crushed boulder surrounded by orange tape, and I wondered what would happen to a car if one of those were to hit it. Far below us, the Eel

River fortified its position without resistance. Unlike the highway and us, it had a very old arrangement with Mother Nature, and therefore not a damn thing to worry about. I stayed that way, my head pressed up against the window, my mind caught in dismal rotation, for over an hour. Rabbit asked me if I was OK at one point, but other than that, remained quiet and still.

"Can I play a little mellow music ... or listen to KGO or something?"

"Sure, man."

"Which one?"

"I don't care."

"Music, then!"

"Fine."

By the time we got to S.F., we were at the end of the fourth CD, I was on my sixth codeine tablet, and my head was throbbing with each of Chris Cornell's shrieks. "Who'd you say this was?"

"Uhhh Pearl Jam ... or Alice in ... I don't remember."

I pressed eject and read the CD out loud. "Soundgarden."

"Yeah, fuckin' sick trout, huh?"

"If that means it sucks balls, then yeah."

"Aw, c'mon Mike, that shit is dope. Grab my wallet out of the box and get me toll money, will ya?"

I handed him three bucks, "So where does Debbie live?"

"46th Ave., close to OB's bro. Too bad you're messed up. You could've surfed VFWs tomorrow."

"What do you know about VFWs?" I always gave non-surfers a bad time for not surfing. "What time is it?"

"A little after six."

"We made good time. Are we heading there right away?"

"Hell, yeah!"

"Cool."

Rabbit took the first right after the Golden Gate Bridge and we snaked through the Presidio and then the mansions of Sea Cliff. I rolled down the window to a cold damp rush of wind on my face, and quickly closed it again. Rabbit had turned on KGO and two people were arguing about whether or not the cops who beat up Rodney King were justified in doing it. The one defending the cops claimed that Rodney had been drinking bottles of Old English 800 and so must have been drunk out of his mind.

"Oh, well of course they had to beat his ass!" Rabbit yelled sarcastically.

Also, the police advocate said, the video George Holliday shot from his window didn't capture Rodney charging at the cops.

"Somehow video never captures that, huh?" I said smiling.

Rodney's team claimed polls taken after the incident showed over ninety percent of Los Angeles residents thought the police used excessive force in arresting him.

"The LAPD has been doing that shit for decades and everybody knows it. Ruthless motherfuckers they are, man," Rabbit lamented.

"Well, they'll get theirs this time."

"No, they won't, bro. They *never* do."

KGO cut to commercials and came back interviewing a little Texan nutjob named Ross who wanted to be elected president so he could run the country like an oil company.

"What the fuck?"

When we got out of the truck at Debbie's, it was immediately clear that she shared the house with others. Or, she was having a party. It turned out to be a little of both. Three girls were shivering on the porch, smoking cigarettes and talking (screaming?) about some like, totally wannabe player who had like, totally tried to get two of them to fuck him at the same time and then one was all, whatever you freak and the other was all, fuck off you cringer and then he was all, fuck you bitches and it was soooooo funny. I figured the gravity of my situation would prevent me from giving a shit about the Magnum P.I. look

I was sporting, but I quickly recognized the folly in that thinking. I followed behind Rabbit, feeling and looking like I'd just
escaped from somewhere I shouldn't have. The girls giggled
when they noticed us, and they most definitely weren't laughing at Rabbit.

"Shut the fuck up, Stacey," Rabbit started in, preempting any
shit they might dish out. "For real, my boy's been thrown out of
a speeding car, shot up, beat up, almost died, and he got stuck
wearing some borrowed clothes 'cuz those that may want to kill
him are probably watching his house, so stop laughing and go
get Deb for me, huh."

She started to say, "Whatever ...," but he interrupted,
"Seriously, Stacey, some terrible shit's just happened to my
bro here and I need to talk to Debbie about her Colombian
friend."

Even though it was a rare occurrence, when Rabbit was genuinely serious, he came off as really serious, and I went from
feeling like a total kook to a badass motherfucker in five seconds. I loved hanging out with Rabbit.

"Oh my God, what happened? I heard that Anita had to go
back to leave ..."

"THAT WAS HER FUCKING NAME, ANITA!"

"Cause her dad was like, in trouble or something, and her
uncle got killed and all kinds of crazy shit."

"What? Is Debbie inside?"

"She doesn't get off for another hour, but you guys can come
in and wait for her. Did you really get shot? What happened?"
she asked, while the other two girls started in with four or five
"oh my Gods" all in a row.

"Are y'all having a party?"

One of the other girls, a blonde, 20-foot tall Amazonian
super model, told us it was girls' night out and they're like, getting "primed" while they waited for Debbie.

"Well, ain't we lucky?" Rabbit smiled and winked. "After
you, Mikey."

Sitting on a pink couch in a girlishly decorated living room were two girls reading lyrics on a CD case, and I realized that all five of the girls we'd just met had the exact same light blonde hair color. I glanced at Rabbit and shared a smile. The girls looked up as Stacey introduced us and I realized they weren't reading the CD case, they were doing lines of coke off of it. Oh shit.

Rabbit began taking off his boots, "Mmm, y'all got a little chop-chop goin', huh? You girls all work with Debbie?" he asked.

"No, me and Kimberly don't," one said, while furiously rubbing her freshly coke- crammed nostril. "We dance at Mitchell Brothers." Considering her manic behavior, it was pretty clear she'd been "priming" for quite a while, and I was instantly turned off. Coke had always been kind of a paradox for me, at times inducing waves of excitement and at other times revulsion; there was never any indecision, no in between. Watching the two girls quiver about in bloodshot, rambling bewilderment, masquerading as conversation, made me want to get as far away from them as possible.

"Sweeeet," Rabbit purred. "Where you going tonight?"

"We're not sure. You guys wanna bump?" Stacey asked, pointing to the CD case. It was Guns and Roses. I noticed there wasn't any music playing and that made me happy. My neck and hand were starting to throb again.

Rabbit, looking at me said, "No party for us tonight, darling."

"Yeah, I don't do blow anymore either. Oh my God, so tell us what happened. Sit down. You wanna wine cooler or something, at least?"

Now that took a little work to refuse, but I did. Thank God she didn't offer me a Guinness.

We told them what had gone down with very little detail while they drank wine coolers and did tiny lines of coke. I was a bit apprehensive to talk at first, but after Rabbit whispered something about them not remembering any of this by tomorrow afternoon, I went along. I thought about the few afternoons

I woke up or, more accurately, passed through the "thank God" side of the vicious coke comedown, with very little memory of what other people had talked about the night before. What I had said was typically very clear and very embarrassing and I'd often wonder why it had seemed so profound twelve hours before. Kimberly then spent a half hour on a two-minute story about her ex-boyfriend who'd been ripped off by cops in Los Gatos. By the time she finished, I had almost fallen asleep. Stacey asked me if I was OK and if I wanted to lie down.

"Mike, you look really tired. You should crash, dude," Rabbit said, walking over to help me up.

"What about Ron and Nerd? What if they go to the Best Western?" We'd told Ken and Jerry that's where we'd be.

"They'll just get a room. And they'll leave a message at the desk, or just wait around for us. We gotta talk to Debbie, Mike."

"C'mon, I have the most comfortable waterbed," Stacey said, and she held out her hand. Rabbit asked if I had my pills and if I needed to take an antibiotic and I said yes and thanks and took Stacey's hand.

She led me up the stairs to the bathroom and gave me a toothbrush to use. After I washed up, I walked down the hall to her room where she was humming and fluffing one of fifty or so pillows. It smelled like strawberries.

"Can I see where you were shot?" she asked.

She looked at me, one dark eyebrow arched mischievously (I remember thinking she'd be very pretty as a brunette, her obvious natural hair color), and I said, "Sure."

I took off the Hawaiian shirt and pointed to the bandage, where a circle of dried blood had developed in the center.

"Ooohh, someone works out!"

I smiled shyly, "Not really. I surf."

"Ouch, did you get the bullet out?"

"It went through."

"Let me see."

I turned around. She put her hand on my back next to the bandage and guided me into bed. "I'll make sure everybody stays quiet, OK? Sleep tight," she said and she kissed my cheek. I thanked her. And before I could consider the sweetness of what she'd just done, I fell asleep.

Chapter 7

JOHN'S STORY

By the time the cop drags me up a set of stairs and throws me into a room my face is drenched with sweat. We must have driven five hours. I figure I'm in the city somewhere. Earlier, I asked if he could take the hood off and just fucking blindfold me, but he wouldn't. He unties the base and yanks the hood off of my head. Yep. There's J.C. Chained up like Hannibal Fucking Lecter (minus the creepy mask) lamely smiling at me. Hmmm, well, nice that you're happy to see me, J.C. Too bad I can't say the same about you. The cop shackles me up, tying all the chains together into a black box at my waist and tells me to make myself comfortable; I'm going to be here awhile. OK, at least they're not planning on killing me anytime soon. He leaves the room, locking the door behind him.

J.C. is no longer smiling. He looks like he's had the shit beat out of him.

I ask him what's going on. They think we know a lot more about the Colombian thing than we do, man. He starts crying. Shit.

I ask what they've been doing to him. Like kind of torturing me, dude!

Kind of? Yeah, like hitting me over and over.

Have you told them anything? Of course, but it's not enough!

Well let's make some shit up so we can get the fuck out of here! He tells me he hadn't thought of that.

We talk as I roam around the room looking for a way out. He tells me there is one exceptionally loony cop that comes around.

The baby face porker who can't speak without saying fucker?
Uh huh, his name is Dixon.

I ask if he at least told them we were supposed to sail a boat-
load of something from Mexico to the states. Yeah, they want to
know where it is ... they think it's money.

I tell him it may have been. That the last time I'd talked with
Anita's dad, he threw out a comment about taking all their cash
out of Panamanian banks.

We stop talking and I watch J.C. as he looks out the window.
He looks scared and broken. I tell him that we'll be ok.

He turns toward me. We might not. I'm sorry, Johnny. I'm
sorry I got us involved in this shit.

I tell him to stop tripping. We'll get out of this.

But I have to admit, studying his smashed up face, I'm not
looking forward to my turn with Dixon. Damn it. I find a space to
lie down on the hard wood floor and my thoughts drift to my dad.
As far as I'm concerned, he's the strongest man in the world. He
got such a shitty deal, he's had to endure the worst kind of shit,
and still, he's kept himself relatively together. Most of the dudes
he's stuck in prison with have turned into full on junkies, but not
him; he's straight as an arrow. Mike and I have dedicated our
lives to getting him out. That's the only reason I agreed to do
this shit with J.C. I could have pulled a cool mil in less than two
weeks. Just like Dad back in '77. It's like a family curse. I think
about how totally crushed he'd be if he knew my predicament.
It'd probably be enough to send him over the edge, finally start
him hitting the smack. He thinks I work in a restaurant. I wish I
would've sent him some dough last week. We usually write him
once a week, and Mike and I flaked because we were getting so
close to harvesting. I hope Mike is okay and that he has enough
sense not to let Dad know what's happening. Hours go by. I start
to fall asleep, but the door opens before I do. Great. It's Dixon.
I look at J.C. and he turns away. Smiling, Dixon steps in front of
me. He has a blackjack in his hand. Fuck. Okay. My turn.

Chapter 8

Stacey must have been at least twenty-two years old, but if you were trying to guess her age based on what her bedroom looked like, you'd probably say thirteen. Posters, photos, and clothing covered everything so that there was not one inch of wall or floor exposed. Although I didn't feel as bad as the morning before, my entire body hurt. I allowed myself to wake up slowly as I glanced around the room, and jumped slightly when I realized Stacey was lying next to me. The faint smell of strawberries was still noticeable, only it had become more like rotten strawberry wine coolers; it was Stacey's breath. Lying there in her little dress, she looked like someone who would sleep through an earthquake, and would no doubt feel like shit when she finally woke up. Looking at her, I was very happy that I hadn't partaken of any of the party favors the night before. At least I had that going for me. I wondered if Rabbit had abstained, but knew that even if he hadn't, he would be fine. He was one of those rare dudes that could exercise restraint at all times. He could drink a few beers, do a couple of lines, maybe a mushroom cap or two, and be in bed by nine. I knew he was just setting an example for me the night before.

I rolled out of the waterbed, sending a wave towards Stacey. She snorted and mumbled something before she froze in the same gape-mouthed position she'd been stuck in. I did my stiff Frankenstein shuffle down the hall to the bathroom, peeking in at an all-naked Rabbit sandwich as I passed an open bedroom door. He was flat on his back, his arms spread out with a blonde head resting on each, and the centerpiece was Rabbit's hard dick aimed straight up to the sky, as if thanking the Lord in heaven for bestowing such a wonderful gift upon it. There were at least four used rubbers spread around the floor. I peeked in to get a closer look, thinking there might be another dude somewhere in the pile, but there was only Rabbit and his boner. I smiled and shook my head; quite unsure of what strategy I should use to wake him. I slammed the door to the bathroom after throwing the toilet seat up and down, thinking that might do the trick and, sure enough, after I had a piss and a face wash, there was a light knock on the door. Rabbit was standing naked at the door as I opened it and he rushed in, practically hitting me with his then half hard-on as he passed me.

"OOOoooohhh GAAWWWD, yeeaaahhhh," he moaned while he leaned over the toilet. "Oh that's good. So good."

"Jesus dude, I'd hate to hear what you sounded like last night," I laughed, quickly escaping any possible overspray. "You're like a goat ... were all those your rubbers?"

"Oh, I had to piss so bad. Where's Deb?"

"What?"

"How long have you been up? Is Debbie downstairs?"

"Was she in there with you, too?"

He gave me a Jack Nicholson smile.

"Fuck! Oh my fucking God, dude you're my hero."

"Hey, I'd have invited you in the mix but I figured you needed the rest. How's your shoulder?"

"It's my trapezius."

"Huh?"

"It's not my shoulder."

"Whatever, bro. Is it OK?"

"I guess, as long as it doesn't get infected."

"Take your pills and get a shower. I'm gonna find Debbie."

"Hey, if you knew we might be coming down here, why didn't you pack some clothes?"

"Dude, I brought guns."

"That's what I mean."

"Huh?"

"We'll have to buy some clothes today."

"Yeah, get ready. I gotta lot to tell you. And we got people to see."

"Who?"

He jogged past me and ran naked down the stairs, totally unconcerned about his incredible shrinking dick.

"Rabbit, where we going?" I shouted after him.

"Get ready!"

I poured a bath, undressed, and slowly climbed into the deep claw-foot tub. Beside it stood a cabinet displaying thirty or so bottles of shampoo. I chose the one with strawberries on it, and cautiously washed my hair. Rabbit came back a few minutes later.

"Dude, are you taking a fucking bath?" he asked through the shower curtain.

"Yeah, I can't shower with all these bandages, man."

"Well hurry up. I wanna shower. I stole a couple a pairs of Marcie's underwear for us," he whispered.

"Whose?"

"Marcie ... the big chick. Don't worry; they'll fit. If anything, they'll be too big and ... they're siiiilllk."

"No way, you freak!"

"Fine, you either free ball it or go around funky till we hit a store. Me, I thrashed my pecker last night, so I gotta give it a little TLC."

"How about letting it rest for 24 hours."

"Funny."

"Not funny. Serious, bro. Fuckin' thing's gonna fall off one of these days."

Just then, Debbie walked in and in a raspy voice said, "Yeah, if there's any justice in the world."

Rabbit slapped what sounded like her butt and hollered, "Hey Debbie, I didn't hear any complaining last night."

"I don't even remember last night," she mumbled. "Get out so I can pee."

"OK. By the way, that's Mike behind the curtain."

"Hi Mike."

"Hello."

"I'm sorry all this shit happened to you."

"Thank you."

"I hope John and J.C. are OK."

"Me, too."

"Will you run the water while I pee?"

"Of course." I turned on the water.

"Thanks."

Thirty seconds later, she told me it was nice meeting me and that she had to go lie down, and that was the first and last time I ever spoke to Debbie.

I dressed and, after a futile search for food in the kitchen, sat down on the pink couch to wait for Rabbit. He came running down the stairs seconds later.

"That was fast."

"I'm starving."

"Me too."

"Fast food, sit down, or coffee shop ... no sit down ... no time, and fuck fast food, gross ... no, nothing like that around here anyway. Let's get bagels at the place towards the zoo, OK? The one where we can sit outside, then we'll get you some clothes."

I let him go on like that, figuring out our plan, knowing he'd do and go wherever he wanted no matter what I said, and I was just fine with that.

Rabbit shouted a goodbye and thank you and we were off. Driving alongside Ocean Beach, commenting on the fog and shitty waves and how the lineup was crowded, regardless. Rabbit began telling me all he'd learned from Debbie, which wasn't much, before Rabbitpalooza (that's what he was calling last night's orgy). He claimed Rabbitpalooza was totally not his idea, but what the hell was he supposed to do? Refuse? Shit.

"OK," Rabbit started in, "turns out Debbie's friend Anita is the daughter of a prominent member of the Medellin drug cartel. Yeah, that's what she said … MEDE-FUCKING-YIN … reassuring, huh? I knew those dudes were serious, but really. And supposedly her uncle got killed by a member of the Cali cartel or some other anti-Escobar group and her father relocated her and her family to Spain. So I guess we'll probably never see her again. J.C. apparently became bros with said dead uncle and was supposedly going to help in some 'operation'." He did hand quotes on 'operation' and we quickly drifted towards the curb. "Shit, my alignment's off. Debbie wasn't too good with the details. But I imagine that's what the whole brouhaha's all about. Medellin and Cali have been at it for years. It's not like that's anything new. So Deb told me she hadn't talked to Anita since the news about the uncle, which was a few weeks ago."

"Well how did she know J.C. wasn't with Anita when you called her?" I asked.

"Good question. She has another friend who was close to Anita and she'd apparently told her."

"It's still kinda weird."

"Ya think? Anyway, the friend is on vacation in Australia so we're left with one option … and it's kinda gnarly."

"What?"

"Go to the house where the party was and see if any of those dudes will talk to us."

"That's psycho."

"That's where we'll find what we seek, Mike."

"Where is it?"

"Back in Sea Cliff. We passed it last night but I didn't want to point it out then."

"Why not?"

"I don't really know. I'm sure it's under surveillance, and I was kinda hoping we wouldn't have to go there."

Hearing that from Rabbit the Fearless was discomfiting. I mean very discomfiting. I was pretty damn reluctant to proceed with something even the mighty Rabbit considered imprudent, but I figured since it was on the way home, I could wait until we were almost there and then beg Rabbit to pass on by and head straight to the sheriff's house. I told him to forget the clothes; that we should grab coffee and get on with it.

Twenty minutes later, my plan in shambles, we were standing outside the gate of a mansion built on a cliff west of the Golden Gate Bridge, arguing about what to do next. Rabbit had parked about a block away in case someone was watching the house—as if it would have made any difference. He'd pulled over in a Safeway parking lot earlier to grab a couple of pistols from the back. He asked if I wanted a semi-auto or a .38 revolver and I told him neither, since I had expected to drive right on by the suicide mission. He handed me a 9-millimeter anyway, and I put it under my seat.

Outside of the gate, I whisper yelled, "Rabbit this is fucking retarded. I know you're 'the king of knowing what the fuck' but right now I think you're wrong. We need to get back."

"Dude, this'll be a wasted trip. This is the source, man. You want to find John or what?! Look, somebody will recognize me."

"Why did you bring the fuckin' piece then?"

"Same reason you should have, Mike! 'Cuz you never fucking know."

"Where am I supposed to stash it? In my Huck Finn belt?" I lifted my Hawaiian shirt.

As he started to laugh, the garage door opened and a Jaguar began backing out. It stopped when the driver saw us. We froze for a moment. Then Rabbit waved, walked towards the passenger side of the car, and stopped a couple of feet short, his hands outstretched as if calming someone. The driver had a pistol pointed at him and seemed to be yelling. As the window came down, it became clear he wanted to know who we were and why we were arguing outside of his gate.

"Dude, I'm sorry, I'm sorry. I was at a party here a few months ago and my homey hooked up with Anita and he's missing and we're just looking for him."

He put the gun down and I began moving towards the car.

"You talking about J.C.?" the man asked, his accent pure Colombian.

"Yeah, man. Yeah," Rabbit laughed nervously.

"You are from up north?"

"Yeah, we grew up with J.C."

He looked at me and asked if I was John.

"No, I'm his brother. John's gone too," I answered shakily.

"*Chinga su madre!* You were helping them with the boats?" He looked nervously down the street. If I hadn't known better, I'd have thought he was just a wealthy white businessman in an expensive suit and car. He looked like Antonio Banderas with lighter skin.

"Uh, no. What boats?"

"You come to the airport with me," he said frantically. "I have to make an airplane. You come there and we talk, but we have to go from here now. It's very dangerous. Get in the car!"

Rabbit and I looked at each other and I whispered, "What the fuck?"

"Let's go for a ride," Rabbit muttered and he opened the car door.

"Dude, no way, he could just be …"

The DEA guys. Again. Before I could blink a fucking eye. They were masterful at appearing out of nowhere. In that regard, their super high-tech DEA training had definitely paid off; I'll give them that. It was as if the van they'd bolted out of had just materialized in position across the street—or had it been parked there all along? Shit.

I recognized the one in front immediately. He had small patch of blond hair on top of his head and a tiny, thin mustache that looked more like a dirt stain on his round baby face. He was pointing a Goddamn machine gun at me and screaming for me to get on the ground. Another cop was doing the same to Rabbit and the third was yelling for the man to get out of the car. Rabbit and I quickly went to the ground as the man rushed up.

"Hello, Mike, you stupid, dumb fucka," he yelled, then kicked me on the side of my face. I thought I felt something break and was consumed with rage.

The third cop was literally squealing at the man in the car but I couldn't see what was happening. Baby Face kicked me in the side; then I did feel something break, and he knelt down, jamming his knee in my back.

"Hands behind your head, fucka," he hollered, sounding like he was hyperventilating, "You're gonna tell us where this shit's going down, aren't you, fucka?"

"I don't know what you're talking about!" I was barely aware of what I was saying.

He punched me in the cheek, and at the exact moment of impact, a gunshot fired off. For a split second, I thought I'd been shot in the face, but I recovered in time to see cop number three lying in the fetal position, screaming and clutching his arm, cop number two blowing the living shit out of the dude in the car, Baby Face racing around the car towards him, spraying the back window in a classic example of "cop panic," and Rabbit, in the grand HOLYSHIT finale, pulling his .45 from his pants.

He fired four rounds under the car at the feet of Baby Face and Number Two, sending them diving over the neighbor's concrete wall. Then he jumped in the car, grabbed the dead Colombian, kicked him out onto the sidewalk, and called for me to get in. I crawled over the blood-soaked body into the passenger seat, and Rabbit floored it in reverse, swerving to avoid cop number three, before I could close the door.

"STAY DOWN! STAY DOWN!" he roared.

I huddled under the dash as Rabbit sped down the street in reverse. Just as the first burst of gunfire hit, he whipped the steering wheel around and back again and I felt us fly sideways and then forward.

"JESUS FUCKING CHRIST!" I screamed.

"You all right?" Rabbit asked. "No more holes in you? Good. We gotta get out of this car."

"FUCK! FUCK! FUCK!"

"Mike, chill out, brother. We're OK. They're not behind us. One of 'em got shot. We have to get out of this car."

"MOTHERFUCKERS! IT WAS THE SAME MOTHERFUCKERS!"

"MIKE! CALM DOWN!"

"What are we gonna do, man? What the fuck are we going to do?" I was freaking out.

The Jaguar's windows were full of holes and there was blood splattered all over the seats and dash. We heard sirens in the distance.

"How 'bout the park? Ditch the car there."

"OK, OK, Jesus, man." I took a few deep breaths, looked around and saw a briefcase in the back seat. After a couple of minutes, I grabbed it and set it on my lap.

"Open it, dude." Rabbit was concentrating on the road and for him that meant an entire 360-degree spectrum. He swiveled his glance back and forth, front to back, and side to side, maintaining as much awareness as the spider-webbed glass would allow. I tried the latches, but the case was locked. Rabbit reached down and lifted his pant leg, exposing a boot knife.

"Use this," he said.

I reached over and pulled the knife out of the sheath. The locks popped and I opened the case. A plane ticket and a sizable stack of one hundred dollar bills sat on top of a mound of papers. Of course, human nature dictated that I pick up the cash first. I thumbed through it and looked at Rabbit.

"Must be over twenty grand here."

"Where's the plane ticket to?"

I reached for the ticket.

"Put the cash in your pocket, man."

I pulled the ticket out of the envelope and read out loud, "Juan Santiago, 12:35 p.m., one way to Cabo San Lucas, Mexico."

"You ever been to Cabo?" Rabbit asked.

Chapter 9

The park appeared a few stoplights away. Rabbit did his best to keep distance between us and the other vehicles, but I imagine there were a few double takes. Luckily for us, the fog was very thick and there was barely any visibility.

"There it is," Rabbit said.

I held my breath until we crossed the last stoplight into the park. The sirens had faded a few blocks back and I hoped that the dirty cops were in fact very dirty and were getting tangled up with the city police. We drove until we reached Stow Lake and parked. There were maybe four people within view, and they were all otherwise occupied as Rabbit wiped down the dash and steering wheel, grabbed the gun and briefcase, and jumped out.

"Let's go."

We walked down to the lake and scooped up water to wash our clothes. Other than Rabbit's butt, we had remarkably little blood on us. I asked how my face looked, and he told me I looked like the Elephant Man, but in a mellow way, like I had a mild case of whatever the Elephant Man had.

I lifted my shirt and felt the spot where Baby Face had kicked me. I winced as I pushed on the broken rib, and pain shot through my body. It was tough to take a deep breath.

"You OK?" Rabbit asked.

"Actually, no. I'm really messed up, man." I checked my bullet hole bandage and it was hanging halfway off and a trickle of blood and fluid was making its way down my chest. I thanked God I'd put my pills in my pocket.

"Hang in there, Mikey. We gotta start walking. Let's get to a bus stop and stay in the woods until we see one coming. We'll be alright. Remember when you and John had to save your dad's ass in Sac? You got this, bro!"

He was referring to a time John and I saved our dad from a bust at a hotel in Sacramento. Dad was middling a huge deal, a hundred pounds, and had been pretty apprehensive all day. Three minutes after he went into the hotel, over twenty cop cars squealed into the parking lot and, defying Dad's orders, John and I ran up the back stairs to the room. While the cops were still busy preparing themselves in the parking lot, we casually walked past them. Dad had me in his arms and held John's hand, so he looked like a normal family man. We were little heroes that day.

"What are we gonna do, Rabbit? Really?" I said, trying to stand up straight.

"We're going to the airport. Hopefully, we'll figure something out after we go through those papers. You got your I.D. on you?"

"Yeah. But what the hell are we going to do in Mexico?"

"I don't know. If anything, we'll be far away from here. I better stash this pistol."

We started walking off the road, but close enough to see which cars were coming. Rabbit climbed a tree and stuck the gun somewhere up there. My body started aching and my knees felt like they could pop out of socket any second. I started coughing and realized I was freezing and that we looked very suspicious with the briefcase. Without it we looked like two sketched out homeless freaks on a mission, but with it, we looked like two sketched out homeless freaks that had just *completed* a mission, like jacked a briefcase out of someone's car.

"We should ditch that briefcase, dude," I said.

Rabbit agreed and he knelt to empty it. He folded up the papers and we stuffed our pockets with them. He pulled a half pint of Tequila out of the side pocket, smiled wide, quickly opened it and downed half of it in three huge swallows. He handed it to me and I finished it.

We walked for a few more minutes. Rabbit came up with a plan that involved new clothes, a shave, and a haircut. When he said haircut, I couldn't believe what I was hearing.

"You're kidding. You're gonna cut your hair?" I asked in amazement. My ribs ached as I spoke.

"Hell yeah, bro. Better than ending up like Mr. Dead Colombian back there."

"Like ... short?"

"Fuckin' A short! Hey, a taxi!" he ran to the road, waving his arms at a yellow cab. Defying the laws of probability, it stopped and the driver gestured for him to get in. We climbed in the back and slammed the door. It felt like it was a hundred degrees in the car and I loved it.

"What happened to you guys?" the cabbie asked softly. He was a young, Middle Eastern guy who spoke perfect English with barely a hint of an accent.

Quickly, Rabbit answered, "Aw, me and my buddy here got in a fight with a couple of assholes last night." He was pretending to be drunk. "We both joined the Army and we're having our last hoorah. We've been partying for two days straight, you know what I'm saying?"

The cabbie congratulated us.

"Thanks, man! Some fucker ripped off our luggage, too! You believe that?" Rabbit pulled out his wallet and gave the cabbie two hundred-dollar bills. "We need to pick up some stuff at a mall or somewhere and then get to a hotel near the airport. We're heading back to Florida tomorrow. Will this hold you for a bit?"

"No problem," the cabbie said with a smile.

I played along with Rabbit's story as the cabbie drove us to a mall and waited in the cab while Rabbit went in. Less than a half an hour later he returned with a mother load consisting of six pairs of khaki pants, six pairs of khaki shorts, two packs of socks and underwear, two belts, a dozen polo shirts, two pairs of flip flops, two pairs of brown boat shoes, two baseball caps, two sporty windbreakers, two pairs of shades, two watches (one gold, one silver), a pair of scissors, an electric hair trimmer, electric razor, various toiletries and medical supplies, two duffle bags, a bag of cheeseburgers and ten bottles of Gatorade.

Our cabbie got out and helped him load the trunk. He had a bottle of Gatorade and a cheeseburger in his hand when he got back in the car. Rabbit handed me the same and I finished it in one minute. I devoured two more and guzzled the Gatorade.

"Oh God, thanks dude. You the man."

Rabbit asked the cabbie what his name was.

"Said."

"Right on. So is there a hotel central around the airport or what?" I asked, knowing full well there was.

"Oh yes. You want a nice place ... or cheaper?"

"Whatever, just drop us at any of them. We're just gonna get cleaned up and hit a bar," Rabbit answered excitedly.

It began raining on the way to the airport, but Said kept the speed at eighty miles an hour anyway. We played our story perfectly until we pulled into a Holiday Inn parking lot. We stopped under the check-in shelter and Rabbit strutted up to the front desk like a rock star. Dressed in a black t-shirt, black jeans, and biker boots, he looked like one. He hollered for Said to pop the trunk when he returned and came to my door and opened it.

"Hold on, Mike. You DO look fucking crazy right now," he said quietly, and with Said's help, pulled the shopping bags out of the trunk.

He handed me a polo shirt and a sporty jacket and told me to put them on. We thanked Said and headed to our room where I attacked the bed as Rabbit headed to the bathroom, warning me not to get too comfortable.

"I thought this was the plan. We chill here until we figure shit out." I said, lying in the fetal position, the bedspread pulled up in my arms like a "wooby."

"We're here to clean up and change and go to the airport. Those dudes are after something major, and they're prepared to kill anyone to get it. What did he say to you?"

"Who?"

"The cop, man. He was yelling at you," he grunted from the bathroom.

"Ahh, close the damn door, dude! He told me I was gonna tell him where the shit's going down."

Rabbit flushed the toilet, "Fucking cops, going down, oohh, it's going down! That's how they describe everything ... it's going down. What a bunch of boners. Well, we know it has something to do with Colombians, cocaine, and boats, so whatever it is, it's big."

"He obviously thinks we know a lot more than we do."

"Yeah. Let's go to Cabo and find out. We got nothing to lose, Mike. Neither of us. Nothing. Who knows, maybe *we'll* pull something off and get rich."

"I don't care about getting rich."

He flushed the toilet again and raced out to the shopping bags.

"We will now transform ourselves into two kooks who look like they've never seen marijuana or any illegal drugs and who would never partake in anything illegal ... other than tax fraud, in their life. You go first." Rabbit began handing me items from the bags.

I never had hair like Rabbit but I'd worn it at least four or five inches long my entire life. I put down the scissors, tore open the electric hair trimmer box and gave myself a buzz cut. When I walked out Rabbit smiled, "Wow! OK, that's actually really badass looking. You look like a Beastie Boy. So whatchya watchya watchya want!"

Rabbit had spread all the papers from the briefcase out on one of the beds by the time I finished.

"What are the papers?" I asked.

He looked up at me; his usually arched eyebrows muscled down into his eyes in complete Rabbit seriousness, "All in Spanish. But I think they're bank statements."

"Yeah?"

"Uh huh. Check it out, *Banco de Occidente, Panama.* Panama, dude. And look at these balances."

I leaned over and glimpsed at the numbers.

"Holy shit, is that forty million?"

"Yep."

"Panama."

"Uh huh, and here's the dude's appointment book. He has, or had, a meeting in Cabo tomorrow." He started to smile.

I stood up and shook my head.

"Fuck it." I looked back at Rabbit. "Tape the bandage on my back. Let's go."

Rabbit confused the hell out of the front desk lady when we checked out. He didn't look anything like the rock and roll warrior who'd checked in less than an hour before. Watching him, I thought he looked like he could be on his way to a God squad pep rally, but when he turned around, that idea fell apart. His Jack Nicholson eyebrows, devious smile, and all around rugged face gave him away in an instant. The dude was a badass motherfucker and no khakis, polo shirt, or bullshit haircut was going to hide that. Me? I suppose I looked like a dude who was on his way to a Christian youth meeting, but only if there was going to be a no holds barred brawl in the middle of it. At least the swelling had gone down and I didn't look like the Elephant Man's little brother anymore.

Rabbit walked towards me, his head back, moving as if he still had two feet of hair.

"Mike, you look like you're ready to rip someone's throat out," he joked.

"I am."

"That's what I'm talking 'bout!"

We climbed into the shuttle and sat down in the back. I was already feeling uncomfortable with the red polo shirt—Rabbit had bought five maroon red shirts for blood stains to blend into, just in case—tucked into my pants, but it was a hell of a lot better than the Magnum Huck Finn get-up. When we reached the airport, we double-checked our wallets for money and I.D. We'd memorized the critical info on the bank statements, and burned them back in the hotel room, figuring a 40 million dollar Panamanian bank statement might be a little hard to explain. We bought two first-class tickets to Cabo San Lucas and boarded without a problem. Of course, we knew it was never a problem getting into Mexico; it was getting back that was the bitch.

Our flight attendant was pretty enough so Rabbit went into the bathroom with his politician hair and came out with it messed up, looking a lot like Jack Kerouac in that famous photo with Neal Cassady. He told me he hoped to screw a stewardess in a bathroom before he died and I nodded and told him of course you do and promptly passed out.

Rabbit woke me just before landing. The cabin was dark except for a few reading lights. The memory of the last few days flooded back like a bad dream as I rubbed my face and head.

We breezed through customs, got some pesos, and charged into the cool Cabo night, hailing what turned out to be the chattiest English-speaking cabbie in all of Mexico, so we didn't get a chance to talk on the way to the hotel. I managed not to hear a word of what he said, and left the small talk up to Rabbit. I was thinking about the only other time I'd been in Baja, on a surf trip John had set up for my eighteenth birthday. Jerry, Nerd, and a couple of other friends drove down in two vans, camping every night except one. That was the night in Cabo San Lucas. We'd started drinking after arriving from Pescadero, where we'd surfed all morning, and were pretty well shit-housed by dinner time. Then we drank Coronas, happily stumbling in and out of bars, until the sun came up. My one and only taste of what it was like for thousands of carefree American college students.

It took a while, but we eventually found a hotel with an opening. Rabbit gave the cabbie a huge tip and asked him if he'd chauffer us around exclusively the next day, and he excitedly accepted. We dropped our bags off and went out for tacos. After a brief disagreement regarding the plan for the remainder of the evening, I returned to the room, and less than an hour later heard Rabbit unlock his door.

I began thinking of John, meditated on his face, focusing on my mission, so to speak, and I remembered how I used to cry like a little baby as a kid and he always made sure he had an arm around me. And yet the only time I saw *him* in need of consolation, I failed him.

We'd been hauling bagged Super Soil down to one of Mom's small patches when we heard the sound of a helicopter. I asked him if we should drop what we were doing and head up the hill. He told me we had nothing to worry about and to keep going. A few minutes later, the chopper long gone, I realized he had been right. He handed me a shovel and I began turning the fertilizer into the soil. He told me our Dad had started the patch I was tilling.

John helped me finish, brought over a tray of "starts" and handed me one. As I gently packed it into the soil, I asked him if he missed Dad and he said yes. He looked at me and put his head down, his curly blonde hair dancing in the light wind. It was then that I noticed he was crying. I wanted to say something, to do something to take away his pain, but I didn't. What I did was pretend I hadn't seen his tears—ignored them, until he picked up a bag of fertilizer and moved on to the next patch. I watched him. Thought about asking if he was ok, but instead, I turned around and went back to work. What a pussy move. I always felt bad for that. And I had trouble falling asleep that night because of it.

Chapter 10

The sun blasted through the balcony sliding door like a search-light, and I immediately brought my hand up to cover my eyes, pounding on the wall with the other to wake Rabbit. He came in as I was finishing my morning bathroom routine and told me he was going to the pool and to meet him at the restaurant in a half hour.

We reacted with a nod when we first spotted each other, still unfamiliar with our new looks, both shaved smooth again and sporting the young Republican look. If the DEA fuckas were to see us seated at a multicolored table overlooking Puerto Paraiso Mall waiting for our food to arrive, they would never recognize us.

"Almuerza con Jesus a la marina what?" I asked.

Rabbit answered with a Spanish word I forgot a second later.

"So we're just gonna go there at noon and look for a dude that looks like Jesus?"

"I don't know, Mike. We could ask out loud. Or maybe they've already heard that Juan is dead and no one will be there. In which case, we stay here for a few days till the money's gone and head back into the shitstorm."

"I don't speak Spanish, and even though you won't admit it, yours sucks. So, how we gonna deal with that?" I said, as I moved my coffee and sunglasses out of the way for my food. I put my shades back on and thanked the waitress. She looked like she was about eleven years old and really pissed off.

"That's why we got Miguel, homey! You gotta trust the Rabbit. We don't really even need a cab at this point, man. He's gonna be our translator ... and guide."

"Oh, so we'll just trust him with all this info. Tell him to tell Jesus that Juan is dead and the DEA is after us and ..."

He put his hand up, "I'll be discrete, dude. Just chill."

"I will."

"Be cool."

"I am."

We finished our breakfast and left the eleven-year-old a hundred-peso tip, but she stayed pissed. The mall was beginning to come alive with loud tourists from Europe and the States, and we strolled through as if we were the same, occasionally stopping at a shop or food stand to check out the wares. Rabbit bought a T-shirt that had a cartoon rabbit smoking a joint and something about getting high in Cabo on the front. He said he couldn't wait to wear it. Because of my injuries, I ended up sitting at a coffee shop for a couple of hours while Rabbit strolled around. I was still coughing a bit and my ribs felt like they were shattering each time. Rabbit came to get me at 11:15, five minutes before we were supposed to meet Miguel in front of our hotel.

He was waiting in his cab when we arrived and smiled widely when we approached him.

"Hey, you guys! Killer day, yeah? Oh man, the waves are big today, too. You guys surf? No, you don't surf ... you like Charlie! Ha ha ha. My cousin is pro, man. He goes to Todos Santos. Big waves. Jump in. You got all you need? Where you want to go?" I hadn't realized he was a surfer the night before but it was obvious when I saw him in the light. He had sun-bleached curly hair and was wearing Billabong surf trunks and an O.P. tank top.

"Miguel, here's a thousand pesos." Rabbit got close to him and put on his serious face. "What we really need is somebody to guide and translate for us today. We're here for business and we're not really sure ... what kind of people we'll be dealing with and whether or not they speak English."

Miguel, looking only slightly concerned, asked, "Drugs is the business?"

"No. No. Not really. It's banking."

"Money cleaning ... as long as there will be no drugs and we are in a public place. Yeah?"

"Absolutely," Rabbit said.

Rabbit offered me the front seat of the old red and green cab and I accepted. He told Miguel a little of what was happening, leaving out key info that would have undoubtedly left him running scared. When we arrived at the small marina, a luxury motor cruiser was heading towards one of the docks, and before we could say a word, Miguel commented on the possibility of that being our guy. Standing on the starboard bow was a clean-cut man who looked to be in his mid-forties. He was wearing slacks and a silk shirt and had a drink in his hand.

Rabbit looked at me and whispered, "Well, if that's not our Colombian, it's somebody else's Colombian."

I laughed, but Miguel started to look nervous and told us he didn't want to talk to the guy.

"Come on, Miguel. Look at all the people, nothing's gonna happen here."

The section of marina seemed to belong to a private resort and there were at least thirty people around the plaza and beach. Rabbit convinced him to at least stand at the entrance to the bar and he, Rabbit, would ask the man if he was Jesus.

"It's easy enough," Rabbit joked. "Here, I'll practice ...Jesus? See."

We stood in the shade of a yellow awning in front of the pink hotel watching a couple of women in bikinis play Frisbee on the beach, until the man got off his boat. He walked down the dock, which was directly in front of us, with a huge fucking bodyguard behind him, and I started feeling a bit nervous. There were three places they could go once they reached the patio we were standing on. Left was the way around the restaurant to the parking lot, to the right was the entrance into the resort's front desk, and straight ahead, the bar and us.

Rabbit swallowed and whispered, "They're coming this way," as the two men walked towards us. Rabbit smiled and waved before they passed and called out, "Jesus?"

They stopped as the man took off his sunglasses and the bodyguard stepped in front of him. He looked at me as if I'd said the name, and I suppressed the urge to point to Rabbit in what would have been a hilarious display of chickenshittedness.

"*Quien esta?*" he asked.

"*Me llamo es Clifford y ellos estan mis amigos Miguel y.. uh ..Miguel,*" Rabbit began lamely.

"Americanos?" he snapped his fingers and the bodyguard stepped in.

"Who are you?" he asked menacingly.

"Oh excellent, you speak English, that makes things easier, um, so Miguel, you can go, I guess," he pointed with his thumb towards Miguel. "He was gonna translate for us but since you speak English ..."

"*Rapido puto!*" the smaller man yelled, either to Rabbit or Miguel or whomever. Miguel scrambled out of there, and I guessed we'd never see him again.

Rabbit stammered on, "We're from San Francisco ... California. We were with Juan yesterday; we were looking for my friend's brother," thumb point to me. "We're totally not involved with whatever is going on, but ... uh ... some dudes tried to kill us and Juan and, but we got away and ..."

"Where's Juan?" With his gold earrings and ponytail, he looked like a giant, sweaty pro wrestler in a suit.

The silk shirt man pushed in front of him and asked, "*Que dice?*"

The bodyguard spoke to him in speed Spanish—as if there were any other kind—and smashed his fist into his palm a few times.

The man answered back and the bodyguard asked, "He wants to know if you're the gringos for the boat delivery ... from the Sheltered Cove."

Rabbit, wasting no time, said, "His brother might have been, but he's been taken by the police, and we're looking for someone who might know why."

"*La policia ... Como!*" The small man suddenly looked ready to blow our heads off, but big boy calmed him down.

Rabbit, trying not to interrupt, snuck in with, "We think they were dirty police, you know, like bad police ... corrupt."

"I speak English."

"I was with his brother and another friend of ours at a party at Juan's, or the house he was at. This was a few months ago. Our friend, not his brother but another guy, was dating Anita, and apparently she got them involved in a job. Yeah, they were going to do something with a boat. Our friend and his brother."

"Anita Valenzuela?" the small man asked, mellowing out a bit.

"Yeah, I think," Rabbit didn't have a clue. "The cops that took his brother are the ones that shot Juan."

"What agency? What police?"

I finally spoke, "DEA ... the same guys who took my brother killed Juan."

"He's dead? Juan is dead? Fucking DEA killed Juan?"

"Well, that's what was written on their jackets ... but man, I mean the SAME guys. At least one of them was. I recognized him."

Big boy spoke to little man for a minute, and then asked, "You assholes have no fucking idea what is going on, do you?"

Together we both said no like a couple of idiot teenagers.

He shook his head and asked if we were hungry. We followed them into the bar and sat at a small round table in the corner. The sunlight beamed in through the windows and we all put our sunglasses on. There were various images of green iguanas all over the walls. Fake plastic iguanas, posters of iguanas riding surfboards, and iguana cardboard cutouts surrounded us. Directly above us was a fishnet filled with stuffed animal iguanas. We ordered drinks and Big Boy's came in a mug shaped like a naked hot chick iguana. It was difficult not to laugh when he took a sip out of it.

By the time we were on our third drink, it was obvious none of us were really interested in eating, and Big Boy, whose name was Jose, and Little Man, also Jose (no Jesus there) began lamenting about the state of their business. We told them every-thing else we knew about the situation, and then some. They were interested in our growing operations and lifestyle. They laughed when we told them what kind of money we made grow-ing weed.

"So much work for such a small payoff," Big Boy marveled. "In cocaine, there is money." It occurred to me that they had no misgivings whatsoever about what they sold; for them, cocaine was a commodity like any other commodity, bought, marked up and sold, just like liquor or fruit, clothing or oil. Rabbit com-mented on the violence and ruthlessness involved and Big Boy disagreed, saying that there were all sorts of positions to fill, not all of them requiring the will to engage in violence. Rabbit and I grinned at that but managed not to laugh. With a buzz kicking in and my body aches diminishing, I was able to trick myself into thinking that hanging out in a Cabo bar with a couple of Colombian heavies was just a little bit cool, despite the horrific circumstances that had brought me there.

I took a drink of my beer and finally had the guts to ask, "So, do you guys know what my brother and J.C. were going to do ... for Anita's uncle and dad?"

Big Boy sighed and rubbed his face, "Things are rapidly changing, the organization is in danger, you know." He asked Little Man a question and Little Man answered yes. I started to think that maybe Big Boy wasn't a bodyguard. He spoke English well and was clearly educated to some degree.

"El Padrino is still able to run things from hiding, but the other organizations are quickly gaining power ... and access.

They have many friends in the DEA. These DEA you speak of, they think they are working for your government, but they aren't; they work for Cali."

I rubbed my head and asked, "What do they do for them besides ... not bust them?"

He sighed, "First of all, Mike, do not be naïve, cocaine is making billions in profits for people. There is so much money. Do you not know what money does to people?"

"*Some* people," Rabbit interjected defensively.

"MOST people. Cali works in many independent groups. They have many legitimate operations, and they are different than us in many ways. They use money, not fear, for influence with government. They say they are gentlemen. They say, 'We don't kill the judges, we buy them.' This is what they say, but they will kill anyone ... and they are determined to crush Medellin. Your DEA probably thinks they are doing a good thing. Destroy Medellin and maybe get rich in the process, but they are no different than all of us. They are just cowboys. Cowboys working with one cartel in order to stop another."

"Why are they messing around with Northern California? You didn't answer Mike's question. What were they going to do? What's with the boat?"

"The Mexican Army killed some federales a few months ago. Do you know of this? They were working with cartels, but since then, President Salinas has severely limited the DEA's ability to function in Mexico; supposedly they can't even carry firearms," he laughed at that, "which is why we are here and not in the Caribbean ... that and Miami has basically been closed to us. Mexico is the new ... what is the word ... conduit?"

"What about the boat?" I asked again, beer balls kicking in strong.

Little Jose said something and Big Jose looked at me gravely.

"Maybe later we will talk about that, maybe we will even show you, maybe you guys can take over for your friend and brother, yes? You are doing all you can to discover what happened to them.

But right now, drink and live life. Enjoy Cabo and do not worry ... there is no need now." He took his suit jacket off, exposing his massive prison tattooed arms, and signaled for more drinks. Little Jose rapid fired Spanish for a few minutes, leaving me utterly clueless. He looked at Rabbit and me as well as Big Jose while he spoke, clearly warming up to us, and ended with a great thirty second laughing fit. I courtesy laughed and pain shot threw my ribcage.

Big Jose asked if I was OK.

"Yeah, but I better eat," I said.

"Yeah, you hungry? Me too, but not here," Big Jose said, and he called out something about a "coche" to the bartender. Five minutes later, we were chilling in the back of a limo on our way to one of Cabo's finer eating establishments. Laughter filled the sound space for most of the trip, and I was struck by the exuberance the two men exhibited. Having never encountered actual Colombian cocaine dudes before, I imagined they'd be serious and dour and never, ever laugh.

We arrived in front of an elegant looking restaurant overlooking the main marina and followed the Joses through the front doors. The maître d' royally kissed their asses and got us to a table immediately.

Rabbit leaned over and did his best Al Pacino as Scarface impression and after laughing, I told him to shut up. We were seated at what was pretty much the best table in the restaurant. With its white tablecloths and crystal chandeliers, the place could have been a typical San Francisco Fisherman's Wharf tourist trap, but in Cabo, it was the bomb. Big Jose ordered wine, bread, and calamari straight away.

We spent over two hours in that restaurant, Rabbit and Big Jose talking and laughing the entire time, while I ate at least four pounds of food. I may have dropped a sentence here or there, but really I just ate the whole time, and so, when we left the restaurant, my buzz was almost completely gone. Rabbit and Big Jose, on the other hand, had been doing shots of Don Julio and were ready for girls.

Back in the limo, Rabbit asked me what I was up for doing.

"I don't know, I'm kind of tired."

Big Jose laughed, "You must be, the way you ate. I don't think I've ever eaten that much in one sitting! Wait till you see where we're going, and I promise you, you will no longer feel tired!"

"How's your shoulder holding up? You want to go back to the hotel, Mike?" Rabbit asked.

Big Jose, who had heard only about my beating, asked what happened to my shoulder.

"I got shot in my trapezius," I said.

"Your what?"

"Right here," I answered, pointing to the hole.

He suddenly looked very impressed, "Holy shit, you were shot by the DEA! That is very fucking cool!"

"Glad you think so," I said a little too sarcastically.

"Shot by the police," he continued to himself, while shaking his head.

Little Jose asked him a question and he answered in Spanish, pointing to my bullet hole.

"*Muy bien*," Little Jose said smiling.

I laughed, "No muy bien, no muy bien at all."

Rabbit again asked if I wanted to go to the hotel.

"Naw, I'll hang out a while." I figured these guys were the best shot in figuring out what was going on.

"Excellent," Big Jose shouted. "To the girls!"

We pulled up to the gentlemen's club a few seconds later, and I was left wondering why we didn't just walk. The Joses had acted like they owned the restaurant where we'd eaten, but in the stripper bar it was as if they were the masters and overlords of everything and everyone inside. They approached a table where a few Americans were seated and over excruciatingly loud techno music, hollered something at them. The Americans grabbed their drinks and scattered like mice. I wondered what Big Jose had said to them but knew that he really wouldn't have had to say anything at all. One of the Americans shouted, "No worries," and I realized he was Australian. He scurried to another table with a confused look on his face.

The club was just like the one other strip club I'd been in. Dark, except for the stage and bar, topless fake-breasted girls roaming around, hustling lap dances, and several drunken slobs staring at them with that horny-dog-ready-to-hump look. Within seconds, girls surrounded us.

"Order me a margarita, Mike! This one ... yeah!" Rabbit shouted as he ran off with a far too perfectly proportioned blonde.

The waitress brought our drinks and a bottle of Tequila. I took a couple of shots before nursing a beer and after a while my buzz kicked back in, so much for taking it easy. The music got significantly softer, and Big Jose had warned the girls not to sit on my lap because I was hurt, and so, other than occasional rubbing of my buzz cut, they weren't paying much attention to me. Two girls were on stage kissing each other while a third pole danced in ways I didn't think possible, and Rabbit was all over the fucking place, returning to the table for a sip of his drink every so often.

"How are you doing, Mike?" Big Jose shouted.

"I'm feeling a little better, those shots help a bit," I smiled, wanting desperately to get out of there and find out what the deal was with the boat.

"What do you know about sailing?" he asked. *Ah, here we go.*

"A little, I have a lot of friends who are pretty good. Rabbit is," I pointed to Rabbit, who was being proper dry-humped by a girl with freakishly huge tits. "Like we said, we do a lot of fishing and sailing up North."

"We have a yacht outside anchored in the bay that was to be delivered to the Sheltered Cove ..."

"Shelter Cove," I corrected him, reluctantly.

"What?"

"It's just Shelter, not Sheltered Cove."

"Oh, OK. In better times, the contents of this yacht would have been delivered in a different way and by different people, but under the current circumstances ... well, under these circumstances, we are not sure what is the best way. We do know that we need gringos for the operation. We had a crew set up before the appearance of your friend and brother. Things did not work out with them and we were stuck without a backup. There is chaos within the organization. Your friend J.C. had gained the trust of Valenzuela, Anita's father, who was to organize this delivery and so it was a perfect fit. Now your friend is gone, along with the men, and our chain of command is breaking down. It seems that Cali and the DEA are aware of the existence of our ... package."

"The package ... is it coke?"

He looked at me for a long time as if lost in thought and eventually said quietly, "Cash. American cash. A shitload of American cash, my friend."

"Dollars."

"A lot of dollars."

"Like how much?"

"Does it matter? When it's tens of millions, does it matter? El Padrino could hire an army but what would stop them from taking the money for themselves. Who can be trusted with that amount of money? No one, really."

"But why John and J.C.? How the hell did *that* happen?"

"Anita was in love with J.C. You said it yourself. Valenzuela must have known. He must have trusted your friend. Your brother and his friend knew about boats and the California coastline; they had access to a secluded bay where the money could be easily transported to a secure area without raising suspicion, and something else you also probably know a lot about, they knew how to hide large sums of cash." He practically sang that last part.

"Yeah, like a bag maybe ... not a ..." I paused for a moment, "a fucking boatload. Really, don't you have people for this sort of thing?"

"Of course! But things have changed. Cali, Los Pepes, DEA, FBI, the fucking Delta Force, these are all forces working against Medellin now ..."

"What's Los Pepes?" I asked.

"They are enemies of Pablo. They do not matter outside of Colombia, they have little impact, but many of these other organizations do."

"I thought we didn't have to worry here ... now," I almost yelled.

"I said you don't have to worry. I didn't say we couldn't be killed at any moment. I just said we don't *need* to worry about it. Tens ... of ... millions, my friend," he said forlornly, pulling a cigar out of his jacket.

He talked like a man who was close to death, and was aware of and at peace with it.

"Jesus Christ," I whispered. "What the fuck was John thinking?"

"He and his friend probably had no idea of the magnitude of what they were getting involved in."

Rabbit slid up to the table and let out a loud hoot.

Big Jose looked at him and then me and said, "I believe your friend is a bit like me. He appears quite fearless."

"You're Goddamn right!" Rabbit wailed excitedly. "Mike, how you doing? You need to get back to the hotel? Jose, what will it take to get a couple of these chicks back to my room?"

"For you, my friend, I think nothing. They seem as interested in you as you are in them," he smiled.

Rabbit began scanning the room as Big Jose puffed his cigar.

"So the boat, what if Rabbit and I were to take it to the Cove?"

Rabbit looked over at me, his grin instantly disappeared and then over to Big Jose. He reminded me of a playful wild animal after noticing a lion stalking in the bushes.

"I don't know you. But I believe you are who you say you are. Jose and I have the authority to approve anything, you understand, but this, this would be out of desperation. My friend, this boat I speak of ... there is not one, there are three."

"Three?" I held up three fingers.

"Yes."

"Well, what were John and J.C. going to do?"

"Probably recruit you, and some other friends ... definitely him," he said, pointing to Rabbit, who had gone into super serious mode. "Chances are they had not yet been told the extent of what they'd be doing."

It became apparent that the Joses were pretty drunk, and I started to wonder if they'd want to kill us after sobering up.

"Whoa, whoa, whoa, hold on now," Rabbit jumped in. "I believe I need to be briefed here. Talk to me, Mike."

I quickly told him what Jose had told me and as would be expected, Rabbit took over the conversation.

"What kind of boats are they? Schooners? Ketches? Why not just motor the fucking money? Or fly it? Or ..."

"Rabbit," he interrupted, "I don't know about sailing. I do know that whoever is doing this must look as if they are sailing for pleasure and own the boats ... we will give you the proper paperwork. The boats are new and sturdy. They are maybe forty feet long, but I don't know what type. Our other modes of transport are too easily compromised now."

"And fucking sailboats aren't?"

"Of course, there is always risk. But they would not suspect we'd use gringos in sailboats."

Rabbit made a smartass half grin face and hollered, "Yes, I think they would. Whoever they are. Have you thought about the fact that J.C. and John were taken by them. Ya think maybe they told them a thing or two?"

"Probably."

"Fuckin' A probably."

"John and J.C. had not yet been here. I believe they knew very little about what was expected of them. The events of the last two weeks have escalated the urgency of the situation. We need to move this cash soon. Would the two of you be ... willing to do this?"

"At this point, I don't know what I'd do. I'd like to find John and put all this shit behind me, but that seems pretty much impossible now," I said.

"We would love to help you get your cocaine money into the States," Rabbit said with what I thought was sarcasm until he went on, "but there's one thing that's kind of important. What do we get out of it if we pull it off?"

"We typically pay ten percent."

"And that would come to ...?"

"Four million."

Rabbit's face lit up.

I quickly said, "I'd just do it out of principle. Those motherfuckers probably killed my brother, so I'd love to fuck 'em over in any way possible."

Rabbit gave me an angry look and said, "Yeah right, but we're not Columbus, Mike. Jose, are we sailing the Nina, Pinta, and the Santa Maria? No. No, we should get paid. We'd need to put together a crew. A massive payoff is the only way to get even crazy motherfuckers to do something like this. We'd need to get back to Humboldt and find ..."

Jose cut him off, "My friends, it is a miracle that we have been brought together. Let's not go any further with this while we are drunk. Choose your girls and we will drive you to your hotel. Tomorrow we will meet at the same place, the Marina, the same time you were there today, and if you are still considering this undertaking, we will talk," he looked at me and continued, "and you ... you need sleep. Sleep is very important for your healing."

"I know."

Rabbit set out to coax a couple of girls to come back with him, and returned with a somewhat heavier Mexican girl with a very pretty face. Guess he changed his mind.

"Would you like a girl to be with you tonight? She could help you with your wounds and perhaps give a blow job?" Jose asked casually, but I declined.

"That is a wise decision. It would have been rude for me not to ask. Vamanos."

Little Jose, who looked like he was about to fall out of his chair, was helped up by a tall woman, who seemed to know him well enough to be annoyed.

"I did not expect to end the night this way. I told myself not to bring up the business of the boats anymore," Jose remarked, looking tired, "but here we are. Too much tequila. Fucking tequila."

We stood up and, along with four or five women, stumbled into the car. Delivered safely to our hotel, we bid the Joses good-night and withdrew to our rooms. Before we split ways, Rabbit hugged me and told me he'd do whatever I wanted to do, that he didn't really give a shit about the money, and I thanked him. But I could see in his eyes that he was thrilled at the prospect. Like I said, Rabbit was always down.

In bed I imagined going for it and pulling it off—getting John back and using the cash to get Dad out. All happy. After an hour of lying awake, I considered jacking off but figured I'd probably die if I tried. Rabbit and his little pretty face grunted loudly, she kept hollering, "Aye, poppy," and "Ju like dis Mexican pooosy?" I chuckled, wondering how the hell he was dealing with that, and eventually fell asleep.

Chapter 11

JOHN'S STORY

This guy standing in front of me is the scariest kind of dipshit. Jarhead haircut, little Hitler looking mustache. Chubby. Is he trying to make sure he never has sex with a woman? Maybe he wouldn't be so fucking angry. How can someone like this get elevated to a position of such authority, I wonder. Easily, I guess. Back in the day, cops were nothing more than toughs and thugs. Things aren't too terribly different these days.

He spits on me as he screams. He has God-awful breath. I distract myself by thinking this guy Dixon is an all around straight up disgusting motherfucker. But I try to be pleasant. I'll tell you everything I know. He asks me where it is. He calls me a fucka. Somewhere in Mexico, exactly where, I swear I don't fucking know. He hits me in the face with his blackjack—one of those little leather-covered things—and I can't help but let out a groan. I think my cheekbone is crushed. Jesus it hurts. I'm not this tough. He cracks me in the ribs a few times and tells me he's going after my brother. Mikey doesn't know anything, man ... he's not involved at all. He tells me someone better find out where the money is real soon. I've fallen to the floor and feel as though I may piss myself. I don't hear the rest of what he tells me before he storms out. I thank God. Then I pray to him to get me out of this.

J.C. helps me to the bathroom. Crazy bastard! Yeah he is, you ok? As I piss, I ask J.C. how the hell we're supposed to wipe our asses with these cuffs on. It's doable. I do my best to wash up in the sink. The door opens and someone throws a burrito in the room. J.C. tells me since he's been there they've only fed him burritos. They're tasty though. Really, J.C.? Tell me you didn't just say that? As we lean into our hands, awkwardly eating, we talk about our situation. What's to say? We're fucked. Proper fucked. J.C. is shaking. Maybe you can convince him to let us go so we can find out more, you think, John? Yeah, maybe, but then we'll probably end up getting killed by the cartel once they make us. We finish eating and I crawl to my spot on the floor. One of my ribs is killing me so I close my eyes and try to meditate. I do manage to access a bit of positive visualization. My ex-girlfriend was packed full of new age-y shit and even though I resisted, I absorbed a lot of it. She was crazy. But sweet. I still feel guilty for breaking up with her. I go there.

To Disneyland, with my mom and dad. Mike and I gather with other children around the teenager sweating his ass off in the Mickey Mouse suit. Dad forgot the camera, but none of us care. Mom smiles. She is happy and radiant, twenty-eight years old. Her long blond hair glows in sunlight. She tells my Dad to stop pressuring me—that I will go on Space Mountain when I'm ready. Mom is intelligent and gentle. Born and raised in the Midwest by tolerant Lutheran parents. She has a B.A. from Boston University and she is strong and opinionated. She was active in the anti-war movement, even as my dad fought. She is loving and genuine. In less than a decade she will be gone. Dad laughs. He is blond, handsome, and powerfully built. He could pass as a Viking. He did three tours in the Vietnam War. He's fun-loving and ballsy. He will be in prison in less than a year. He picks up my brother and me. Walking alongside Mom, he carries us down the path. We are a family. All together. Happy.

I've done this before. Usually when I've been too depressed or stressed out to fall asleep. I always visualize the same thing. I know it's kind of lame. Disneyland. Oh well, it usually works. I fall asleep.

Chapter 12

I woke up with a vivid memory of the dream I'd had that night. In it I was just a tiny kid, maybe three or four. Mom and Dad were with me as if nothing had ever happened to them. John was there too. We were at Disneyland. I was too young to remember that trip. What I knew of it I got from John. He talked about it a lot. I think it was the best day of his life or something. I lingered in bed a few minutes, touching my bandages, trying to open and close my cut hand. I heard Rabbit and Pretty Face start to get busy again and lurched into the bathroom. After bathing and drying off, I listened for them for a few seconds. I jumped when Rabbit pounded on my door and loudly asked if I was awake.

"Yeah dude, are you alone?"

"Uh huh, she split. Lemme in, man!"

I opened the door, and he came flying towards the bed, falling headfirst in a baseball-type slide.

"Woohooo, bro! Hey, I didn't want to get all crazy last night, but Mike, he said four million, dude! And I think he was serious. I mean, I liked the dude, and I think this thing is for real, man!"

"Well, let's meet them and see what's up. Maybe they'll kill us right away and we won't have to worry about shit anymore," I said while putting on my little preppy khaki short shorts.

He opened the white curtains, flooding the room with sunlight as he began laughing uncontrollably.

"I was too gone to really comprehend the magnitude last night. We could live the rest of our lives worry free, Mike. Rich and worry free. Now, who can we bring into this?" he asked grinning.

"Practically everybody. Jerry for sure, Ron and Nerd. Man, I wonder if they're OK. Young ... how many dudes would we need?"

"Four besides us. Two per boat, you know. I wonder where we can get some weed?"

"I don't know. Probably the Joses, as long as they don't kill us."

"They're not gonna kill us!"

I believed that too. The Joses seemed so sincere and so stuck in their own private debacle that I really trusted them. Still, I figured our chances were about fifty-fifty.

"What time is it?" I wondered.

"A little after eleven."

I looked at him with raised eyebrows.

"Dude, we slept in. We got in pretty late last night," he continued.

"Yeah, but I went right to sleep. You had your Mexican pooosy freak fest for who knows how long," I said smiling.

"You heard that shit? I know, right? And I picked her 'cuz I'd actually decided I felt like a little one-on-one sweetness last night ... so much for that!"

"That was hilarious. I'll meet you at the restaurant."

He hopped up and did a little happy dance out the door. I finished my routine and headed out to the restaurant. The same angry little girl was pointing to something on Rabbit's menu when I walked in and she looked up at me like she'd just as soon stick needles in my balls than wait on me.

"What's wrong with that kid?" I laughed as I sat down.

"Her name's Esmeralda and I think she hates gringos," Rabbit whispered.

"She's so severe. Jesus."

Rabbit tried tipping her twice what we had the day before, but it did no good.

We arrived at the hotel marina late, a few minutes after twelve, and discovered the Joses were nowhere in sight. I began to doubt the entire scenario, figuring once he'd sobered up, Jose had regretted telling us so much about their business, when Rabbit pointed out the luxury cruiser coming our way.

"Wow, holy shit," I said.

"El Dispuesto," Rabbit whispered, beginning to bounce out of excitement.

"Huh?"

"The name of their boat, see?" he said pointing at it as it backed into a slip.

"What's it mean?"

"I don't know."

This time only Big Jose disembarked, and when he approached, he told us Little Jose was still drunk and asked to be excluded from the day's business.

"How are you, my friends? Still feeling as brave as yesterday?" he asked while extending his hand.

I shook his giant hand and told him not quite.

"Bullshit!" Rabbit hollered. "We're as brave as ever. Question is, are you?"

Jose looked perplexed, "In what sense?"

"You still think you can trust a bunch of young gringos for this?"

"Rabbit, I have no doubt you have the cojones, and well ... what else do you need?" He studied Rabbit for a long time and then looked at me. "But if you fail, you will most likely die. You do know this. If you do not make the drop off, you will either already be dead or have tried to escape with the money ... in which case. ..."

I nodded silently.

"Those close to you, family, friends, etc. Do you understand?"

"With a four million dollar payoff, you really think we'd even consider that stupid shit? Really?" Rabbit said.

"No, I don't. Which is why using men such as you became a possibility in the first place. Before we discuss details, do you want to see?"

I stuttered, "See it … them … see the boats?"

"Yes, Mike. They are here in this marina," We stared dumbly. "Well?"

"Yeah," I said. "Hell, yeah."

We started walking towards the rows of docks, Jose in front of Rabbit and me, when Rabbit blurted, "Are you fuckin' kidding me? You have them here … here?" He pointed to the docks. "No one watching them?"

Jose stopped and pointed to a window on the fifth or sixth floor of the hotel. There, a man staring out into the marina waved, and I was reminded of the level of sophistication the guys had going. I asked Jose what exactly the dude was doing, even though it was obvious.

"There are two other men in that room. They are practically the finest snipers in Colombia. They take shifts. One well positioned man can defeat a small army if they don't know he is there."

"Well, we just saw him," Rabbit whispered.

"Those men don't know, but they are decoys. The *finest* snipers in Colombia are on the top floor … and you will never see them," he didn't point that time, "and they have a direct line to El Padrino."

He continued toward the docks. The sun beaming off the water reminded me of my beautiful, destroyed grow room and how the lights would blind anyone entering at night. I looked back at the stucco pink building, beginning to feel a little paranoid, and suppressed the ridiculous urge to wave.

Jose stopped at what Rabbit called a bitchin' 42' schooner and held out his arm, "After you, my friends."

We hopped onto the clean, white boat, Rabbit first, and I commented on its beauty.

"I told you they were high quality," Jose responded.

Rabbit laughed, "Well, considering what they're carrying …
yeah, they'd better be pretty fucking seaworthy."

We moved out of Jose's way as he approached and unlocked
the door to the cabin. He beckoned and we followed him down
the stairs into a galley featuring state-of-the-art mini-appliances,
granite countertops and teak cabinetry. At the end of the galley,
a wall of cleanly wrapped cash rose to the ceiling. Rabbit and I
shared a "holy fuck" look.

"Wow, there it is. So I guess it'll be close quarters," Rabbit
grinned.

"Not so bad," Jose answered. "This is all of it. It will be
divided between the boats. There will be room for sleeping."

Rabbit rubbed the countertop, "Oh, there won't be much
sleeping. We'll wanna sail day and night. Make the trip as quick
as we can. If we hit weather in California, and chances are we
could, we could be proper fucked."

"We are aware of that."

"How soon do you need us back here with a crew?" I asked,
wondering whether or not Nerd and Ron had made it, thinking
they probably hadn't.

"As soon as possible. If you don't return in, say, seven days,
we will have to begin putting together another arrangement."

"Fair enough," Rabbit said. "How do we contact you?"

"We'll get to that. First, let's go for a sail," Jose smiled.

"Really? Now?" I muttered.

"Mike, I am trusting you with tens of millions of dollars; I
need to assess your sailing abilities."

"Makes sense," Rabbit said.

"I will need to check the others when you arrive with them as
well …" Jose started as Rabbit sped up the stairs, clearly excited
at the prospect of being able to do what he loved most, which
was showing off.

He performed like a champ, effortlessly backing out of
the slip and motoring toward the bay, ordering us around
like a couple of dipshit deckhands, getting the boat heeled

at almost forty-five degrees like we were in the America's
Cup, following the right-of-way to the T, and coming about
perfectly when it was time to return. After we were safely tied
up two hours later, he looked at me and whispered, "Did I ace
that or what."

I smiled and allowed him to bask in his glory.

The three of us headed into the bright bar where we'd started
out the day before and, over Coca Colas, ironed out the details.
Rabbit and I would return to the States, and while maintaining
absolute secrecy, recruit four of the most capable dudes we knew
and set up a safe house for the money. Of course, Rabbit and I
knew that finding our friends was first priority and the secrecy
part of that plan might end up compromised. We'd return as soon
as possible and walk to a palm tree just before the docks, turn
and wave, walk to the bar, and wait for Jose. We'd check the
forecast, buy provisions, and get gone.

"If after you signal our man in the window, I do not arrive
within an hour, continue on your way."

"On our way," Rabbit muttered sadly, "to what?"

"Back to your life," Jose answered.

"Yeah, right," I whispered.

We finished with business and Jose ordered shots of Don
Julio for us to toast to our arrangement. With the remnants of
last night's party and a belly full of eggs, it took everything
I had to get that shot down. We stood up, said our goodbyes,
and headed to our hotel to gather our things. An hour later
we were at the airport buying our tickets home. With little
debate, we settled on catching a flight into Eureka from San
Francisco. We were more than likely much safer in the city
than back in Humboldt, but every bit of instinct told me to
go north.

We had surprisingly little trouble getting through customs; a fact we attributed to our new, preppy college-boy looks, and had dinner at SFO while waiting for our Eureka connection.

After boarding, we discussed how exactly we were going to go about accomplishing everything that needed to be done, but we got nowhere in that discussion. Ultimately, we had no idea what kind of crazy shit we were about to find going on in Humboldt, so it seemed a bit premature to plan more than one step ahead. Our first goal was to find out if anyone had heard from Ron or Nerd, and whether or not the DEA had traced Rabbit's pickup to his property. If they had, Young and Jerry might also have been in a world of trouble. I thought we should check Ken and Martha's first, but Rabbit thought we should head directly to his place.

It was dark by the time we landed. Fog covered most of the runway and the small airport. We stepped off the plane into the wet Humboldt night and headed for the shuttles. We made it to Hertz car rental a few minutes before closing and rented a Ford Explorer. Rabbit asked if I wanted to drive.

"I don't want to move my arms," I told him. "And besides, you're the better driver."

"Nah, dude, you drive good."

"I didn't say I didn't drive well; I just said you drive better."

"Yeah, I guess you're right."

We made our way to Garberville slower than usual due to the fog, and when we stopped for coffee, we were happy to discover that we were unrecognizable to a couple of dudes we knew. We didn't talk much on the way to Rabbit's. At one point he went over the plan again, which was mainly to get some guns out of the ground, have a quiet look around, and nothing more.

We pulled onto a small dirt road about a quarter of a mile south of Rabbit's, making sure that the car couldn't be seen from Wilder Ridge Road, and began making our way toward his property. The rain had let up and the night was dead silent. Occasionally, we'd turn towards a noise in the woods, freeze in place for a couple of seconds, and continue on. By the time we reached the gate, which was closed and locked, I wished I had a real jacket and a pair of boots.

Rabbit gently shook the chain and whispered, "I wonder if Jerry even made it here."

"Who knows? Where are your guns stashed?"

"Way down by my water pump. You don't have to come if you don't want to; it'll be rough in the dark ... in these shoes."

I looked up at the sky, "At least there's some moon. Let's just take it slow."

"Right on."

We headed down the driveway. I became increasingly confident that we were indeed alone on his property but still remained cautious. We took the trail leading to the pump.

"Remember when your dad installed that pump for my ma?"

"Yeah ... sort of ... no, not really."

He slipped on the gravel.

"Fuck these shoes!"

When we reached the pump, Rabbit walked to it and turned.

He began counting steps as he paced, first forward and then in other directions until he reached what sounded like a hollow box. He dropped to his knees and began clearing dirt and leaves off the top with his hands. I squatted across from him and began to help.

"Rabbit's stash," I said. "Is this passed down from your ma?"

"No way. This is my own private spot, one of 'em anyway. I dug this when I was like eleven or so."

"Really?"

"Yep," he pulled open the door and, after feeling around awhile, pulled out a burlap bag full of pistols. "Here, hold this."

He began rummaging for ammo and I asked him where he'd gotten all the guns.

"Remember that biker my mom was with just before she got sick?"

"Yeah."

"He was a real piece of shit you know, fucked with my mom pretty bad. He was holding all these for some Hell's Angels dudes. I took them from his shed in Redway a few weeks after she kicked him out."

"You evil little fucker!"

"Fuck that asshole. I hope they fuckin' ate him. Hand me the bag."

He pulled out two semi-autos one at a time, popped out their clips, and handed them to me while he stuffed bullets into the magazines. He handed me a clip, and I slammed it into the grip full Hollywood style.

"Easy," he whispered. He filled another clip and handed it to me. "Put this in your pocket."

I stood up, asked him what caliber gun I was holding, and pulled back the slide.

"Mike, no. Here, hand me that." He released the clip and emptied the chamber. "You don't want a round in the chamber with this thing down your pants, OK? This is the safety, by the way. Don't forget that. It's a Beretta. A nine-millimeter. I got bags of them."

"Jesus man."

I stuck the gun down the back of my pants and then, immediately realizing how uncomfortable that was, tried the front.

"Fuck, this is uncomfortable. Dude, this is bullshit." I thought of all the movies I'd seen where the hero carries his piece around in his pants. "You got a holster or something?"

Rabbit laughed and said, "Actually … actually, I do. I got a bunch of them. But doesn't it feel cool carrying it that way?"

"Oh yeah, I can't wait to blow my dick off!"

"Hold on," he dug back in the buried box for a minute and came up with another bag, one full of various gun holsters, and tossed it to me. "There … holster that sidearm, soldier!"

I rifled through the bag, pulled out a shoulder holster, and threw the bag back to Rabbit. He watched me as I adjusted and strapped it around my shoulder.

"You need help?" he asked. "You look like you're in pain."

I was, but I told him I was OK. When I was done, I practiced drawing a few times and Rabbit, noticing how much more efficient and easier to conceal the holster made things, decided he wanted one, too.

He returned the bags to the hole, laid the top down, and covered it with dirt and leaves. I stood up and shivered. The gun felt cold under my jacket. I hoped my body heat would warm it eventually. I looked up at a small clearing in the grey sky; the stars looked like they were trying to squeeze their way into view through the dense clouds and fog. I barely heard the clamor of Rabbit coughing and spitting as I silently prepared.

"What do you think is gonna happen, Rab?"

"I have no idea, bro ... I have no idea."

We made our way along the trail, stepping as lightly as we could, until we noticed the light coming from Rabbit's trailer. Passing the house, Rabbit peeked in and whispered, "I can't see. I can't tell if my plants are still there."

"How old are they?" I asked, trying to distract myself, my nerves needing calming.

"Brand new. Starts."

Coming around in the woods from the back of the trailer, we realized the kitchen light was on. Rabbit told me to pull my gun.

Chapter 13

"They're sneaky motherfuckers," said Rabbit. "If they got any-body posted up here, they're probably in the brush somewhere waiting for us to do exactly what we're doing. Fuck it. I'm going to the door. They want info so they'll probably try to draw down on me first."

"Are you fucking kidding me? INFO! They tried to kill the shit out of us!"

"Not really, man. Think about it. They ... dude, let's not talk about this now, OK? Get behind that boulder over there. You'll have total visibility. I've always wanted to say this ... COVER ME."

He turned and marched towards the front door as if all was normal. When he peaked in through the window, he ducked and went to his hands and toes, as if he was ready to sprint. I stood up. He put his hand in a stop position and waved for me to get back down. Slowly raising himself back up to the window as I became aware of how much lighter the night had become. If someone was in there, Rabbit would be visible to him. He looked in two directions back and forth a few times and slowly mon-key-walked around to the back of the trailer. A minute later, he emerged from the other side and ran towards me.

Breathing fast when he reached me, not because he'd been running, but because he'd just seen two heavily armed cartel-looking motherfuckers sleeping in his living room.

"Holy shit, dude," he panted.

"The DEA fuckers?"

"No, man, no. They look Colombian, but who knows. They're dressed in camo, man, and they got M-16s. For real? Christ."

"Let's get out of here," I said, but the look in Rabbit's eyes told me he had another idea. I began shaking my head. "No, no, hell no, Rabbit. You're my bro, but you *are* crazy. Let's get gone."

"Mike, think about what we could find out. This is a gift. We got the drop, man. Let's tie these fuckers up and get Vietnam on 'em, find some shit out."

"Rabbit, no."

"I thought you were pissed off, dude. C'mon. This has just been handed to us. One is lying on the couch ten feet from his gun, and the other is lying in the beanbag. My mom's beanbag, Mike! Mother *fucker!*"

That changed my mind. The image of the beanbag was more persuasive than any of Rabbit's bullshit. That was the beanbag that my dad would throw me onto, and John would usually sit in when he was visiting. It was part of Rabbit's hippie heirloom, a piece of his mom's sad legacy, defiled by some evil cartel cocksucker.

I put my head down, closed my eyes, and let the anger in, "Alright ... how?"

"Right through the fucking door. I'll kick it in and draw on the one on my ma's chair. His rifle is right next to him. I'd blow his head off straight away but I don't wanna get blood on the chair." I have no idea why but I chuckled at his calling the beanbag a chair.

"Stand away from him, Mike. Don't get close to him. If he moves, smoke him. Seriously, are you able to do that?"

"I don't know."

"You gotta do better than that, Mikey. Make sure your safety is off. Chamber a round."

"Huh?"

"Pull your slide back ... cock the gun."

"Oh. Yeah."

"You ready?"

"Yeah ..." My heart and breathing, along with my mind, began to race.

"You sure?"

I nodded and stepped into the clear. Rabbit quickly moved in front of me and I followed him to the door, staying low to the ground. He slowly peaked in the window and motioned for me to do the same. In a barely audible whisper, he asked if I saw them and I nodded.

He stepped back and said, "On three."

I was consumed by adrenaline by the time he kicked the door in, leaping into the trailer faster than I'd ever done anything in my life. Rabbit tossed beanbag dude's rifle behind us before the guy even opened his eyes, and I kicked couch man's away before he could sit up.

"STAY DOWN, MOTHERFUCKER! STAY THE FUCK DOWN!" I yelled at him, while Rabbit barked his own profanity-laced orders at the other. They put their hands up without us telling them to, and I was relieved to see they looked genuinely freaked out by what was happening.

"Alright, alright, alright," Rabbit sang as he backed up towards the kitchen, "keep your fuckin' hands up ..."

As Rabbit reached down to open the drawer for the duct tape, beanbag dude whipped his hand down to the pistol holstered at his waist. I was still drawn on couch man and didn't have a second to think. I heard a blast from behind me. A hole appeared on the man's throat and blood sprayed the beanbag and wall behind him. His hands went up to his neck and he started to make a horrific gargling sound. Couch man was shouting in Spanish. I wanted to tell him to shut up but shock and horror stopped me. The wounded man began reaching for his waist again. I opened my mouth to yell for Rabbit when another shot blasted out my eardrums. Beanbag man's head blew out from the back, Rabbit appeared and tore the beanbag out from under the dead man, saying something like, "Get the fuck off my chair!" Shaking, I tried to keep the gun leveled on couch man.

Rabbit looked back at me, "Mike, you OK?" I stood there dumbly.

"Mike?"

Finally I mumbled, "Yeah, yeah ... holy shit, man! We killed him."

Couch man started to holler something in English, and Rabbit flew over, slamming him in the head with the butt of his pistol, shouting, "Shut the fuck up right now!" The man's face began to flood with blood. "*I* killed him, Mike. Don't trip, bro. *I* killed him, OK? Do you understand that?"

I nodded.

"I killed that piece of shit," he whispered while backing up to the kitchen. "Keep on him, Mike. I'm gonna tie him up."

I had a difficult time keeping myself from glancing over at the bloody remains less than ten feet away from me. I did notice the beanbag really didn't get a whole lot of blood on it, and I was oddly happy about that. Couch man had put his hand on his head where Rabbit had smacked him and was looking at the floor in silence.

Rabbit set his gun on the countertop, walked over to the couch, and began wrapping the man's hands behind his back.

"What's your name? *Como se llama? Habla Engles Puto?*"

"My name is Carlos," he said angrily. "I speak English. They don't send us unless we speak English."

By the time Rabbit was done, the man's hands were absolutely glued to his back by twenty or so layers of duct tape.

"That should hold. Mikey, wet down a towel and throw it to me. I'm gonna wipe Carlos the helpless dumb motherfucker's face for him." I holstered the gun and went to the sink.

"Wow, this is killer. This is totally fuckin' rad. So where should we start? What do you think, Carlos? How 'bout what the fuck are you doing here?"

I tossed Rabbit the towel and he wiped Carlos' face, but fresh blood trickled down it. Rabbit tore a piece of the towel off and taped it around the top of his head and jaw World War II style.

"How's that Fuckface? Better?" Rabbit got right in his face.

"Who are you working for?" Carlos glared back at him and told him we were dead men and to go fuck ourselves.

Rabbit growled, "We don't have time for this shit." He exploded into the kitchen, tore open a drawer, and yanked out a giant Norman Bates-looking kitchen knife.

I asked him what the hell he was doing, but he blew past me and slammed the knife deep into Carlos' thigh. Carlos and I screamed together.

"Dude, whoa! What the fuck!?"

He was back in the kitchen in an instant, grabbing another knife, when Carlos squealed, "Stop! Stop! OK, I'll tell you! Please! Please! I'll tell you!"

Rabbit stood in front of him; knife poised over his other leg. He raised the knife higher as Carlos closed his eyes, and swiftly jammed it into the couch cushion. Carlos hollered like someone trapped in a nightmare. As horrific as it all was, it was clear Rabbit's tactic was effective—but I could never have done it.

Rabbit shouted over Carlos' bellowing, "Who do you work for? You workin' with the DEA?"

Carlos began slobbering and blathering, "Yes, yes of course. We work with any and all enemies of Pablo! We were supposed to capture any person to come to this place and bring them ... we were supposed to be in the trees but we got tired of the cold!" He put his head down.

"Where were you gonna bring us?"

"You are one of the people to move the cash, yes? Do you know what kind of people you're working for?"

Rabbit laughed, "Yeah, yeah, we're all fuckin' scumbags as far as I'm concerned, Carlos. You, me, the DEA ... but right now you're in my fucking living room ready to kidnap me." He picked up the knife again and said slowly, "So where were you supposed to bring us?"

"To a whorehouse in Oakland. Near the bay, off of Broadway ..."

Snapping out of my stupor I interrupted, "A whorehouse ... what!?"

"Yes, you know for storing goods and ..."

"Oh, a *warehouse*," Rabbit laughed.

"Yes, yes ... please pull this out," he groaned.

Rabbit took hold of the knife and twisted it. Carlos shrieked.

"I think we'll leave that in there a little longer," Rabbit said.

"Whose warehouse?"

Carlos grimaced and muttered, "Callihan, agent Callihan. That's the only name I know, I swear to you. He's DEA. He works with my boss. They want the cash, man, they're after the cash."

I stepped up next to Rabbit and asked, "What cash?"

"C'mon, you know what cash! They would not be going after you so hard if you didn't."

"Pretend we don't. What do you know about it?"

"Just that there is a lot of it and it is to come to the U.S ... by boats, by gringos ... by your people."

Rabbit laughed, "Our people. That's good. What happens in the warehouse? Are there people being held there?"

"I don't know. I've never been there. I don't know what they do there. It's DEA. It's not ours."

"And who exactly are you talking about when you say 'ours'?" I asked.

"*Perseguidos por Pablo Escobar.* Los Pepes. People persecuted by Pablo Escobar. We work with the authorities. DEA, Search Bloc, the military ..."

"You're just out for revenge?"

"Yes."

"And the DEA?"

"They want money ... and to destroy Pablo Escobar."

"What happens when they get him? You think they're gonna let you assholes keep truckin'? They'll jump all over your shit the minute he falls. Alright, three questions: one, the warehouse, what's the address; two, Callihan's full name and what he looks like; and three, did you ever see any other gringos who were involved with this shit?" Rabbit gripped the knife again, threatening.

"I don't know the address, but it is on Broadway," Carlos answered. "I haven't been there. I believe Callihan's first name is John, but I swear I don't know what he looks like. And no, I knew that Callihan began going after them, after everyone; he wants this money very bad. Now please, pull this fucking thing from my leg ... please, I don't know any more."

I stepped in front of Rabbit and yanked the knife from Carlos' thigh. Blood bubbled out of his pant leg like a hot spring.

"Mike, now we gotta tape that shit up," Rabbit said, obviously annoyed.

"The inquisition's over, you fuckin' sadist," I fired back, the reality of having just engaged in murder and torture sinking in.

"I'm sorry, Mikey, I'm just pissed off." He picked up the towel and tore off another piece while Carlos groaned. He performed the same quick duct tape procedure and washed his hands in the sink.

I studied the body sprawled on the floor, doing my best to suppress the panic and revulsion, but after a powerful stench reminded me that corpses often shit themselves, I was overcome by nausea.

"Rabbit ... Rabbit," I called out.

He came to me and asked if I was OK, but I was already throwing up. I ran to the sink and, feeling as though I was going to fall over, reached for the faucet. Emptied my stomach and fell into an intense crying jag, a thousand tragic images invading my consciousness with every shudder. I cried for my brother, I cried for my mom and dad, for J.C., for Rabbit and his mom, for Ron and Nerd and Jerry and everyone I'd ever known, and I suppose

I cried for the man who Rabbit had just shot. I cried so hard I thought I was going to die. It felt as though my soul was clawing and hammering its way out of my body.

My entire body was cramping when I came to, the kind of pain that doesn't seem possible, and I wondered if my muscles had torn themselves from my bones. Rabbit was speaking frantically but I couldn't hear a word he was saying. He was gently slapping my face. He looked worried.

Eventually, I heard him asking if I was OK and I answered no.

I sat up and put my hands to my face, "Oohhh, how long did I go on like that?"

"A long time. I've never seen anything like it. I think you had some shit pent up, Mikey. I thought you were going to die, I really did."

"So did I, bro." My body began to loosen up and I looked at Carlos. "What happened to him?" He was unconscious, lying back on the couch.

"He started laughing at you so I knocked him upside the head again. He's alive ... but he may have a little brain damage when he comes to."

I looked at him.

"He's lucky I didn't kill him, Mike. That would be the wise thing to do. This is the life we have now, dude! This is our fuck- ing reality! This motherfucker has seen us. He knows what we look like. I *should* smoke him ... but I can't ... and I bet we'll regret that before this is over. I really do. But you do need to accept this, bro. *This is our reality*. You feel me?"

"Of course. I just ..."

"Can you get up?"

"Yeah." The pain left me wondering if I'd be able to walk to the Explorer but I powered onto my feet. Rabbit grabbed a duffle bag and packed up some cash, a few CDs, and the men's guns and ammo. Carlos woke up and Rabbit leaned over him.

"It may take you all night, but you'll get out of that pickle eventually, Carlos. *Adios … hijo de puta.*"

We walked slowly up the road. Rabbit stopped at the top and turned around, his eyes moist with tears, gazing out at the land where he'd spent his entire life. We remained silent, but I knew what he was thinking: that he'd probably never see it again. Poor Rabbit. Such was the price of friendship, the price of loyalty. What a tremendous sacrifice. I put my arm around him and we continued on, our lives permanently altered.

By the time we reached the Explorer, we'd decided on a plan. Rabbit still thought the Sheriff was a bad idea. He stood outside of the car for a couple of minutes while I closed my eyes and laid back in an attempt to give him privacy. He was having a "moment" of his own. I'd bawled my head off for God knows how long, so I figured I'd leave him alone to do what he had to.

I felt like we were justified in killing that man, we really were defending ourselves, but I still wondered if I'd ever feel fully absolved. For normal people, regardless of the circumstances, the enormity of taking a life is impossible to reconcile. The psyche is irrevocably twisted and torn.

I jumped when Rabbit opened the door and hopped inside.

"Wow, this really, really does suck, man," he said. He was rubbing his eyes.

"No shit. We should drive somewhere else to crash."

"Yeah, of course, let's just pull off of King's Pink somewhere." He started the car. "Goddamn I'm thirsty. I didn't think to grab anything. Did you drink any water after you passed out?"

"You mean fainted?"

"We don't need to call it that."

"I drank a little. Shit, we have nothing to drink. I have to take my antibiotic."

He looked over at me, "Are you in pain? You still have Ken's codeine?"

"Yeah, he actually gave me a shitload ... I'll give you a couple."

I passed him a couple of pills and he swallowed them. I bit my tongue in order to stimulate a little saliva flow and forced the pills down.

"These will probably make my stomach sick, as empty as it is," I whispered.

"Roll a joint. Pre-empt that. If we can get through the night, we'll stuff our face with doughnuts in the morning."

"I can't roll unless you pull over, dude. I'll get sick."

Rabbit pulled over and I quickly rolled a sloppy joint. I lit it with the car lighter while he pulled back onto the road. Uncharacteristically, I let the smoke linger in my lungs for a couple of seconds before exhaling. It had been awhile since I'd last smoked weed and the smoke felt like it was gently scratching an itch. I smiled.

"Pretty good, huh?" Rabbit asked as I passed the joint to him.

"Uh huh."

He hit the joint for at least a minute, taking it in intervals but ultimately holding every bit in, until he released a huge rumbling cough.

"Take it easy, Cheech. See, that's why I don't hold my hits, man!" I pointed out.

"Yeah ... what a waste," he retorted.

"Like we've ever had to worry about that." I thought about something my brother used to say, something he got from the Fabulous Furry Freak Brothers cartoons, "Times of weed and no money are much better than times of money and no weed." Though meant as stoner humor, it made sense in Humboldt County, where the two things are essentially the same.

I took a second hit and passed on a third wanting to stay somewhat focused and not fall into a THC induced paranoia. Asking if I minded some mellow music, Rabbit put in Cat Stevens' Tea for the Tillerman. We drove, listening and occasionally humming along, while the weed and gentle lyrics soothed our minds and offered a more tolerable perspective on the ugliness we'd just experienced. Hiding my face in my window I managed to keep from tearing up until Cat busted out with *seagulls sing your hearts away, 'cuz while the sinners sin the children play, oh lord how they play and play, for that happy day, for that happy day!* After that, I went a big weepy one and tears ran down my face. Like I said, I was always waiting for the good part to start, and here I was, at what seemed like the end. Close the fucking book on Mike, I thought. I sniffed as I tried to compose myself by recapturing some of the anger, and Rabbit reached over and tousled my buzz cut. So much for hiding my tears. He pulled off the road and killed the engine.

"This music getting to you, Mike? It's me, man. My ma used to sing a lot of these songs, remember?" I didn't, but I said yes. "She had an awesome voice. You know she was in a band before I came along and fucked her life up?" he went on while I balled up a shirt for a pillow and laid my head on it. "That was the problem with all of our parents, Mike … us. You know that. We were. We fucked it up. The Age of Aquarius and all that shit, the dawn of individualism … self-realization. They were so busy trying to figure themselves out, you know, who they wanted to be, who they wanted to be with … left little time for us … sex, drugs, and rock 'n' roll. All of a sudden the fifties were over and you could just be a total fucking freak, be whatever you wanted to be. And that's great, but could there have ever been a group of people more into themselves than the fucking baby boomers? You can't just explode that kind of freedom onto a culture over the course of one generation. There's gonna be a glitch, a giant fucking hiccup. That's what we were. We just ended up cramping their style. I mean, really, if anyone should not have ever had children, it was the generation who ended up having the most ... all that fucking ... all that fucking. They get orgies and drugs, and what do we get? Fucking AIDS and just say no. That's just bitchin'. Fucking hypocrites. We're a generation raised by the most ... self-absorbed, self-centered bunch of hypocrites to ever walk this Earth ... subconsciously ... collectively harboring all this ... resentment towards their kids ... or at least the fact that they had to take care of 'em, and they wonder why we're not gushing with gratitude towards them, so grateful to be brought into this ridiculous shithole. Aaahhh, it is what it is. We'll be worse."

"I'm never having kids," I yawned, silently amazed. Rabbit was known to go off sermonizing in this way and whenever he did, regardless of what he was saying, I was always impressed.

"Hear, hear ... it's too wild a world, man. It's such a wild fucking world, Mike."

"That it is."

"That it is. That it is. Goodnight, Mike."

"Night, Rabbit."

Chapter 14

I woke with a throbbing head and neck ache. Rabbit jumped awake when I opened the car door.

"Shit, it's freezing," he whispered as he rummaged for the keys. He started the engine and cranked the heat.

"Did you sleep at all?" he called out the door.

"I guess," I answered, my piss steaming as it hit the ground, "a little."

"I'm starving! It's after seven, let's get down there, bro!"

"You think we should at least try driving past Ron's house?" I asked.

"No, man, no way. If those dudes lost Ron and Nerd, they'll be lookin' for them. If they were-"

I interrupted, "OK, if Ron is gone, Jack Randall is gonna know. Jerry's been running around for the last few days, so how many people you think he's told? I'm just saying, I bet Randall already knows everything … we just gotta figure out a safe way to see him."

Rabbit leaned back and gently nodded his head, "Mmm, maybe you're right. Maybe you're right." He flipped his wavy black hair off of his forehead—he'd already developed a modified shorter-haired version of the Rabbit hair flip—and began rubbing the stubble on his chin. I noticed that, more so than his short hair, it was his smooth shaven face that made him difficult to recognize, but with the black shadow of stubble surfacing, his face had begun taking on its old shape and character. "Let's just see what Dara can tell us and go from there. For all we know, it's already been blown up and everyone's looking for us."

Rabbit slowly eased the Explorer down King's Peak Road, continually tapping the brakes, as he ranted on about a variety of things that really pissed him off. For example, it was turning out to be a sunny day, and that pissed him off because he thought we'd be less likely to be identified in the rain. We stopped midway down the mountain to pull off a redwood branch that had fallen prey to lightning. The sun shot through the trees like a film projector, creating slivers of light and half-light that shimmered in the moist air. Even with sunglasses on, I was occasionally blinded by the spectacle. Once we reached Shelter Cove Road, Rabbit had voiced practically his entire catalogue of things that pissed him off and seemed to be relaxing. Though he didn't speak of it, I supposed the dead man decomposing in his living room was likely the chief culprit for his shitty mood, and with that thought, I had the first of what would become a lifetime of ugly flashbacks.

"You alright?" Rabbit asked. "You look like you're trippin'."

I wanted to say, I am. I wanted to say, we should have at least buried the Colombian, but all I got out was, "Let's not talk about it, OK?"

"Mike, as far as I'm concerned we never have to mention any of that shit ever again," he said, though we were both well aware that we probably would.

"Right on. Check out that buck!" I pointed to a decent sized deer standing on the hill ahead of us. Rabbit slowed down as we passed it. "Oh man, jerky for days!"

He shook his head, "I could never understand how dudes as mellow as you and John could kill a fucking deer. They're like so … majestic."

I shot my first when I was twelve, and since John put the big Native American, livin' off the land, cycle of life spin on the whole experience, I didn't hate it. We used to butcher them in the garage and give away most of the meat.

"You didn't seem to complain when you and your mom were eating our jerky."

"Those were good grinds. Still though, I don't think I could shoot one."

I reached up and touched my bullet hole, "Yeah, well ... me neither ... not anymore."

"God, I'm fucking starving. I hope Dara's got some scones this morning. That's what I'm in the mood for. Oh hell, yeah! Maple scones. Doesn't that sound awesome?"

I didn't answer. I couldn't really think about food. Rabbit was a master at distracting himself.

When we pulled into the gravel parking lot of the general store, two middle-aged men were climbing into a newer Ford pickup. They were pulling a sweet Bayliner speedboat that didn't look at all outfitted for fishing.

"What the fuck is that?" Rabbit whispered. A week before, neither of us would have given those guys a second thought.

"Joy riders?"

"Sheeeiiiit."

We waited for them to leave before we got out and climbed the stairs into the old store. Dara was in her early forties but looked like she was in her late twenties. She had the long exotic face of a European super model; pale and statuesque, she teetered on the border of beautiful and bizarre. Her features were such that by changing the shade of her skin, she could pass for any race or nationality. She had a stately demeanor, the result of her Ivy League education that had always intimidated me. After all the years I'd known her, I still felt like a dipshit in her presence, and rightfully so; compared to Dara, we were all dipshits.

"Dara?" I called out when I realized she wasn't behind the counter.

"Ssshh. She's probably in the back," Rabbit whispered.

Dara appeared from the bathroom door and quickly lifted her finger to her lips in shush fashion. "Hi Bob! Nice to see ya!" she fired off with a dead serious look on her face. We stared at her, dumbfounded. "It's been a long time. You gonna do some fishing?" she continued, while scurrying over to the counter. She picked up a pad of paper and pen and began writing frantically.

After a couple of long seconds, we finally caught on to what she was doing—fucking dipshits—and I said, "Yeah, yeah ... gonna see what's bitin'! How ya been?"

"I've been quite well, thank you," she held up the pad. *Feds have been in here. Probably bugged.* We nodded our heads. "Who's your friend?"

Rabbit, ever the actor, stepped up and held out his hand, "Tom Culwell, very nice to meet you."

"Likewise," she ignored his hand, writing on the pad while continuing her idle conversation. "This your first time to Shelter Cove?"

"Yes it is. Bob's been trying to get me up here for years. He says you can't beat the fishing."

"Well, he's right. You got a charter set up?" she held up the pad. *Did Ron and Randall find you?* I shook my head. Rabbit made a victory fist and we both smiled. Ron had made it.

"Nah, we're gonna play it by ear. See who's down there." I reached for the pad and wrote *Nerd and Jerry?*

She shrugged and took the pad, "That'll work. You picked the right time. This last storm was pretty heavy, no one was going out." She lifted the pad. *Something major happening. Ron and Randall went to motel in SF. You need to get away from here.*

"Yeah, I was ready to turn around yesterday," Rabbit laughed, reaching out for the pad.

"Well, what can I do for you? Would you like some coffee or pastries?"

"Absolutely. What have you got?" Rabbit held up the pad. *When did they leave?*

"I have raspberry scones just out of the oven."

"Yes! Two each, please ... and coffees to go."

"Comin' right up." *Three or four days ago.*

"Thank you so much." *Nothing else?*

She began bagging scones while Rabbit poured coffee into paper cups.

"Here you go! Still warm." She took the pad. *No, be careful.*

"Mmmm, those smell goooood!"

"Oh, they are delectable."

"Well, thanks again. Say, what time do you close again?"

"That depends on how my husband feels. You remember Dave—but usually around seven." *REALLY. Be careful.* She looked at us with glaring sympathy, like we were men on our deathbeds.

"See you then, maybe!"

"Nice meeting you!"

"You too. Good luck." She blew us a kiss as we stepped out the door. Rabbit sighed deeply after he started the engine. We looked at each other and then back at the door, where Dara stood watching.

"Fuck it. Let's go."

Five hours, three bags of Cheetos, and one terrifying speeding ticket later, we were pulling into a parking spot a few blocks from the Best Western Rabbit had told Jerry about. We figured we'd run our limit with the rented Explorer in Clifford Kazinski's name. Rabbit hopped out, grabbed our bags, and began jogging along the sidewalk, leaving me stumbling along behind him. Rabbit was standing outside of the front desk when I approached the building. He looked angry and anxious.

"They didn't stay," he hissed. "They asked for Joe Gibson but they didn't fuckin' stay," he ran his hands through his hair.

I put my head down, "Waste of fucking time, man."

"What should we do?" I motioned toward the stairs. The motel was small, two stories and maybe thirty rooms, but there was a pool and hot tub. "Should we drive back, crash here tonight … or what?"

"I don't know, man. Shit! I feel like a beer. You wanna get drunk?"

"Sure," I answered, unable to come up with a better idea, at a complete loss. Rabbit got us each a room and went off to buy us swim trunks. I headed to the front desk to find out where the closest liquor store was.

I found a pretty middle-aged lady working the desk and I smiled nervously when she greeted me. Surprised Rabbit hadn't mentioned her. She looked like an aging stripper or call girl, like she might have been a gorgeous angel had she chosen another road. I asked about the store and she asked what we had planned for the evening.

"We're gonna hot tub. My friend, Clifford, who you met, he'll probably go out later. Me, I'm pretty tired."

"You look like it. Were you in an accident?"

"Yeah."

"Well the hot tub's on and the pool is heated; it might feel good to soak a bit."

"Cool, so ... liquor store?"

"Oh yeah, sorry ... about a block away, that way" she pointed down the street. "Let me know if you need anything."

I thanked her and took off for the liquor store. At the store, I bought a twelve pack of Guinness, a bag of Cheetos, two giant cigars, and a Styrofoam cooler. The man at the counter smiled as he rung me up. "Nice day for this huh?"

"I think so."

"Enjoy."

"Thank you."

Back at the motel, I dumped ice in the cooler. Rabbit and I put on our new trunks and headed for the hot tub. A young father and his two daughters were playing volleyball in the pool. Ignoring the NO ALCOHOL sign, Rabbit set the cooler down and opened two bottles with a knife. The sun's reflection made me squint as I slowly lowered myself into the water. I was about to sit down when I noticed the sexy front desk lady had a clear shot of me.

I raised my bottle to her, correctly assuming she didn't give a shit about the no alcohol rule, and sat facing the pool instead. Even though I wanted to, I didn't want to seem rude by putting my back to her altogether.

I took a swallow of beer and shut my eyes. In the distance, probably in one of the rooms, a radio was playing a Spanish station. I couldn't hear the lyrics; the accordion and inflection of the DJ's voice gave it away. The traffic on the street hummed, squealed, and occasionally honked me out of my reverie. In the middle of my third beer, I felt a buzz kicking in and I took a deep breath, welcoming it. The father and daughters joined us. I gave him a beer and he told me their story. His wife's father was in the hospital, dying. They'd been staying in the motel for about a week. He was an unemployed logger from Coos Bay Oregon who hated tree huggers. Rabbit told him we were tree huggers and there was no reason to hate us. The man smiled politely. Maybe because he liked us, but more than likely because Rabbit and I looked so much like men not to be fucked with.

We stayed there until our skin was pruned beyond recognition and, after gathering our trash, went in for showers. When I finished, I gently dabbed my face and body dry and got dressed. I called sexy front desk lady and asked her to call us a cab. She told me she was off in a half an hour and would be glad to give us a ride.

"Sure ok, that'd be awesome. We're not really sure where we want to go though."

"Well, what do you guys want to do?"

"Drink."

"I'll help you with that."

"Cool. We'll come down in a half hour."

"Make it twenty minutes. The next shift usually comes a little early."

"Ok."

Sexy lady was still behind the desk when we stepped into the office. "Hey, you look better," she said, smiling. I actually felt a little sick from the Kong Dong cigars I'd bought, brilliant idea that was. She paid barely any attention to Rabbit, which made both of us feel like we were in the Twilight Zone.

"Thanks, I feel better," I lied. "Should we come back?"

"No, we can go. Next shift's here, she's in the bathroom. My name's Lynette, by the way. C'mon."

"I'm Mike." I thought she'd make a perfect Snow White. The skin on her arms was like porcelain, not a noticeable pore, hair or freckle. I realized the only thing that made me think she was at all tore up was her age and the fact that she was working the front desk of a shitty motel. She was really quite lovely. Of course, the five beers I'd just slammed may have aided in that newfound perception.

A few minutes later, she pulled off a perfect lightning speed parallel park on Columbus Avenue. I quickly stepped in front and opened the door for her. Walking in, I was struck by the splendor of the place. It had a full-on bohemian artist vibe going, but maintained an elegant flavor with stained glass chandeliers, a thick oak bar, classic posters and photos on the wall.

We sat at the bar and I started pounding drinks. Rabbit quickly struck up a conversation with a couple of women, leaving me alone and somewhat nervous. After a bit of blathering about ex-loves and the state of the world, Lynette asked me what I was looking for.

"What am I looking for ... you mean like, oh my big search, what life-"

"No Mike, I'm talking about now—you're looking for something ... or someone."

I felt the alcohol open the floodgates and let loose. "My brother. He's gone. I can't tell you what happened but, he's missing ... and I need to find him."

"Is he in trouble?"

"Yes."

"What's he like?"

"Everyone loves my brother, John, including me. Very much. He's just a REALLY good dude, tough as fuck and a really good dude. He'd do anything for anybody. And he always ... my Dad's been in jail since I was like five and my mom died when I was thirteen ... but John always took care of me."

She watched me with a sad, soulful expression, "That's sad. My Daddy was an alcoholic. You know, I was pretty fucking young when it occurred to me that one of the strongest factors affecting a child's happiness is the drug of choice of their father."

I quickly moved the conversation to the lighter side, and we went on trading jokes and funny stories, until I felt entirely comfortable with her. I discovered the lines on either side of her mouth had developed from years of smiling and they became beautiful to me. I confessed that I thought she might have been a stripper when I first met her. She slugged my shoulder and I managed to stifle any reaction to the pain shooting through my body. I told her I thought she was beautiful and she thanked me.

After two hours of talking, she put her hand on the back of my head, "I have to go, Mike."

She stood and said goodbye to Rabbit, who was by then thoroughly stuck on one of the girls he'd been talking to. He told me we'd now be heading to a nightclub; the thought of that made me cringe.

"Dude, I'm going to stay."

"Really. Okay, I'll stay with you," Rabbit said, looking heartbroken. I told him to go ahead, I didn't care.

"You sure, Mike?"

"Yeah, go ahead."

"Ok, don't get too shitty. I love you, man." With that, he hugged me and followed the girl out the door.

The place began filling up with loud yuppies around six o'clock, and I decided to search for a quieter place. I found a little coffee shop a couple of blocks down the street and slipped in for a cup and a pastry, hoping to sober up a little.

After a cup and a scone, I thanked the counterman again and shuffled back into the night. Searching for another bar, I relaxed deeper into a tranquil haze, the past and future slowly gliding away from my awareness, until I reached the summit of the alcohol buzz, that perfect section just before the downhill slide. I could have gone back to the motel and passed out. I should have.

Instead, I followed the voice of a chanteuse into a perfect little shithole at the end of the North Beach strip. Inside, I found the scene I was looking for, one in which I was immediately the novelty. No more than six people, all well over forty, sitting sideways at the bar, facing a fallen beauty as she surrendered her dreams and sang for them. In her mid-fifties, she looked like one who was not going lightly into old age. Her hair was dyed copper red and she wore bright red lipstick. She looked like she'd been pretty, but years of failure and disappointment had chiseled that away. She leaned on the piano, her cheap red dress falling off her shoulder, and threw everything she had into a classic jazz song. Whether in the throes of buzz perfection perception or she was exceptionally good, I thought her singing was sublime, and I mumbled, "This is the one."

"Say again?" It was the bartender, black, friendly, and sad looking, nothing like the loud young bartender at Vesuvio.

"Oh, I've just been looking for the right bar ... I think this is the one ... to post up in for a while."

"Glad to have you ... but you sure? You may get bored here, son."

"No sir. As long as I got a beer in front of me ..."

He smiled, "I see, you wanna get high then? Wanna get drunk?"

"Yes, I do."

"Well, what'll it be then?"

I looked at the taps. "No Guinness?"

"We ain't in Ireland, son!"

"Just give me a plain old shitty American beer," I slurred.

"How 'bout an Anchor Steam? It's American, but ain't nothing about it shitty!"

"Bring it on, good sir!"

He handed me the glass. "Start you a tab?"

"Please."

"So what happened, you get in a fight?" he asked, his tone honest and sincere.

"What's her story?" I pointed to the singer. "She's got a beautiful voice."

"Yes she does. Name's Sharon Jones. She had a bit of the glory in New York City for a time, but the world got the best of her. I'm sure she'd have liked things to have turned out different— but I'll tell you, that woman puts her heart and soul into every damn song she sings up there. She's been with that piano player there for most her career."

"That's her husband?"

"No, no, just been with him. Her voice will bring you to tears, you wait, she'll have this whole place cryin'."

I laughed.

"You wait and see; you look like you're on the edge as it is."

"I suppose I am." I downed half my beer.

He watched me closely and said, "You know I got a grandson 'bout your age. He got caught up in L.A.; Compton, that's where I'm from."

"Straight out of Compton," I rapped, smiling.

"Oh son, don't even start with that shit!"

I laughed and put my hands up, "I know, I know ... I had to, though."

"He's a smart kid, got real potential, but he went and got himself in serious trouble few months back and I'm afraid we're gonna lose him."

I stopped laughing. "How?"

"Same way I lost my boy, his daddy, he's been in the penitentiary for almost ten years now."

"What happened?"

"Cocaine, that's what happened. My boy got caught up in the early eighties, got himself a murder rap; I brought Jeffrey, that's my grandson, I brought him up shortly after."

"I thought you said he was in L.A."

"He is ... he caught his case down there, that's where he's being held. I thought he'd have a better chance up here, but I was wrong. There's only so much a man can do, you know what I'm sayin'?"

"I do."

"I did so bad with my boy; I thought I could redeem myself by making things better for Jeffrey, but wasn't nothing I could do. My wife, bless her heart, she said we ought to get out of the city, move to a small town, and I'd tell her, as soon as we win the lottery we gonna do that! Nothin' else I could do except try and teach him what's right, but you know, sometimes, most the time, that ain't enough. Boy's gonna be a product of his surroundings, can't keep 'em with you all day."

"Where'd ya live?"

"Down in Bayview."

"I don't really know the city that well."

"Bayview ain't much different than Compton."

"Is he in for murder, too, your grandson?"

"No, but he may as well have. He's caught up in a crack distribution ring. They're trying to put these boys away for twenty, thirty years. Gotta wonder what's more harmful, crack or the law, you feel me? The so-called remedy's worse than the sickness."

"Does he have a good lawyer?"

"Sheeeiiiiit, he ain't got money for a lawyer. None of those boys got money. You watch the news, listen to the police, and you'd think these crack dealers makin' millions off a misery, but you tell me then, you tell me why they all still livin' in the projects? Somebody makin' money, but it sure as hell ain't those boys."

"It's the Colombians."

"Say again."

"The Colombian cartels, the source, they're making the millions," I caught myself slurring.

"That's right! Damn straight! And the white people middling all the deals, them too."

The singer announced she was taking a break, and everyone clapped.

"What does she do on her break?" I asked. "Can I buy her a drink, or give her a fat tip or something?"

"What's your name son?"

"Mike."

"Mike, I'm James. Lemme tell you something, two things you never got to ask a lounge singer you can do for them, buy them a drink or give them money. Never."

"Well James, I *am* new at this."

"I know. I know you are son. But try not to get too used to it, ya hear?"

Sharon made her way towards us, stopping to accept each patron's individual form of praise and gratitude, kisses, hugs, and handshakes, until the ancient shell of a man five stools down from me, called out, "James please get Sharon an Absolute martini and another for me."

"Sure thing, Hank, but this youngster here beat you to it ... in fact, he's buying the next round for everyone."

Like a chorus line, they spun in unison and I raised my glass, a little embarrassed. All but the couple who'd ordered drinks had no clue that I was even there. They thanked me and raised their glasses back. The old man looked pissed off and I felt bad that I'd just thrown salt in his game, as Sharon languidly made her way to where I was sitting.

"Thank you, handsome. Now who would go and do a thing like this," she touched my bruised forehead, "to a face like that?" She had a mild southern accent and a voice so deep I wouldn't have believed it was her singing if I hadn't seen it.

"Oh, any number of assholes, but it's a long story. I really like your singing. You have a really awesome voice."

"Thank you very much, that really means something comin' from a young man."

James set a martini in front of her and leaned over the bar, "How you feelin' tonight Sharon, sound like an angel up there!"

"Thanks sweetie, you know me as long as I got an audience, I'm happy. Charlie on the other hand he's bein' a real pain in the ass tonight. Can't you tell?"

"No."

"Me neither," I said.

"He's all over the place! Bastard's been drinkin' since noon."

"Me, too!"

"You working today?"

"Nope."

"Then sugar, you got every right to been drinkin' since noon."

She laughed and walked away, and that was the first and last time I spoke with Sharon the dive bar chanteuse.

"Can I get another one?" That was probably my twelfth beer, and from there, everything became a bit blurry. I remember Sharon getting the small audience singing along with her for a few songs and me humming along without a clue until the chorus, which I'd eventually picked up, and everyone applauding themselves at the end of each tune. Although proper shitfaced, it all sounded pretty horrible to me and I wished she would have kept us out of it. A room full of drunks singing sea shanties or Irish drinking songs was bad enough, but you get them wailing away at *Bye Bye Blackbird* and you got a full-on train wreck on your hands. James told me stories of his days in Folsom, though I don't remember why he was there. Sharon went home with her wasted piano player. And one by one, the other denizens and I converged in the middle of the bar, brought together by common drunkenness, hollering away as if we'd known each our whole lives, grateful for the company. I felt like I was nearing lights out, so I had James call me a cab. I had the cabbie drop me off at a 24-hour doughnut shop a few blocks from the motel. I felt like doing something nice for Rabbit and I knew doughnuts in the morning would make him giddy. After buying two dozen assorted and a half-gallon of milk, I was stumbling down the street towards the motel, daydreaming about the next morning and the joyous look on Rabbit's face as I pulled them out from under my bed. I noticed our rental car parked on the street, and in a fit of drunken brilliance decided I'd look really cool if I were to kick the bumper.

That would have been all good and fine had it not been under surveillance.

Chapter 15

They waited until I was back at the motel, struggling with my room key before grabbing me. Two of them, guns drawn, demanding I get on the ground with my hands behind my head. Oddly, I couldn't bring myself to ruin my doughnuts, and I began to gently lower them down.

The cop closest to me—who looked just like John Denver—yelled, "Drop the box mother fucker, drop it right now!"

Wow, that's no John Denver. Is that a Texas accent?

"Hands behind yer head, you li'l sunofabitch!"

Yep.

Within seconds, I was thrown into the back of a van with F. Bueller Electric painted on the side. I wondered if it was a Ferris Bueller reference—like some joker cop thought it'd be funny. It kind of was.

And then it hit me. Sheer terror. Rabbit had shot a man, killed him. We're done. Close the fucking book on Mike and Rabbit. I heard John Denver talking on the radio. He told someone the address of the motel and the room number. We'd been waiting a few minutes, when a voice came over the radio and told the cops to go ahead, that they'd be there in a minute. John Denver told them to "be very careful with the other asshole; he's extremely dangerous." I desperately wished I could have sent some sort of message to Rabbit, but there was nothing I could do. As we passed the front office, I wondered what it all looked like to the lady who had replaced Lynette at the front desk.

Denver's partner reached back and put a black hood over my head. After considering that for a moment, I became almost pants-shitting scared. I hoped I was headed to a real jail and not to the Oakland warehouse, but that hope was crushed the minute I recognized the rhythmic bumping of the Bay Bridge sections as we drove over them. John Denver and his partner occasionally spoke some random bullshit. A Tom Petty CD was playing, and they spent a good five minutes discussing his greatness. I felt like telling them that Tom Petty had undoubtedly been a drug user at some point in his career, as was every other rock hero they might worship. Maybe get them to see the light, soften up a little bit. Yeah, right. Cops have to avoid ambiguities and reject anything that might muddle their fervor towards their mission. If they didn't they'd be lousy cops and probably end up fired. Or they wouldn't be cops in the first place.

Eventually the other cop said, "Hey Mike, you know we got a lot to talk about, you know that, right? You gonna be straight with us?"

I wanted to tell him to fuck himself, to eat shit, and suck John Denver's dick, but, of course, like a giant pussy, I answered, "Definitely."

I tried preparing myself for whatever form of beating or torture I would soon be enduring. I tried projecting myself into a happy place. I tried praying. But it wasn't until I thought of John and my Dad that I became angry and, with that, some semblance of courage began to develop. It wasn't until then that I recognized that anger was the most important ingredient in my questionable blend of bravery. Without it, I'd have been totally fucked.

We reached the warehouse. Someone opened the door and threw me onto the pavement. This is really, really gonna suck, I thought.

Under my breath I whispered, "Ouch," and I wondered what the hell I'd done to deserve this.

"Where's Callihan?" John Denver asked someone.

"I don't know? You're big boys … you can find him."

"Where the fuck is he?"

"Easy, General Lee!" The voice was laughing, "I'm just razzing you. He's in his office."

John Denver and his partner guided me up a flight of stairs and into what seemed like a brightly lit hallway.

"Fucking CIA asshole, I hate that guy," he mumbled, pushing me along.

After hearing him say *CIA*, I really felt like the end had come. I tried to muster a little hope, but I knew that these were an "end justifies the means" bunch of assholes, and because of that, merciless. I shut my eyes, preparing for the worst.

"Here he is, Lieutenant," John Denver said, sounding frustrated—the CIA man's attitude had gotten him all butt-hurt.

"Take his hood off," another man interrupted.

My eyes slowly adjusted to the fluorescent lights as I opened them to see a brightly lit office carpeted with what looked like Astroturf. The white walls were bare except for a mirror and huge bulletin board covered with photos of gnarly looking dudes hanging out together, shaking hands, walking down the street, exchanging bags, and doing whatever other shit dudes like that do together. Although I only had a quick glance, I noticed all the photos had names and dates written on them.

The man leaning back with his hands behind his head struck me as the real deal, early forties with long dark hair and a week-old beard. I thought I recognized him from somewhere but figured he just looked like someone from a movie, the kind of guy who could kill everyone in the room with his bare hands.

"Mike, I'm Special Agent Jonathon Callihan."

His calm voice and intelligent demeanor put me at ease.

"Hello," I said dumbly.

"Do you know why you're here?"

"Uh … no?" I answered like I was asking a fucking question, immediately realizing how terrible I was at this.

"This will be much easier for you if you're straight with me, Mike." He leaned forward and, folding his hands on the desk, lowered his voice. "Contrary to what you might think, the criteria the Drug Enforcement Agency has in place for potential recruits is not terribly stringent."

He paused for a moment and continued, "I've been at this a long time, Mike. There are a myriad of reasons applicants are looking for a position in law enforcement, but one that is becoming more prevalent every year is that the recruit is in some way predisposed to violent behavior. Now, I'm sure you're not a bad kid but I have a job to do and, frankly, your life is worth nothing more to my superiors than your usefulness to them." He stood up and opened the door. "If you don't start talking to me in five seconds, I'm going to ask agent Stevens to beat the living shit out of you until you do."

I was no longer put at ease by his intelligent demeanor. "Because of the money? The money in the boats?" Pussy.

"That's right. See how easy that was? Your brother and his friend, Jim Carmichael, made an incredibly bad decision when they got involved with Colombian drug cartels."

"Do you know where they are? All I want is to know where my brother is."

"Is that right? Is that why you and Clifford Kasinski were standing outside the home of Alberto Valenzuela and shot at my men while they were attempting to arrest you?"

"Arrest us? They were trying to kill us before ... They shot me in my trapezius!"

"Your what?"

I pointed to my bullet hole, "In my trapezius muscle!"

"Ouch! ... Is that why you traveled to Cabo San Lucas shortly afterwards? Just wanna find your brother, my ass."

"Yes! Is he here?" I shot back, wondering why he hadn't brought up Rabbit's murdered Colombian, thinking he probably didn't know about it.

"No."

"Do you know where he is?"

"No, no I don't. He was released shortly after he was apprehended. I was in Mexico so I didn't get a chance to see him directly, but I was told by my men that he agreed to do what he was instructed to do and that we lost communication almost immediately. He either went AWOL or was killed. I thought you might be able to tell me."

"No one's heard from him. What about J.C.?"

"Later. What did you do in Mexico?"

I hesitated.

He repeated, "What did you do? Look, we know your crew was being tapped to move this money, OK? You need to tell me what you know, Mike."

"The man who was killed, whose car we escaped in, he had an appointment book. We went to an appointment he had in Cabo and met the dudes he was supposed to meet. Otherwise we would've had no idea what was going on."

He laughed and raised his eyebrows, "Good God, you guys *are* crazy ... you should consider joining the agency. We are always in need of men who actually have a pair."

I wasn't sure what he was talking about. I was scared shitless. But then, I wondered if perhaps I did have balls and because I'd grown up with true bad-asses like Rabbit and my brother, I just hadn't yet realized it. The thought made me momentarily happy.

"Man, I'm telling you, John didn't tell me a thing about any of this. I wasn't involved at all."

He sighed. "I'm not really sure your brother was either, to be honest with you. Jim, or J.C. as you call him, was in the recruiting process when we brought him in. We're not sure how far he'd gotten. Who did you meet with? Was it any of these men?" He pointed to the bulletin board, "Go ahead. Stand up."

I walked to the bulletin board and, after pretending to study the photos, said, "No. I don't see him."

"Are you sure? What did he say his name was?"

"Rico," I lied.

"No last name?"

"No."

"And what did you talk about?"

Again, I hesitated.

He went on, "Ok, let's jump ahead. You are going to leave here and assemble a crew. You will structure a new arrangement with either the source you've obtained in Cabo or one that we will provide for you. You will bring the cash into United States territory where you will then surrender it to us. In return, you will be paid a generous sum ... and we won't charge you, Clifford, or your brother with conspiracy to distribute cocaine, resisting arrest, attempted murder of a law enforcement officer ... murder."

Shit. He knows.

I sat back down, "That's ruthless."

"Yes, it is."

"Why don't you guys just go get the money?"

"So you know where it is."

"No."

"Even while engaging in an operation as secret as this one, we are sometimes presented with certain ... restrictions. If it's in U.S. territory, it's all ours."

"Where does the money go?"

"Tell me what you learned in Mexico. Wait, hold on, you want a soda?" he got up and moved towards the door. "Somebody grab me a couple of Cokes." A few seconds later, John Denver was at the door holding two sodas and, judging by his sneer, it was obvious he wasn't too thrilled to be playing waiter to me. I thanked him after he handed me one, and he glared at me in silence. Callihan took his soda without saying a word.

"What did ... what did you say his name was, the man in Cabo?"

"Rico?" I almost forgot what I'd told him.

"Yeah, what did he tell you?"

"He told us they've had difficulties bringing cash and coke into the U.S. and that they're trying to ... they're trying something different."

"So he trusted you?" He seemed surprised.

"Yeah, I guess. He was pretty drunk."

He quickly asked, "You drank together?"

"Yeah, we had dinner and hung out at a strip club ..."

"Goddamn," he grinned and looked at me with what seemed like genuine admiration. "You boys got right in there. Did he know about your brother?"

I was feeling increasingly nervous talking to him, wishing I hadn't said anything about our time in Mexico. My mind was simultaneously attempting to process his demand that I deliver millions of dollars belonging to the motherfucking Medellin cartel or be at the mercy of the United States criminal justice system. Either way, I was completely fucked.

"A little, he knew about the arrangement. If I bring this money to you, what then? I'll be a fucking dead man."

"No you won't. These are men whose organization is on the verge of collapse. We could send you somewhere, if necessary."

"What if something goes wrong? What if we don't pull it off?"

"That depends."

"On what?"

"On the situation, Mike. Look, you're not in any position to negotiate here. We set the terms, understand?"

"Uh huh," I looked at the bulletin board. "Would you guarantee our uh ... what do you call it ... immunity, if we at least tried and we don't make it?"

"Again, that depends."

I put my hand on my forehead. It felt like I had the elephant man thing happening again. It was incredibly sore.

"Mike, you're basically fucked here. I'm sorry, but this is how it works."

I continued rubbing my forehead.

"Mike?"

"Huh?"

"You realize you really have no choice."

"So you're forcing us to do illegal shit?"

"Call it whatever you'd like. It's a process ... an extremely effective process."

"Well, it didn't seem to work on my brother or J.C." I said, hoping he'd drop a little more info on me.

"Well, like I said, I'm not sure what happened to them. I was told J.C. was embarrassingly pliable, but that your brother, on the other hand, seemed almost professionally evasive. He was apparently eager to protect you. Sounds like a good big brother."

"He is. How do you know he's ... how was he supposed to stay in touch with you guys? What was he supposed to be doing exactly?"

"Same thing you will, Mike. Put a crew together, orchestrate a deal, and -"

"No, I mean how do you know he's not doing that? How was he supposed to stay in touch with you?"

Callihan raised his eyebrows. "Just a telephone. He was supposed to call me so we could talk and continue calling me once a day. He never called. Not once. So, he's either hiding out somewhere hoping this shit blows over or, I'm sorry to say, but quite possibly ..."

He raised his shoulders clearly uncomfortable with what would've come next.

"Why do you say quite possibly?" I asked, practically ready to cry.

"Because he knew if he didn't do what he was told, we'd come for you."

"And J.C.? What made you so certain he'd play ball?"

"He was scared shitless."

"So when was the last time anybody saw them?"

"They were dropped off at the Powel Street BART station a few days ago. I would have thought that the Medellin boys made them, but as far as we know they never even made contact after we released them. We've had all the key players under surveillance for months; that's how we came upon J.C., and unless they played us, they were as perplexed by their disappearance as we were."

"So you didn't have them wearing a wire or anything? No tracking device type thing?"

"No, no they'd have been executed within minutes if they were found wearing a wire. We don't need to gather evidence on these guys. We want to cripple them by confiscating their assets. Their power is in their profits. Take that away and they have nothing. We're just talking about one load here. There's a hell of a lot more where that came from. Panama used to be a safe haven for their cash but that's in the process of ending. The Medellin Cartel is on its way down. How well do you and your friends know how to sail, navigate ... in the middle of winter?"

"Well enough. I know dudes that are much more capable than I am. I know it's prime cruising time in Baja right now, but not so much north of L.A."

"We'd rendezvous well before that, off of San Diego. You'll have a transponder. Just get there, drop anchor, and wait. We'll take care of the rest." He reached into his desk and pulled out a folder. "Here, memorize these numbers. Once you have, you can go."

I opened the folder and, after pulling out the one page it contained, I began to read. There were only a few things for me to memorize, and I was able to do it in less than two minutes. Three phone numbers, one for Callihan, and two for two other agents—his bosses I figured—a couple of dates, and a set of coordinates. I told him I got it and he quizzed me.

Afterward he said, "Those men that got chased down your driveway can come out of hiding now. I tell you they dropped completely out of sight. It's got my superiors thinking we're dealing with a serious set of professionals here. I still can't believe Dixon lost every one of you."

"Dixon, is he the chubby baby-faced dude?" I made it a point to remember that name.

"That's him. Everyone you recruit will be sufficiently compensated, you can tell them that. But you're a tight bunch up there. You all look after each other. It shouldn't be too difficult convincing your boys to help you out. Christ, from what I've seen of them, they'll probably jump at the chance."

Realizing I had forgotten about Rabbit, I quickly asked what Callihan was planning to do with him.

"Nothing ... honestly, you exhibited a level of reason I didn't really expect, so I gave the order to leave him be."

"What do you mean 'level of reason'? You thought I'd be harder to ... to deal with?"

"Not necessarily. You're obviously a bright kid, Mike; it's not so much fear as a thorough understanding of your situation ... that's what I was looking for."

"So what, that's it?"

"Yep." He stood and called out the door, "Stevens! Stevens, we're done in here."

John Denver appeared and asked Callihan if he wanted me hooded again.

"Yes," he looked at me. "Sorry, Mike, under orders. Can't have you knowing the location of this place."

"I understand."

Stevens went off to retrieve a hood.

Callihan sighed deeply.

"What?" I asked.

He stared at me for a few seconds and asked, "How's your dad holding up?"

"You know about my dad? Okay, I guess. Considering."

"It's a shame he's there."

"Yeah," I answered, not at all knowing what to make of this Callihan. Hearing a DEA agent say that about my drug dealing Dad was surreal, to say the least.

He continued, "The man does three tours in the shit and that's where he ends up. It's a fucking shame."

"Yeah ... we're you in 'Nam?"

"Around the same time as your Dad. Navy SEAL. I ran special ops."

John Denver returned with a hood and Callihan stood. Holding out his hand, he told me to stay in touch and to make sure I called him daily at 6:00 p.m. I was led out and into the van. On the drive back to the motel, I realized the adrenaline had sobered me up in a big way. I felt groggy but that buzz was long gone. I thought about Callihan and wondered if his threat to have me beaten was a bluff. I felt like it was. He actually seemed like a decent guy. A good cop. Wow.

After being dropped off at the motel, I stood in the parking lot trying to get a handle on everything that had just happened. I looked up and noticed a silhouette of two people walking close together materializing through the scarlet fog. If not for the sound of the woman's laughter, the sight would have been downright eerie.

When Rabbit saw me he let out a hoot. Then he told the woman walking with him, in a somewhat quieter voice, "That's my friend. He worries about me. Mike, what *are* you doing up?"

Once they were in full view, I noticed the woman looked to be in her mid-forties and was wearing a business suit, not exactly consistent with Rabbit's usual lady du jour but still quite sexy. He stepped up to hug me.

"Rabbit," I whispered, "Rabbit, we gotta talk."

"Mike, this is Angie! She's a lawyer from Georgia! Isn't that weird?" he hollered between snorts of laughter. Angie stood straight and held her wedding ring up in full ladylike fashion. While giving her hand a delicate wiggle, I whispered, "They took me in, dude. We need to talk now, bro."

He stood staring at me for a few seconds, focusing on my face, eventually understanding. He politely rejected Angie—called her a cab and remained attentive until she was out of sight, then followed me into the room and sat down on the bed rubbing his face. "That chick was a pro. Martinis, dude, holy Mary mother of fuckers, martinis. Ok Mike, tell me."

Chapter 16

I lay in bed, watching as Rabbit got up and stumbled to the bathroom, mumbling what seemed like a fairly sincere apology in advance for what was about to come, which was a ten minute symphony of farts, gags, and groans. Until he emerged, his face clean-shaven and hair gelled. Ranting about all that needed to be done in the next few hours and chiding me for still lying in bed.

"Dude, you are unbelievable," I laughed, "aren't you hung over?"

He smiled, "not anymore. All in the head, Mikey! It's all in the head. Now lesgo! Up and at 'em!"

Four hours later, after sleeping through most of the drive north, Rabbit woke up. "Fuuuuuuckk," he moaned, as if it had three syllables, "I think I was still kinda drunk this morning, maybe."

"Yeah, you were pretty fuckin chipper," I replied. "I think we should hunt down Ron and Deputy Randall ... what do you think?"

He nodded.

We drove to Ron's house in Shelter Cove. I opened the car door, relieved to be out in the open. The sun was an hour from dipping into the Pacific and the temperature was quickly falling. We walked to the door and began pounding on it, certain that no one was inside to hear it. The idea was that we would begin at Ron's and make our way towards Randall's house, stopping anywhere we thought Ron, Nerd, or Jerry might be hiding along the way. Since Ron's house was exposed to most of the other homes in Shelter Cove, we lingered outside for a while in hopes of someone seeing us. I slowly paced, stretching periodically, while Rabbit played Hacky Sack.

Eventually, I asked if we should head over to Jerry and Nerd's.

"Yeah, I guess. I wonder if anyone has seen us? And if they'd fucking recognize us if they did?" Rabbit asked.

"Well, definitely not you. You know we can use the phones now ... why don't we go down to Torrio's and call people instead of driving all over buttfuck hell?"

"Yeah, I guess so, huh. But we should only call people who we're gonna tell ... who we're going to ask to help," he replied, still Hacky Sacking.

I realized we hadn't come up with a definitive list of whom we were going to ask. It wasn't like we were going to be doing them any favors by getting them involved.

"Right, right ... well, Ron, Nerd, and Jer are already there, so really we only need one more."

Rabbit continued to kick the Hacky Sack and grunted, "Young."

"Has he ever sailed?"

"No, but he's crazy as fuck."

"There's a good chance we're just gonna get blown away no matter what happens."

"Yes, there is."

"You're ok with that? He's like your little protégé."

"Dude, he's no dipshit. Young can make his own decisions."

"What about Honda ... or Linkalupilus?"

"Link." He froze and caught the Hacky Sack. "Fuck yeah! There ya go. Link knows his shit, too."

"I know. He sailed a bunch of ganja to Hawaii just for the fuck of it."

"He has done some serious shit."

Linkalupilus, as he was known, had lived in Humboldt off and on for four or five years. He was a curly haired hobbit-like man in his late twenties who had a fun loving, gentle nature, knew how to grow pot and had many friends in both the surfing and sailing scenes of Santa Cruz.

"Do you know how to find him? I don't even know where he lives."

He put the Hacky Sack in his pocket and started for the car. "It looked like there was a little swell at Deadman's. Let's drive by Nerd's and then go check. At least see who's down there."

Just before I opened the car door, I noticed a flashing light coming from the window of a house above the golf course. I looked up and pointed it out to Rabbit.

"What the fuck," he said, "somebody's doing that with a mirror or something. They're signaling us man! Check it out, they're fucking signaling us from that ... old dude's. The lawyer, what's his name?"

"Gene. Gino Pistelli. Yeah, Ron knows that dude! That's Ron, man! Let's get up there!"

We jumped into the car and Rabbit squealed into Gene's driveway. Less than a minute later, a clean-shaven, red-haired Ron marched out the door and started into a light jog towards us.

"Jesus fucking Christ, where the hell have you guys been?" he asked, giving us hugs.

"Why are you out in the open?"

I started to answer. Interrupted by a hopping, hooting bald and bearded Jerry, black haired, mustachioed Nerd (also hooting), old Gene and Ron's dog Ruttiger.

We all yelled, "DUDES!" a few hundred times until we finally settled down enough for me to reply to Ron's question. "We've been in custody, we don't have to worry, they're not gonna do anything to us right now. We got a lot to tell you guys."

"A shitload!" Rabbit shouted. "It's crazy man, fucking nuts!"

"Well then, let's get inside," Ron said smiling at me. "I'd say a spot of drinking is in order ... Gene, open a good one huh?!"

"You got it, Ron," Gene answered excitedly in a thick Chicago accent, while we followed him into the house.

I didn't know much about Gene Pistelli other than that he was an Italian widower from Chicago and, even though he'd never been out to sea in his life, he was fascinated by anything nautical. I'd been in his house quite a few times with my Mom and Ron as a kid but had never seen it as an adult. I had always thought of it as a kind of amusement park. We all sat around his dining room table in plush red velvet, wood, and brass chairs. The room would have been a perfect set for Captain Hook's quarters, with telescopes, model ships, anchors and bells, wood, red, and brass everywhere. He even poured the wine into silver goblets. Ron toasted our return and asked for the rundown.

Between the occasional outburst of anger and laughter and the mixture of the two, it took Rabbit and me an hour to tell them everything that had happened to us. By that time, we'd gone through seven bottles of wine, five boxes of crackers, and a few giant chunks of cheese and salami. Everyone had become buzzed enough to feel confident and ready to fly to Mexico and do whatever the fuck we needed to do to keep Rabbit and me alive and out of trouble. The problem was "whatever the fuck we needed to do" was laughably vague and only became more so as the night wore on.

Jerry, energized and fully animated, hollered on about pushing those motherfuckers (the boats) right on down to Costa Rica and living out our days fishing and surfing.

Ron, turning to him and interrupting his own sentence snapped, "Uh huh, excellent plan Jerry, are you talking about the two or three days we'd have until somebody shows up and murders us?"

"If we stayed low key, no one would ever find us!" Jerry continued, appealing to the rest of us.

Ignoring him, I started in, "We have to appease this Callihan guy; that much is certain. He said we'd get paid."

"That's hard to believe," old Gene said. "You know, it seems that this operation might be a CIA thing and could therefore, technically, be legal ... unless it blows up and Congress decides differently. And if that were to happen, like Iran Contra, it would have already been done, history, all done. These guys basically have full immunity. Mike pretty much has to do whatever they say."

Ron uncorked a bottle and grunted, "But how do we do that? How do we hand over all that cash and expect to get away clean? We'll all be killed. I still can't believe J.C. garnered that kind of trust ... you really saw all that money?"

"Yeah, man, a pile, a massive stack."

"Let's take half and stash it, what's his name ... Callihan, he doesn't know how much money there is. We bring them some cheese, make him happy and take the rest and head to Europe. I mean, Jerry's got a point," Rabbit hummed calmly, holding his goblet like a drunken king. "We should take care of ourselves, but it may be a bit smarter to get the fuck out of Latin America, you know, head to France, Hossegor ... and hello, let's not forget about John and J.C.! We gotta find out what happened to them."

Ron stood up to pour wine. "Of course, Rabbit. That's priority. We all know that."

Everyone nodded in agreement.

I realized I was late calling Callihan.

"Oh, shit, I gotta call Callihan!"

Ron stood and handed me the phone. "Don't tell him much. We'll go see Deputy Randall tomorrow, get his advice ... here, as little as little as possible."

I took the phone and looked at Gene.

He shrugged his shoulders, "Oh hell, I don't care if you call from here. I'm eighty eight years old, what're they gonna do to me?"

Ron asked if I wanted privacy and I shrugged. "No, I don't give a shit."

I dialed the number and Callihan answered on the first ring, "Getting lazy this early on ... not a good sign, Mike."

"I know, sorry I'm late."

"Fine, but I need you to be on time. I'd rather not sit in the office waiting for your call every night. A few minutes later and I would've missed my show."

"Are you serious? What show?"

"*Coach* ... I watch *Coach* on Wednesdays."

"That's a funny show."

"That's why I watch it. So, on time tomorrow?"

"Yeah."

"What have you done so far?"

"Well, I think I have most of a crew together already."

"Splendid. When you have, call with their names and Social Security numbers. I need you guys in Cabo no less than five days from now."

"Okay."

"On time tomorrow."

"Yep."

"By the way ..."

"Yeah?"

"You know, Gino Pistelli was a pretty famous defense attorney back in the day. He made the *Chicago Tribune* almost every other week. My dad was a cop in Cicero at the time."

"Huh?"

"Tell him hello for me." He hung up.

I paused, my mouth hanging open stupidly, and slowly put the phone down.

"Wow," I whispered.

"What," Ron started. "What did he say?"

"He said to say hello to Gene. His dad was a cop in Chicago. He knows we're here. Gene, you remember a cop named Callihan?"

"I remember at least ten cops named Callihan, you kiddin' me!"

"They must've had somebody watching my house," Ron mumbled.

"Well, it's happening, he wants us in Cabo in five days. You all sure about this? I mean, really?"

"Of course." "Hell yeah." "Fuckin A."

Rabbit picked up the phone and began walking towards the Kitchen, yelling, "We need one more. Me and Mike, Ron helps Jerry, and one more for Nerd. We were thinking about Link."

Everyone agreed he'd be perfect, but just as I was about to ask if anyone knew how to find him, Gene quietly asked, "What about me?"

Gene was quite strong and fit for his age but he was up there in years. He did look like he'd been athletic in his younger days and he had a head full of thick white hair. No human could look more Italian than him. We all stared at him in confusion.

The rest of us at a loss, Ron said tenderly, "It could get dicey. It'd be really hard on you, and ... and Gino, you're afraid of the water, remember?"

"I've read every Goddamn book about sailing ever written. I'm old, Ron. Let me play a part in this. A first and last adventure for old Gino, huh? What do you boys say?" The quiver in his voice and moisture in his eyes made it impossible for any of us to refuse. Finally, Ron put his hand on Gene's shoulder. "That's it then ... we have our sixth sailor." And we all began to laugh.

We toasted Gene and continued the revelry. Unlike the week before at Ron's, the night was joyous, full of cheers and back-slaps, jokes, smiles, and music—Tony Bennett, Sammy Davis, and Sinatra—we were at Old Gino Pistelli's, after all. And it was he who mostly held forth that night, recounting stories of old Chicago and memories of a better time. Listening to him, I gradually realized why my Mom and Ron had enjoyed his company so much. He was wise, and his manner and wit exuded an old school elegance that was completely foreign to me. It also occurred to me that since I never had much of a relationship with any of my grandparents, I had remained wholly uninfluenced by the wisdom of that generation. I drunkenly asked him if he'd be my adopted grandfather and he told me that he already was. Minutes later, Jerry started to cry and Ron began talking to himself. Rabbit and Nerd smiled silent smiles through rolling currents of smoke. We carried on for as long as we could, one by one abandoning consciousness, until the last bit of us gave way, gentled down by the wine. And unless I'm mistaken, I came in second that evening; stumbling to a couch and mumbling goodnights, leaving Old Gene, awake and graceful, as the night's champion.

Chapter 17

JOHN'S STORY

It's been a couple of days. It's not looking good. These DEA agents are definitely not on the up and up. I wake up this morning feeling as though one of my busted ribs is beginning to jam itself into my lung. I tell J.C. about it. Can you breathe ok? Yeah, I guess.

But really I can't and I'm worried about it.

I think about Mike. If I don't make it through this, he'll be devastated. Ruined. Mike's had such a tough go of it. I remember how often he used to cry. Sometimes, I thought he'd never stop. I know he's really not cut out for the outlaw scene and I sometimes feel guilty for allowing him to be a part of it. He would have done just fine going to college. He's a smart kid. But other than a short phase when he thought about law school, he was persistent in helping me put together what we needed for Dad's pardon. Man, we were getting close. So fucking close. I'm sorry, Dad.

Mike's always trying to get me to agree to visit him. Dad has strictly forbidden it. I tell Mike we have to honor that. But if we get out of this, I think a visit will be in order. It looks like it'll be the only way we'll ever see him again. Dad almost had a prisoner transfer set up just after our first and only terribly fucked up visit with him, but that got shot down after he stabbed another man in self defense. In his letter, Dad told me he could have killed the man but hadn't, out of pity. Either way, the incident shot out his chances of ever getting into a U.S. prison.

My thoughts are interrupted by screaming coming from somewhere else in the house. I sit up. Start sliding myself towards

141

the door when it's thrown open by Dixon. He looks rabid, out of his fucking mind angry. Moving toward me. He kicks me in the ribs and tells me my brother has just fucked up big time, trying to shoot him and his men somewhere in the city. I'm in too much pain to speak. It becomes apparent that whatever happened, Mike has escaped unharmed and I'm happy for that. Proud, even. That's two for zero, Mikey! Hell, maybe you are cut out for this. I wonder who's with him. Hopefully, Rabbit. If so, maybe there's hope after all.

Dixon takes a few more shots at J.C. before he stomps out of the room. I can't help but curl up in the fetal position. Having trouble breathing. Something's wrong with my lung. J.C. is crying. Dixon, that piece of shit psycho, would not care one bit if we die. I try to calm J.C., even though I'm on the verge of tears myself. Positive visualization is no longer working. Disneyland's a blur. Get us out of here, Mike.

Chapter 18

I woke up with a gnarly hangover. For me, hangovers were always easier to deal with if the party was good. Like a cost/benefit sort of thing, I'd have endured a three-day hangover for that night at Gene's. He was in the kitchen making breakfast with Ron. The smell of eggs made me a little nauseous, but I shuffled in anyway.

"Mikey, how ya feeling? You okay?" Gene asked. "Ron's telling me he can't even see straight."

Ron nodded his head and rubbed his face, "Fucking red wine."

"I'm not sure yet," I responded honestly. "Give me a few minutes to find out."

"Your shoulder okay?"

"It's my … yeah, it's getting better."

They both smiled and we all agreed it had been an epic (drinking) session, but that it would be the last one for a while. Now, we had to stay straight and keep our minds clear. Gene proposed we lay off the weed as well and we agreed, although that would have to wait until tomorrow. One by one the rest of the crew woke up and came into the kitchen, each feeling as shitty as the next, no one but Gene escaping unscathed. I asked him how it was that he felt so good and he told me that red wine was in his blood, adding that he'd only had four glasses.

We all sat and ate what we could. Ron mentioned talking to Randall.

"I'd like to go to my places first, you know, check them out, get some real clothes," I said, dying to get out of the khakis.

We decided to go our separate ways and meet up at Ron's later that day. Rabbit gave me a ride down to my pickup, still at Ron's, and refused when I offered to follow him to his house in case dead dude was still there.

Well aware of what my day could end up looking like, Ron told me to return as soon as I could. He thought it would be a good idea for the two of us to see Randall together. He aimed the remote at his Bose and Forest Tempest's fifty or so synthesizers began roiling about. I cringed and he told me I didn't know good music when I heard it. I laughed on my way out.

"Be back by one!" he hollered.

Rudy followed me out to my pick up and gave me a leaping face lick before I opened the door. I told him I'd see him later and pulled onto the street. Planning on stopping off at the General Store to let Dara know that we were ok, but after spotting Rabbit's Explorer in the parking lot, I decided to drive on by. I remember being quite happy that he'd stopped there, figuring that he was much better qualified for the public announcements at that point. I was too uneasy to pull off an "everything's ok" show. A mile later, over the hill, the air turned foggy and gray and I began daydreaming about lying next to a beautiful girl in front of a fireplace in a Lake Tahoe cabin, big wooly sweaters, hot cider, jazz music, and everything else you'd find in a lame-ass cologne commercial. Then, I shook my head and cursed myself for being susceptible to such crap. Fucking television.

As soon as I turned onto the driveway, I remembered that most of my clothes were at our other property and there wasn't really any reason to be there. Ron's pickup was laid to waste a little ways in, just as Ken had described. I jumped out, walked to the driver side door, and began reenacting the scene in my head. Ron and Nerd had told us that the cops had lost control of their vehicle and that had given the two of them time to escape. They had run downhill like me but ended up going south, to the house of a junkie Nerd knew. They'd even suffered through a touch of hypothermia themselves.

The Ford had at least a thousand bullet holes in it. "Fucking idiots," I mumbled as I reached out to close the door. Pausing when I noticed my bloodstain on the seat. Resisting the urge to reach in and touch it, I walked back to my pickup and stood for a moment, listening to the wind blow through the tops of the redwood trees. I raised my head to them. The rhythm of their movement, like a familiar song, held my attention for a few moments. Not wanting to end up in tears, I decided not to go to the house.

I turned my truck around and headed towards my property on Wilder Ridge. Since Rabbit had given me the rest of Dead Medellin Colombian's cash, I figured I'd keep the money that John and I had stashed at Mom's. In Garberville, I picked up the new John Grisham novel and got a money order to send to Dad. At the post office, I discovered I had a letter from him and felt bad that I was late with correspondence. I threw the letter on the seat and continued on.

At our property, I stepped out to find the air significantly colder than at Mom's and I put on my sporty Nike jacket for the last time. The sadness that had settled over the place, like a weathered shroud, made everything look different, older and unfamiliar. All the hope that the place had represented was gone.

Stepping inside, I noticed that the carpet around the front door was soaking wet and beginning to smell of mildew. I tried closing the door, but the blown out jam prevented it. There were a few rotten items left in the refrigerator that I threw out the window; then yanked the cord from the socket. Figuring if I were to make it through this, I could try and get something for the property someday, though it would take years for it to regain any value. Busted land is considered damaged goods in Humboldt County. I changed clothes, filled a garbage bag with clothing and toiletries, and headed to my pickup.

Even though he'd told me not to, I decided to check in on Rabbit. Back on Wilder Ridge Road, I took a left towards his house. Halfway there, it began to rain. My wipers were perfectly synchronized to Fugazi's *Waiting Room*. *"I am a patient boy ... I WAIT, I WAIT, I WAIT, I WAIT ..."* I sang along, paying attention. Relating to the lyrics more than usual. Rabbit's gate was open and I drove straight through to his trailer, where I found him tearing up carpet, cursing with each yank. The couch had been dragged outside and set on fire, though the rain had extinguished the flame before it could burn much, and the beanbag was emptied, its fuzzy skin hanging on a busted lawn chair.

He looked up and asked me what I was doing there.

"I figured I'd see how things were here. I stopped in at the property," I answered shakily—the inside of his trailer made me nervous. "So was he gone?"

"Who?"

"Who do you think?"

"Oh! Yeah, yeah, they must pick up their own garbage."

Rabbit grunted as he began pulling on the carpet. "They left a hell of a mess though, how's your ribs and shoulder ... or trapezius, can you help me pull this out?"

"Sure, yeah ... give me a corner." I took hold of it and began pulling with him. Together we managed to strip the entire living room down to the plywood and we tossed it all on top of the smoldering couch.

"Fucking rain!" He shouted. "I want this shit gone from this world right now! Mike, will you go grab a tank of gas from the track?"

"Sure."

"There should be a few tanks in the garage, under the workbench. Grab the fullest one. This shit has got to burn!"

It was clear that he was pretty worked up so I figured I'd do whatever I could to help him. Obviously, trying to purge the remnants of the horror show from more than just his house, he needed something symbolic to happen, and as I drove to his garage, I realized I did, too. I grabbed two half full gas cans and turned around. He had them out of the bed of the pickup before I even came to a stop.

The wind picked up, angling the rain into our eyes, soaking us sideways. Above us, the storm bombarded the roaring, dancing redwoods, creating the illusion of an uninterrupted explosion, like a bomb stuck in detonation. Rabbit began to growl as he tossed gasoline from the can. I followed behind him silently, furiously pouring and shaking until the can was empty, and waited, squinting in the rain, while he went into the house for flame. Returning bare-chested with his shirt on fire in his right hand. We yelled as he tossed it onto the pile, the two of us nearly engulfed by a ball of fire; flames stabbed wildly into the wind and rain, as if fighting for their survival and Rabbit, as if fighting for his, raced toward them. He howled as he dove headlong into the fire and out the other side. Covered in mud and soot, he rolled to his feet and raised his arms. Like deafening applause, the rumble prevented me from hearing myself roar, as I put on my own show and ran into the blaze. We went on, taking turns plunging ourselves into the fire, joining in its snarling, violent performance, until all three of us were exhausted. I was left filthy and oddly at ease by the time I got in my pickup to return to the cove, pleasantly preoccupied by the task of assigning various spiritual deficiencies that could be repaired and bolstered by such a ritual. It wasn't until an hour later, as I began to climb out of my truck that I realized how much pain I was going to be in. Not from being burned—the rain prevented that from occurring; or my bullet hole—that was healing up nicely; but my ribs. It felt as if I'd just been kicked a few more times. Fuck it, I thought, it was worth it. Ron came rushing out as soon as he saw me.

"Jesus Christ, Mike, are you okay?" he shouted. "What happened?"

"Nothing, I ended up helping Rabbit burn some stuff at his place. All the bloody shit-"

I didn't need to say anymore. Silent and understanding, Ron gestured towards the garage, where I undressed and threw my clothes into the trash. Jerry, Nerd, and a few other worried friends were gathered at the round table and I passed them, wearing only whitey tighties and a heavy frown. I was down the hall and in the bathroom before anyone could speak. A few seconds later, Nerd was knocking on the door and I told him I was fine, to talk to Ron, and to please leave me alone.

After showering, I grabbed a cup of coffee and joined the crew around the table where Ron was holding court. Everyone looked at me sympathetically, mumbling "hellos" and "how ya holding ups" and after a few "fines" and "I'm okays," I asked Ron if he was ready to go to Eureka.

"Yeah, sure, let's do it. Alright, the rest of you guys stay away from now on. You know what's happening so just keep away 'til all this blows over okay? Nerd, you just stay here ... Rabbit'll be here soon. We'll be back around six."

"Right on," Nerd answered.

"And Nerd ..."

"Huh?"

"No party tonight."

"I know, alright dudes, you heard the man. Time to get the fuck out!"

Ron turned to me after the boys shuffled out the door. "You alright? Really?"

"Yeah, thanks, man. So are we meeting Randall somewhere or what? I mean, I don't know if I'll feel right walking into the fucking Sheriff's station."

He picked up his keys and replied, "Why not. Who gives a shit at this point? Are you worried about what Callihan might think or you just freaked out by the police station?"

"Both."

"Well to hell with it, it might shake them up a bit if they knew we got a cop friend."

"Yeah, right. They'll be shakin' in their boots. Big bad Jack Randall's on the case!"

Nerd interrupted, "C'mon Mike. Ron's always been close to Jack, he's willing to help, so what the fuck. He *is* a cop man. He has access and ..."

"Yeah and no authority whatsoever."

Nerd reminded us to make sure we returned by six for my phone call and I thanked him. Ron asked me if it was okay if Gino came along.

"Hell yeah," I answered, "I fucking love that guy!"

"Me, too."

Two minutes later, just as I was feeling my appetite return, watching Old Gene digging crackers and cheese out of a grocery bag, it couldn't have been truer—and both Ron and I made sure we let him know that. I listened to Gene, and fed on cheese and crackers for an hour and a half without saying a word, learning something every minute. I learned that Reagan's drug "czar" went on to start a urine testing company and ended up making millions from it. A few weeks after he left his post, Congress conveniently passed a bill mandating random drug testing for federal employees. I learned that Nixon was basically just interested in developing a federal police force that could exist and operate outside the normal boundaries of law when he formed the DEA, and that the Bush family had an ample stake in a company that manufactures the low grade, exorbitantly priced food sold in federal prison commissaries.

"I wonder what was really going through the S.O.B.'s head when he showed up on TV tough talking drug dealers," Gene said. I learned that, in his opinion, drug use and drug markets had nothing to do with morality and everything to do with socioeconomics; that it was an age-old trend occurring whenever and wherever three key ingredients intersected—supply, demand, and poor people—and that no amount of policing would ever change that. He told me Al Capone really was a crazy motherfucker.

"My dad owned a small restaurant that Capone would eat at every so often and I'll tell you, my dad was a tough son of a bitch, but when Al Capone was around, he could barely speak. And hey, Al Capone's a perfect example. If the yahoos in Washington would've staved off the madness of prohibition, we'd never have heard of Al Capone."

"I hear that," Ron mumbled, as we pulled into the parking lot of the Sheriff's office.

Two cops eyed us suspiciously as we passed them on our way to the glass entry.

Gene gave them a big smile and they lightened up. "Hello officers," he said cheerily. "How ya doin' today?"

They both nodded and smiled, answering together, "Fine, and yourself?"

"Oh not bad, not bad ... cold. Have a good one."

"You, too, sir."

We walked into the station. Ron asked for Randall, gave his name, and before we had a chance to sit down, Jack Randall, smiling, balding, and waddling, stood before us, extending his hand.

"Ron, good to see you; you must be Mike." He grimaced. "I'm told you have a problem, son."

"Yeah."

"Well, let's go to my office ..." He looked at Gene.

From behind, Jack looked like Santa in a cop suit. He was jovial and sincere, and I immediately liked him. Unlike the others we passed, where everything was neat and the walls were covered with photos of wanted men, Jack's office was messy, and the only photos were of his family. Instead of harsh fluorescents, he used antique lamps for lighting, so that everything inside appeared softer, less severe than the rest of the station, putting my nerves at ease. I wasn't sure what rank or position he had but it was obviously enough to get him a small office. One wall seemed to be entirely dedicated to paintings, drawings, and other art projects given to him by his grandchildren. In his early sixties, I thought Jack seemed old for a cop, but what the fuck did I know? He asked Gene to close the door behind him and told me to start from the beginning.

I looked at Ron and he nodded. "It's OK, Mikey, it's safe."

As I spoke, Jack remained totally attentive, occasionally shaking his head and looking at Ron, not once interrupting me. When I finished, he moaned and rubbed his face.

"Jesus," he sighed, "this is crazy. Son, if it weren't for Ron, I reckon I wouldn't believe a word you just said, it's that incredible ... it's that damn incredible. I have to tell you boys, I'm vexed, I don't know what kind of advice to give you all. When I went with you the other day, Ron, we were looking for Mike here, we had a clear goal. Now we got ... this is just one hell of a Goddamn pickle!"

Ron looked at me and said, "I know. I'm sorry, Jack but ..."

"No, don't be sorry. I've known you a long time, Ron. You did the right thing, you did. And I'll do what I can, I just need a little time to process this, you know how the Feds feel about me already."

"I do, and I appreciate you risking-"

"Oh hell, I'm retiring next year anyway, I ain't worried about that, it's just, they're not exactly forthcoming with me when they're conducting legitimate operations, let alone this kind of thing. I got to figure out what I can do and how to do it. It'd be great to see 'em all get indicted but hell," he laughed nervously, "how to make that happen, I don't know, I certainly don't ... I tell ya this is a bit above my pay grade!"

"The thing is," Gene wondered aloud, "all this is probably being done with CIA cover. I don't know what that really means from a law enforcement perspective, but I would think any sort of legal action, unless it originated from the very top, would be inconsequential. I agree with you there, but any information you could compile, anything at all that could help these boys make a proper decision, would be helpful."

"A proper decision? Either damn way they're breaking the law ... I certainly can't advise them to do one thing or the other. But what if we take it to the Press, or a congressman for that matter, that's an option, and if so, we gotta think about how much trouble Mike and the boys could be in. It's really hard to say."

"If the charges were substantiated and indictments were handed down, then I would think these guys," Gene gestured towards Ron and me, "would be offered a deal, at least some level of immunity, but at what cost? They'd have to go into witness protection."

I jumped in, "Well, we're gonna have to come up with some form of protection no matter what we do, right? I mean, no matter how this unfolds, powerful, bad dudes are going to want us dead or in jail."

Jack agreed, "Yep, and that's where this gets terribly messy. This agent Callihan is authorized to lie, fabricate evidence and God knows what else to accomplish his immediate objective, which seems to be disrupt Medellin's cash flow or, more accurately, *divert* Medellin's cash flow. Who knows who he's answering to ... and then there's the loose cannon ... what did you say his name was?" He looked down at the notes he'd taken.

"Dixon."

"You got ways to find out about these guys," Ron said. "What sort of resources do you have to check on DEA or federal operations?"

"Other than them telling us ... not much. We usually deal with their agent in charge and sometimes his number two but that's about it. When DEA's around, even if we ask them to be, it's their show. They use my guys for manpower. Same goes for Camp, MET, even the ATF. If DEA is involved, they're calling the shots. In other words, I'm never really in any kind of position to start asking questions." He sighed deeply. "And if I start snooping, if I try and find out what these boys are up to, their positions, what office they're out of, hell I don't know what that could lead to."

"Again, I wouldn't want you to get into any kind of trouble, but what I'm thinking here, I'm wondering at what level this is authorized, this is some serious corruption," Ron started quietly. "What if you call some of these top dogs and they don't have a clue what you're talking about? Maybe that would ignite some kind of internal investigation."

"How corrupt is it? Really? They're doing their part in the systematic dismantling of the largest cocaine distribution organization the world has ever seen," Gene argued. "Plenty of folks might not call that corruption. Their methods on the other hand ... well it's CIA, nothing else needs to be said about that."

"But maybe it would get enough people asking questions to get them to let these boys alone. I imagine they got plenty of other options, it's strange that they don't just take some Special Forces outfit down there and take the damn money." Jack began writing as he spoke.

"I told you, he said they can't do that. I know it's weird but that's what he said ... that they had restrictions," I reminded them. "He said a few things I had to wonder about, left me thinkin' he wasn't being entirely straight with me. I mean the whole thing was so bizarre."

He laughed and agreed, "I'm sure you've had quite a few bizarre conversations the last few days. You certainly got yourself in quite a pickle, son, you surely did."

"That I did, that I did."

"I have to say I'm a bit surprised you and your friend ..." He looked at his notes again. " ... Rabbit, there, had actually considered taking on this task for the cartel before you were brought in by the DEA. You realize how ..."

"Not really," I interrupted, not entirely lying. "I want to find my brother. I don't know what Rabbit and I would have done, especially if we had found John. The fact is though, the Joses, or uh, the cartel guys, didn't threaten us in any way, the DEA did. That's what's so fucking crazy, oh excuse me, they're the ones forcing us to do this now. For all I know the Jo ... the cartel guys have found some other way to get the money here and Callihan's gonna screw us for it."

Ron stood and walked to the window, "I imagine this Callihan has a few irons in the fire. It could be a bluff. Shit, John and J.C. may even be in a holding cell in that warehouse."

I told him I didn't think so. Jack agreed and asked us if we wanted any coffee.

"Please."

He picked up his phone, demanded four coffees, and asked me how my shoulder was holding up.

"Trapezius," Ron said quickly. "He prefers to call it that."

"Because that's what it is. It's not my shoulder."

A skinny young cop walked in before anyone had a chance to laugh and courteously passed out our coffees. Served a drink by two different cops on two different occasions in less than a week, trip on that, I thought.

"Anyone want sugar?"

"No."

We sipped our coffees and discussed the next couple of days. Jack told me to make my Callihan calls and that he would also make a few calls himself. "I can't promise anything but I'll see what I can do. I suppose I could even put out an APB on your brother, see what kind of shit that stirs up but I don't think that's wise. I'll check the database; see what I come up with. Ron and I will keep each other posted; he's got a direct secure number to me."

Gene and I looked at each other with raised eyebrows upon hearing that, signaling that I wasn't the only one harboring suspicion that Ron's seemingly unbustable operation had something to do with his friendship with Jack.

During the drive back to Ron's, I slept. My neck ached when I woke, with Ron gently shaking my arm, and I sucked in a gob of drool as I popped my head up.

"We're here?"

"Uh huh."

"Where's Gino?"

"We dropped him off. We let you sleep, you were out, man ... thought I wasn't gonna be able to wake you."

I grimaced as I moved towards the door, easing my legs out. "Yeah shit. I'm tired. What time is it?"

"Five thirty. You got a half an hour to pull it together."

"What if he asks about Randall? He'll probably know we were there some fuckin' way or another ..."

"Just tell him what Jack told you to tell him. That he was a friend of your mom's and you wanted his advice. I'm sure we weren't followed though. I know they got somebody posted somewhere in the Cove but I don't think they're following us around anymore."

Rabbit, Nerd, and Jerry were all gathered at the table drinking coffee. They stood up when we stepped through the door, and Rabbit asked how it went with Jack.

"I don't know," I sighed. "Pretty good, I guess. I mean, he's gonna do what he can you know, maybe find out how legit their operation really is or, uh, actually I'm not really sure what the hell he's gonna do. I don't think he knows what the hell he's gonna do, huh, Ron?"

"Yeah, I kinda got that impression," he agreed.

Rabbit shook his head. "Man, I told you that was a waste of time. Let's get to Cabo and bring the fuckers what they want and call it a day. Seriously, if Callihan makes this look like a bust, what can the Joses say? They can kill us, I suppose, but they shouldn't."

Ron laughed. "Rabbit just because they shouldn't, doesn't mean they wouldn't. But you've got a point. Mike, when you talk to Callihan, ask him about that, how it can be made to appear ... like a bust, something completely out of our control."

"Okay."

"Did you guys talk to the Cabo Colombians about that?"

"About what?"

"About what would happen if you got busted?"

"Well yeah, sort of ... basically, if they didn't get their money, we were dead. That's pretty much what I got out of it," I said, as Rabbit nodded.

"Great."

"Yeah."

Nerd jumped in, "Well, we will when we see them, right?"

"I guess. We don't want to sound like we're planning on it ..."

"Well, yeah. But at least we'd know if we should bail or not."

Rabbit looked at me and asked, "Did the Joses say anything about IDs, like how they were going to confirm our identities and shit? They didn't, did they?"

"No, not really. But they probably will. They wanted to know everyone's name and assess their sailing abilities, remember?"

"Yeah."

Ron rubbed his chin. "I wonder what they're gonna think of Gene?"

Rabbit answered, "You mean the fact that he could drop dead and fuck everything up? I thought of that. I was thinking we should bring Link in. Gino can come along, still feel like he's doing something but you know, it'd be in a more passenger type capacity."

Ron nodded. "Yeah ... Nerd, you and Jerry should track Link down tomorrow. Mike, you should make your call now, huh?"

"Oh, yeah." Rabbit handed me the cordless.

As the phone rang, I wondered if Callihan was bullshitting about his TV show. He answered on the second ring.

"That's better, Mike."

"Punctuality ... I can do that."

"So whattya' got?"

I gave him everyone's name and Social Security number except for Link, whose involvement, in that instant, I decided to keep secret.

"I don't know if bringing the old man is such a bright idea."

"He really wants to come."

"Weird. So let's say two nights 'til Cabo. Call when you get there. What is that? Monday? You remember those coordinates?"

"Uh huh ... you want me to repeat them?"

"No, we'll confirm everything later."

"Why'd you have me memorize all that shit if we were just gonna talk on the phone every night?"

"Just to see if you could."

"Nice. That's totally awesome."

"I know. Hilarious."

"So, hey, is this whole thing gonna look like a bust or what? We're just a little bit concerned about the cartel you know ... not that you really give a shit, but could we make it so it seems like that's what happened?"

"It'll look like a bust, Mike."

"Uh huh, anything else for tonight?"

"That's it ... tomorrow."

"Yep." I hung up the phone.

Ron looked at me, waiting for me to speak.

"What?"

"What'd he say?"

"Nothing new, said you guys should go on ahead to Cabo, get things rolling."

Rabbit had been heating up a frying pan and was beginning to drop burgers into it. He hollered over the sizzle, "When will you know if Randall has done anything for you guys?"

I rubbed my bullet hole and shook my head. "I don't know."

"Me neither," Ron said quietly. "It's not too late, let's get to Torrio's and call him."

"If you guys are gonna do that, do it now!" Rabbit hollered. "These'll be ready in two licks of my wand!"

It was dark when we stepped out into the mist. I started the truck and threw it in reverse. Just as I began backing up, Jerry showed up waving his arms in the glare of the headlights, calling, "Get some ketchup!"

"Alright ... anything else?"

"No beer tonight, huh?"

"No, man."

"How 'bout some Fruity Pebbles?"

"Okay."

He chased us down the street screaming for us to get milk, and we both agreed Gene was onto something when he told us to lay off the weed until this all blows over.

At Torrio's, Ron headed for the phone and I went in for food. Ron was still talking when I came out. I threw the bag in the cab and walked towards him. He looked up and motioned for a pen and paper. After failing to find anything in my pickup, I ran into the store and grabbed a pencil and a deli menu. Ron nodded and scribbled for a couple of minutes before hanging up the phone.

"That was fast." He smiled.

"What'd you find out?"

"A lot. Full names and addresses of a few agents. C'mon, let's get back."

On the way, Ron told me what else he'd learned from Jack. Callihan and Dixon were legitimate DEA agents and had been in the San Francisco Bay Area for the past two years, working mostly coke and heroin cases, but they had recently spent a lot of time in Los Angeles.

"Did he know why?" I asked.

"No, but he assumed it has to do with our thing. They can shuffle these guys around departments, he said; have them help this task force and that task force, run super undercover operations. Jack said himself, it's pretty terrifying, the massive funding and lack of oversight some of these operations have."

"Hell, yeah, it's terrifying, especially that nutjob, Dixon."

"Who's that?" Ron interrupted, pointing to a white Chevy Blazer parked in front of his garage. My stomach sank.

I aimed my headlights at the vehicle as I pulled in and whispered, "It's them."

I killed the engine and looked at Ron. He nodded. "Well, let's see what they want."

We found the boys sitting quietly at the table, each face pushed into its own distinct version of dread and disgust as they faced the man whose back was to me.

He didn't need to turn around.

Chapter 19

"Hi, Mike."

I walked around the table and pulled out a chair. "Agent Dixon."

"I'm glad you're finally here. These fuckas are so rude! You know they didn't even offer me a seat."

"What do you want?"

"See, right there's what I'm talking about! You guys' mothers must not have had a clue, too high to teach you any fuckin' manners." He looked at Rabbit. "Fuckin' hippies."

Rabbit, appearing to be on the verge, looked up and beyond Dixon. Ron stepped into his gaze and stared him down with a "don't" look. Rabbit didn't.

I sat down and repeated, "What do you want? I already talked to Callihan-"

"Fuck Callihan!"

"Okay." I felt like I was dealing with a twelve-year-old. He basically yelled when he spoke. His facial expressions were forced and didn't coincide with his statements, as though he'd not yet developed adequate coordination for conversation.

"Does Callihan have your brother?" he spat.

I exchanged glances with Nerd and Rabbit, who were sitting directly across from me.

Ron sat down next to me, "Do you?"

"No shit, Sherlock!" His forehead wrinkled as he opened his eyes disgustingly wide.

"Where?" we asked.

"That depends," he said, attempting to look sly.

Jerry hollered, "What the fuck dude? C'mon, what's your angle, already?"

Dixon's face turned red as his battered, fragile ego took control. "Watch it, fucka. You watch how you talk to *me*."

Quietly, as if he were speaking to a child, Ron said, "Agent Dixon, if you have John, then we will certainly try and be more respectful." He gave Jerry the *look* and went on, "Unlike you, we have no experience with this sort of thing; we don't know the protocol, who to trust ... we're all scared and confused." I glanced at Rabbit. He was grinning. Ron knew how to play an idiot like Dixon. "We're just trying to get our friend back, trying to get our lives back ... so whatever you need from us, man, if we can do it and it means we get those things back, then let us know."

Dixon sighed and folded his hands. "First of all. You don't fuck with me." *Yes, we got that, moron.* "Second, if you do, I'll kill you. I'll kill you and John and J.C. and any other fucka I want." *Nice, psycho.* "Third, you do not tell Callihan about this." *ABOUT WHAT, YOU FUCKING ASSHOLE!?* "Fourth ... okay, fourth is it. You need to bring the boats to me."

Rabbit asked him where that would leave things with Callihan.

"Well, that will be your problem. Callihan's all talk. He ain't gonna arrest nobody for real. He just wants the money. I have John, I'm the one to deal with," he answered, while pulling a Polaroid out of his shirt pocket. I was thinking about how, without provoking a tantrum, I could ask him to prove he had John, when he slid the photo across the table. It was of John holding a copy of the San Francisco Chronicle. Ron leaned over for a look. "That's yesterday's."

As we quietly passed the photo around, it occurred to me that up until now none of us had been taking Dixon's visit very seriously and that we'd better start. The photo came back around to me. I couldn't help but smile. John was sitting on a hard wood floor holding the newspaper at his belly. He looked like he'd had the shit beat out of him, but there was a subtle smirk on his face that only I'd recognize. I felt like it was there just for me. His right hand held the paper in such a way that his middle finger was sticking up beyond the rest. That was probably for Dixon. I looked up at the smiling faces of my friends and we all began to laugh. John was alive.

Dixon put his hands up. "Have your little laugh now; if you don't do as I say, he'll be dead."

I kept looking at the photo and asked, "So, now we deliver the money to you?"

"You want the least amount of trouble you can possibly get, yeah? Well, I'm more trouble than you can imagine, so I'm the one you gotta listen to, fuck head! You don't ask the questions, I do!"

"Ok, can I ask one ... like where we're supposed to bring 'em now?"

"We'll intercept in Mexico. I'm not sure yet, probably near Pescadero ... I ain't takin' any chances with you losers."

Ron took the photo from me. "Guess you're not bound to wait until it's in U.S. territory, since you're basically undermining ..."

"What'd I say about the questions?"

Ron tossed the photo on the table and put up "chill out bro" hands.

Dixon went on, "I'll give the order to let him go as soon as we have the money. Callihan won't do shit. I'm telling ya, whatever badness needs done, he has me do anyway. If you tell him about this, your brother won't just die ... I'll torture the motherfucker. You have my word on that. And I won't think twice about going after anybody else." He stood up and began buttoning his jacket.

"So that's it? How do we stay in touch with you? I'm supposed to get everybody to Cabo soon."

"Oh, I'll figure something out. I'm gonna be your recurring fucking nightmare," he laughed as he walked out the door, slamming it behind him. And there it was, Agent Fat Ass

Idiot Psychopath Dixon took back his rightful place as arch-fucking-nemesis.

Rabbit broke the silence. "We should follow that piece of shit and blow his fucking head off. That happened too fast. We could have held him here and called Callihan "

Ron interrupted, "Yeah, but can we trust Callihan? Trust any of those motherfuckers? Shit! Shit!" He cranked the volume of his stereo to drown out our voices in case the house was bugged.

I sighed, "Jesus Christ, what now? Where the hell does this leave us?"

"Fucked. Fucked. Fucked."

"Thanks, Jerry."

"That was fucking insane."

"He's fucking insane."

"No shit!"

"Fucking Psycho."

"This is fucked."

"So fucked."

"What the hell are we supposed to do?"

"What a fucking nutjob."

"I think he's retarded, like really!"

"How'd he ever get out?"

"What the fuck?"

"Crazy ass motherfucker!"

"We should call Callihan."

"Call Jack."

"Call Callihan and Jack."

"Jack first."

"We can't call Callihan."

"Can't tell him."

"Why not?"

"Dude, he has John!"

"Psycho."

"Stone psycho"

"So get Callihan to him first."

"He said he'd torture him."
"Crazy fuck."
"Jesus Christ!"
"Fuck!"
"This is psycho!"
"What the fuck?"

We tired ourselves out circling through various versions of that dialogue and, after realizing we were getting nowhere, decided to crash. Jerry and Nerd headed to their place while Rabbit and I camped out at Ron's. I held the photo of John in my hand while we sat on the couch.

Rabbit reached over and I handed him the photo.

"I can't wait to find John," he said. "You remember how he used to take you to the Cove to surf after school even when the waves were shit?"

"Of course."

"You ever think about what a pain in the ass that was for him? That's the kind of shit your dad would have been doing, but John sacrificed his time to sit on the beach and watch you scramble around the mush looking for something to jump on. He did that for you. You realize how he took care of you, right?"

With that, I was reminded of Dad's letter and I ran out to grab it. I sat next to Rabbit and opened it. Nothing could have prepared me for what it said.

My Dear Sons,

Something has happened that has rendered me without use of my hands. This is the handwriting of my very good friend Eddie Chance, but these are my words. And they will probably be my last.

I've spent the last fifteen years doing everything in my power to remain strong and maintain my sanity, but I've come to realize that I've run out of resources.

Internally and externally, completely depleted. In a word, finished. A life can take only so many mistakes before crumbling, and I tell you boys, I reached my maximum long ago. Please understand there is nothing left for me to hold together.

John, when you were born, you came into the world without a tear. Your capacity to appreciate everything you have, without dwelling on that which you don't, was immediately apparent. Your resolve and your strength was certainly something to marvel at, kid. What's more, you exhibited a level of generosity and selflessness I hadn't thought possible for someone as young as you. I remember watching you hand out brownies at your third birthday party. You were so concerned about the differences in size, worried that some kids might not get a fair share, that you tore small chunks of your own and gave them to the children who you thought hadn't gotten a large enough piece, until you were left with nothing. Nothing. That was the kind of boy you were. Meanwhile, that little shit Rabbit was sneaking around the table trying to steal bites off of everyone's plate. After your mother passed away, you wholeheartedly took on the duty of taking care of your brother, you continued to write letters, and though you must have felt abandoned, never did you have a harsh word for me. That's the kind of man you are. And I'm so deeply proud of you. I have only one thing to request of you John, and that is to stay out of trouble. I know you tell me what I want to hear. I do. Whatever you do from this point on, please stay relatively within the boundaries of the law. Don't end up like me. This is my final request of you, son. Please honor it.

Mike, you are also something to marvel at. As a young boy, your sensitivity and power of perception was almost unworldly. Your mother and I couldn't hide anything from you. You were always so easily affected by those around you, like John, full of genuine concern, and you were completely open about it. My God, you once cried when I came home after a day of fishing empty handed. Not because you wanted fish—you hated fish then—but because you felt sorry for me. You were only four years old, Mike. Four years old. Just a few months before you lost me. I'm so sorry I missed out on your childhood, your life. But I know you've grown into an incredibly kind and gentle person, just like your mother. You never passed judgment on me. You sent books. You stayed loyal. You couldn't know me, but you always loved me. I remember a time back when you were interested in going to school, and at some point that faded away. Please reconsider it. I know that you have so much to offer. I couldn't be more proud of you.

I want you boys to understand how much I regret what I did. I would do anything to go back and change things. I often think about the day I got the letter from Carmine Lucchese, may he rest in peace, and I can't help but daydream hours away through different scenarios. It's a meaningless exercise, but one that I can't help but indulge in. Meaningless because the decision to take part in his deal had already been made, hardwired in my DNA at birth, programmed into my psyche over the course of a poor childhood, reinforced by a hellish war, and finalized by the responsibility of raising a family. I've met enough smugglers in here to know that I'm not much different from them—my circumstances no more or less extraordinary than theirs, and I've accepted that. There are exceptions but, overall, these are not evil men. Nor do they think there is anything innately evil about what they were doing. What makes them willing to take such risks? It's rarely one thing. It's always situational, but rarely is it a fluke—one single act of desperation—as a lot of these men have convinced themselves.

It takes time to develop, a spectrum of experiences, a combination of factors too vast to fully comprehend. No one is born willing. I don't feel shame or guilt, in no way disgraced. I've suffered enough. I feel no need for atonement. But I do feel regretful— with such intensity that it seems there should be another word for it. Regret at its most extreme becomes something else—a different kind of emotion altogether. I don't know how else to explain it.

Your mother did everything she could to talk me out of it. She was an exceptional woman. Never forget that. She is the reason you are who you are. She is why I am so proud of you. She could have moved on, should have moved on, but she prioritized you boys. She sacrificed a lot. I know I don't have to tell you that. You know how much she loved you.

But it has come to this, and I beg the two of you to understand that I truly have no choice. I can no longer survive in here.

Remember us, your mother and me, and know that we will always be with you as long as you want us to be. Keep us close. Never forget who you are. You are just what your mother made you—strong, honorable, generous, and most importantly, kind. Make wise decisions and you will be able to stay that way. Be loyal friends. Take care of those in need. Let your kindness guide you. Become good husbands and patient fathers. Take my mistakes and lessons with you. There is real wisdom there. Let you be wise beyond your years. Do these things. I love you both so very much. Please do these things and be happy.

Forgive me my sons, Goodbye.

After reading it, I couldn't move, unable to speak or cry, like a statue, stunned into paralysis. I barely remembered having Dad in my life but, nonetheless, always took comfort in the idea that we would one day get him released and become a family again. In a way, I'd come to take him for granted. His letters came regularly. His writing was that of a strong and wise man—it gave me the impression that he was super-human. He had a tough childhood. He survived 'Nam—lost in fucking Cambodia for weeks, carrying around his busted up future partner-in-crime, Carmine Lucchese. He was a bad ass. And he had always made it patently clear that above all else, his priority was the well-being of his sons.

Rabbit suggested that maybe it wasn't from my dad, possibly someone fucking with us, but I recognized the voice and style of his writing. It was Dad. As confusing as it was, I knew it. Rabbit woke Ron, who immediately got on the phone in a noble but futile effort to make contact with an official at Bang Kwang prison. I did what I could to help, but remembered how difficult it had been for my mom to ever get any information out of Bang Kwang. Eventually, we gave up. Deciding that Ron would take the first flight out of San Francisco in the morning, bound for Thailand. There really was no other option. Then I washed down a Valium with a pint of beer and fell asleep.

Chapter 20

"C'mon Mike. We got an idea. Mike get up, we got a plan." Rabbit was gently shaking my arm; a hot cup of coffee rested on a small table next to me. "Drink up. We should be on the road like ... now."

I slowly sat up, reaching for my ribs as I let out an exaggerated moan. "What time is it?"

"It's late."

"How long have you guys been up ... fucking Valium, that shit really got on top of me."

"You needed it. Get up now." His voice dropped to a whisper. "Ron and I have been talking."

"About what?"

"Sshhh." He shot into the other room and back in seconds. *Galactic Explosions* signature panned flute intro suddenly filled the room. I put my hands to my ears and grimaced.

"Uuuhhggg."

"I know, bro. Can't take any chances though ... keep your voice down."

"So, what are you guys thinking?"

Ron came in with a plate of buttered toast. Because his black beard had begun growing back, his dyed red hair took on an unnatural punk rock sort of look. I told him he looked cool and he made an immediate beeline for a mirror, apparently thrilled by the compliment.

"Listen, Mike, I know this seems crazy, but we want to find John?"

"Yeah."

"You hate this Dixon fuck?"

"Of course."

"Rescue operation."

"Huh?"

"Listen, Ron's going to Thailand, he'll stop your Dad if it's not too late ... Meanwhile, we'll stop Dixon. We can do this. The guy's way off the reservation, acting on his own. He's got nobody to go to, so fuck him. Let's get John and J.C. back."

"Serious?"

Rabbit smiled and said, "As an STD." I recoiled.

"Think about it, Mike, we got Jack on our side, we know Dixon's address; hell, we know everything about him now, we follow him around until he leads us to John and J.C. and-"

"Alright, let me take a piss and wash my face. You guys gotta give me a minute ... just give me a minute."

"Yeah, of course. But hurry, we gotta get you to Eureka," Rabbit whispered excitedly, helping me up. "They're gonna think we've gone to Cabo, we'll be ghosts, man. It's gonna be the coolest shit we've ever done."

I did my morning thing, changed my clothes, and returned to the planning committee.

"Why am I going alone now ... what's the rush? What makes you think they're still watching us?"

"Probably they're not. Maybe just Dixon ... who knows? But if anyone is, this'll throw 'em off. Splitting up, I mean. If we make them think we're gone, we can take the day and do whatever we want. Now go pack a bag."

I grabbed the garbage bag full of my clothes and stuffed it in one of Ron's carry-on bags while Rabbit handed me a piece of paper with an address on it. "That's close to the bridge. Get a room under Randy Fiddlesweed and hang out by the pool. We'll be driving down later."

"Randy who?"

"Or whatever, we'll find you there easy enough ... we'll drive down later, after we've got everyone together. Your ticket's waiting for you in Eureka. Miss your connection in S.F. and get a cab to the motel. Don't worry about your dad, bro. Ron will handle it. He's the fucking man!"

Ron told Rabbit to make sure nobody got killed—that none of this would be worth anything if someone is killed.

Rabbit answered, "No shit ... see you in a few, Mikey."

Before I could question their plan I was sitting in the passenger seat of Rabbit's rental while Ron drove just slow enough to keep us on the road. It was encouraging to see him looking less worried and more determined than before. Other than a few homophobic redneck types, people respected Ron. He had always been considered a stand-up guy, keeping his shit together through thick and thin, and I wondered if this would be the thick that ended up fucking his shit up. I asked him how all of this was going to affect his plans to retire.

"Well, it's definitely gonna speed up the process, I'll tell you that. If we get through this, I'm out of here. Costa Rica, matey. Find me a nice Costa Rican man, set up a little place outside of Pecos or Tamarindo. Lord, I hope I reach your dad in time. Why now? What could have happened that after all these years to make him want to kill himself now?"

"I don't know. Maybe he was attacked. He says his hands are all jacked up. He's lost hope, I guess." I dug into my bag and pulled out the last of my antibiotics. "He's finally lost hope."

Ron raced to the airport, ending with a sprint to the gate, yelling for them to hold the door. I flopped into my seat, out of breath. The stuffy businessman in the seat next to me inched away so I looked over and nodded as he forced a smile. I knew his type, and I suppose he knew mine, so we didn't speak to each other. The flight attendant came by with the drink cart once we were airborne and I resisted the urge for a beer. Just twenty-one years old, I still found a thrill in ordering alcohol. The businessman ordered a glass of white wine and nursed it for the entire flight. Watching him from the corner of my eye, I began to envy his control. I imagined he was cautious, frugal and organized, perfectly placed in this society and exactly

where he wanted to be. Just as I began picturing his hot young
trophy wife, I stopped myself and remembered Mom's rule
about judging people. Everyone you meet, no matter who they
are, has experienced or is experiencing some level of misery,
whether confined to their psyche or right out there for the world
to see; it goes with being human. For all I knew, that stuffy
businessman had just lost his balls to testicular cancer. I found
myself staring at his groin while I pondered that and quickly
snapped my eyes back to the magazine I'd been reading. Didn't
want him leaving the plane thinking I was the toughest looking
fag he'd ever seen.

I was glad to find San Francisco sunny and warm. I took off
my hoodie and stuffed it into my bag, savoring the feeling of
the open air on my arms. Jumped in a cab and gave the driver
the address of the motel. He was an older Vietnamese man. I
asked him what life was like in Vietnam, but he didn't seem terribly interested in talking about it. Instead, he spent most of the
drive telling me about the best "titty bar and ho house" in San
Francisco. I couldn't really tell if he was talking about one place
or ten, and I really didn't care.

    I headed straight to the motel, got a room, and in less than
two hours, Rabbit, Nerd, Jerry, Link, Young, and his cousin
Skye showed up. Skye was an ex-marine who got kicked out
of sniper school after getting busted with an eighth of weed.
Rabbit came in for a hug, and I told him I was ready to come up
with a plan.

    "That's good, Mike." Skye said, walking over to us. "Cuz
that's exactly what we're gonna do." He held out his hand and
we did the double shake.

    "It's good to see you, Skye. I haven't seen you since you got
out," I said.

    "I was kicked out."

    "Yeah, I heard. I'm sorry."

"Probably for the better. After Desert Storm, I realized ... aahhh, probably for the better, now I can freelance, right?"

"Yeah, man, thanks for coming."

I greeted the rest of the crew, and we loaded into the room for planning, where everyone, including Rabbit, deferred to Skye. Before they came, the boys had picked up disguises and maps. Jerry began passing out wigs and big sunglasses while Skye taped a map to the wall. I joked that we looked like professionals.

Skye responded, "I *am* a professional, man. So eyes forward."

We all looked at the map as he continued, "The target, who will hence forth be referred to as Douchebag, lives alone in Berkeley, I know, can you believe that shit? Here in the hills." He pointed to a section of the map. "We're gonna post up here and here, alternating vehicles every two hours. Parking is fucked up there, so we may have a problem getting spots with good vantage, but whatever. At least we'll be covering the exits. If we feel like we're getting too much exposure, we'll move to plan B."

"What's plan B?" I asked.

"I'll take a position in a tree or something, use a scope to watch his house, and we got these bad boys to keep in contact." He held up three giant cell phones. "If and when I confirm a visual, I'll direct you."

We all oohed and aahed over the cell phones and Jerry wondered out loud why none of us had one yet.

"Because they don't work back home ... so what's the rest of plan A, or either plan, do we just follow him?" I asked.

"That's right."

"How?"

"Three teams, Team Angus will be Rabbit, Jerry, and Link. Team Beck ... Nerd, and Young, and Team Clapton will be you and me. You guys can decide on who you're gonna have drive but I'll at least say I'm of the opinion that Rabbit, Young, and I should be the drivers."

Jerry put on a long blonde wig and asked in a woman's voice, "Maybe I should try picking him up at the bar?"

Rabbit threw a plastic cup at him and the rest of us faked ha ha ha's. Rabbit, opening up a duffle bag, said we'd be lucky if we actually caught him at home; that he could still be in Humboldt, for all we knew. He pulled out two forty five calibers, held them up cowboy style, and continued, "But if not, I can't wait for phase two ... operation Douchebag Dead!"

We all looked at him, waiting and hoping he would say he was kidding. He did.

"He may be kidding, but the possibility of shooting is very real," Skye lectured. "Each and every one of you has to be aware of and prepared for that."

As he walked over to the duffle bag and picked up a gun, I noticed that he had lost weight since I last saw him.

Skye had always had a muscular build, but now he looked more wiry and overall fit, like he could easily run a marathon. His brown hair had outgrown his jarhead by about an inch, but he still looked very clean cut, as did the rest of us, except for Young. With his handsome young looking face, he almost kept up with Rabbit in the girl department, and was the only dude I knew who'd stand a chance in a fight with him. At six foot three and two twenty, with thirty plus street fights under his belt, Rabbit greatly outdid Skye's five foot eleven frame in strength, size, and real world experience but, thanks to his dad, a 'Nam vet and a Bruce Lee fan, Skye had been training in martial arts since he was seven. Punching and kicking was like a second language to him. Guys like that are hard to touch in a fight. And you really don't want to get touched by them.

"All you guys know how to shoot rifles well enough, but a pistol is a totally different thing. They're much harder to aim. I also got two vests, a few smoke grenades, a bad ass assault rifle, sort of legal, and a few other ..."

"Yeah!" Nerd laughed, as he and Jerry began digging through the duffle bags. "cowabunga!"

"It's ooh ra!" Skye hollered.

"Huh?"

"Ooh ra! We're not surfing, Nerd!"

"No shit."

"So, let's hear it, you fucking hippies!"

Everyone let out an ooh ra, and Skye smiled. Each team was given a map and various forms of firepower. We took turns shaving and put on bright red lipstick. After that, we helped each other get our wigs just right, tossed our wallets on the table, and headed out the door. As I jumped into the silver soccer mom minivan, I noticed the motel manager watching us from inside the office; I waved. Confused by his seemingly tepid response until I saw my reflection in the mirror. From the neck down, we were dressed in our regular clothes—me in jeans and t-shirt, and Skye in camo cargo shorts and tank top—but our faces and hair had gone full drag.

Skye backed out of the parking spot and pulled behind Team Angus. With thumbs up all around, we pulled onto Bryant and toward the Bay Bridge. I told him about everything that had happened to me and he listened, shaking his head and groaning periodically. Afterward, I thanked him for helping.

"You kidding? I'm honored. I've known you guys my whole life. I know I took a different direction and all but, hey, that doesn't matter. It's all about brotherhood, you know?"

"Yeah, man."

"You get that in the military, man. Big time. When dudes are in war together—I guess that's kind of what's happening with us right now—the only problem with the military is respect and authority is handed out without any *real* merit. By that I mean earning respect, like people have to in the real world, earn it, not get it because you have a degree or a certain amount of time in. You wouldn't believe some of the dipshits I had to take orders from, man. If a guy's got rank, you listen and kiss his ass, that's the way it is. I'm not saying they shouldn't have a ranking structure. They've got to, but too often it's automatic, undeserved, you know? Take Rabbit, man, he's got everything necessary to be a great soldier, but he'd never be able to kiss enough ass to last twenty four hours. Then you get some dipshit fresh out of officer school; some guy who can barely run or shoot but is a master ass kisser and, bam, he's pullin' rank. If I was ever to be stuck in the middle of a real war, you know, like 'Nam, I'd take Rabbit any day. Hell yeah."

"You don't think Desert Storm was a real war?"

"Are you kidding me?"

"Well, I don't think so but, hey, I don't want to insult you. You were there."

"Mikey, that shit was a fucking joke. Air strikes, man. We barely did shit. It was all air strikes ... and then we came in and took prisoners, I have no idea why, they all just ended up gettin' released after we left. Nothin' really changed there. You know we got all these Iraqis to help us, like, rise up against Saddam, Kurds and Shiites and then we just bailed on them. Left 'em to get slaughtered. Free Kuwait. Stabilize the region. It was a joke."

"You saying it was a joke because there was no real action or ..."

"No man, there was action, plenty of it, for the people getting the shit bombed out of 'em! It's just ... all the talk of honor, it's always about honor ... honor, honor, honor, we engaged in one of the most disproportionately balanced battles in the history of mankind and we go on celebrating our honor and glory as if we'd stormed the beaches. I mean, I know it wouldn't have been done any other way, I know that, I'm glad we had limited casualties, I'm glad I'm alive and all my friends are alive, but did so many of the enemy have to die, really?" He stopped quickly, almost running a red light, and I noticed that he looked very angry as he went on, "I came back from there feeling like ... like, I don't know. In terms of strength and firepower, it was like a grown man fighting a child. Honorable, my ass. There is no honor in a war like that. I became pretty disillusioned after Desert Storm."

"I'm sorry."

"Hey, it made it a hell of a lot easier dealing with my dishonorable discharge, I'll tell ya that. I already felt dishonorable. But I'd signed up for sniper training. I thought I could handle that. At least then you know who you're killing, you may not look him in the eye, but you're not dropping a five hundred pound bomb on a building full of people that he may or may not be in. Oh well."

"What are you gonna do now?"

"You mean if I get away with helping you crazy motherfuckers? I got some ideas. My dad thinks I ought to open up a karate school in the city, that'd be cool. I'd have to grow a little to get some capital. I got a buddy who's working in Hollywood as a consultant. I'll figure something out. What about you, man? You gonna try anything out or just keep growing?"

"Oh Jesus, I don't know. I thought about law school, you know, but I've just been working with John, trying to get enough scratch to get my dad out. I feel like I've been struggling with that too much to give much thought to anything else, like I just haven't had the time."

"I can't imagine what that's like for you guys. If it weren't for my pops, I probably would never have joined the marines, you know. He made that an easy decision."

We got on the Bridge and Skye began telling me about the scene in *The Graduate* when Dustin Hoffman is racing back to Berkeley to pull the girl from the church. In the scene, Dustin Hoffman is driving on the top deck of the bridge while going east. We were going east, and we were on the bottom deck. Apparently, they thought it would make a better shot and a stronger overall impression on the audience having him on the upper deck. We wondered if they'd paid a lot of money to close the bridge for that shot and, if so, how they got the studio suits to go along with it. We passed the portion that had been repaired after the Loma Prieta earthquake and we each recounted our personal Loma Prieta experience.

Thirteen minutes later, we were parked less than a block away from Agent Douchebag's house, sitting in the back of the minivan, taking turns watching for him. Even though it was in the hills, Marin Street turned out to be a busy motherfucker, and Dixon's house was tucked beneath three giant redwoods, blocking our view of the entrances. He also didn't seem to have a driveway or garage so, like many people in that area, he'd have to find street parking. That basically meant he could be parked more than a block away from his house.

To deal with the boredom we played games like Count the Volvos (we counted a lot) and Hacky Sack basketball. We tried to use the cell phones and learned that they were worthless up there. After two hours of nothing, Team Angus pulled up beside us and Jerry peered through the window.

"Dudes, pull up to Beck. We'll take this spot. The phones don't work up here."

"We know. If he leaves, more than likely he'll be headed towards the freeway. They'll work down there. Whatever, there are only two directions he can go. We'll head up. Did you find a spot at the circle?"

"Yeah, it's mellow down there. Okay, later." We drove up the hill a block and a half, had the same discussion with Team Beck, and sent them toward the circle at the base of the street. After counting Volvos got too easy, we began counting Free Tibet bumper stickers, and then ultimately a more difficult variation, counting Volvos with Free Tibet bumper stickers.

We'd counted seven by the time I saw him. Dixon was climbing up the hill with what appeared to be serious difficulty, looking every bit like the crazy asshole that he was. Wearing aviator shades and a tight tucked-in black t-shirt with a cartoon bulldog saying *Lead, follow, or get out of the way*, he struggled on in pseudo-tough guy mode, with his arms out as if they were Arnold Schwarzenegger's. Watching his belly dance as it hung over his denim short shorts, I began laughing before I could point him out to Skye. More than the outlandish spectacle, it was seeing him out of uniform that caused my laughing fit. Without it, and the authority that came with it, he'd become much less threatening to me. He was just a man.

"What?" Skye asked, looking out the window. "Oh, shit!" He began laughing.

"Oh, this gets funnier," I told him with raised eyebrows.

"You're kidding me! Oh my God that's him ... what a fucking weirdee!"

"We told you!"

"No wonder Rabbit insisted on being strapped!"

"For real, man. Dude is a stone nutjob."

"Scary."

Even though he was across the street from us, we ducked from the window as he got within a hundred feet, and Skye pulled out his mini spy mirror.

"Ok, hopefully, he hops in a car soon," he began quietly. "Don't want to have to turn around in case he takes off from one of these side streets. Shit! There he goes! Ok, let's go, Mikey! The giant black Chevy pick up ... fucking figures. Let's go."

After climbing into the front seats, we adjusted our wigs and waited. Dixon pulled into a driveway in order to turn around and we waited as he inched forward and backward a few times. A line of cars had accumulated in both directions by the time he finished his turn around.

"That sure is a practical vehicle to drive in the congested Bay Area," I said.

"Uh huh ... I'm sure it makes his dick feel bigger, though!" We were about six cars behind him when we pulled onto the street. Jerry and Rabbit had seen us coming down the hill and had their windows down by the time we passed them.

I glanced out and said, "Black Chevy," as we slowed beside them.

Rabbit, looking like a fiercely ugly woman, hollered, "I thought that was him ... what a fuckin' goober!" and pulled out behind us. As we reached the circle at the base of the hill, I noticed Nerd pouring something out into a flowerbed.

"That's Nerd, what the fuck is he doing?" I asked.

"Oh man, is that piss! Not now, Nerd!"

Dixon was nearly at the base when Nerd noticed us and began walking in the opposite direction. Eight busy streets converge into one common circle, and Nerd decides to dump his piss right in the center of it. At least he had the sense to face the other direction when he saw us. Dixon entered the circle seconds after and continued straight down Marin Street towards the freeway. Skye kept us a few cars behind him while I tried the cell phone again. Young answered after the third ring.

"Cool, they're working ... was that piss?" I asked.

"Mike, I told him to stay out of the circle but he wouldn't listen. Still, what are the fucking odds, man? That was him in the lil' pecker truck, wasn't it?"

"Yep!"

"We figured. What a fuckhead."

"Well, he must not have made Nerd, he's not smart enough to pretend otherwise ... probably would've gunned him down right in front of everyone straight Scarface style."

He laughed, "For real, man. Anyway, does Rabbit know?"

"Yeah, we told him."

"He must be stoked."

"Hell yeah, it's pretty lucky we got him so fast. Let's hope he gets somewhere quick."

"Well, the odds are still slim, Mikey. Don't get your hopes up yet. We may have to go to plan C."

"I gotta make my Callihan call in a couple of hours ... wait, what's plan C?"

"Ask Skye, he's the man with the plan."

"Okay, I'll talk to you in a few minutes."

I hung up and asked Skye about plan C. He was watching the road ahead intently; ready to floor it and run a red light if that's what it took to stay on Dixon. I noticed his lipstick had smeared across his cheek after he rubbed his mouth with the back of his arm.

"Plan C?"

"Young said we had one ... if Douchebag doesn't lead us anywhere."

"Oh, yeah, well ... then we kidnap the motherfucker."

"No shit?"

"Why not? We're gonna be in the shit no matter what we do." A light turned yellow and Skye gunned through the intersection just before it hit red, leaving Beck and Angus behind. After we blew past San Pablo Avenue, the main drag running parallel to the freeway, I got on the phone and let Beck and Angus know we were in fact getting on the freeway. As soon as we figured out a direction, I called them back.

"West."

"Right on."

And so we drove west, back into the city. Skye and I kept the chitchat to a minimum, concentrating on maintaining a visual of Dixon, which, because of his teenage-style high speed driving, turned out to be quite a chore. I spotted him shoot over three lanes toward the Civic Center exit and quickly pointed ahead.

"I see," Skye, grunted as he looked back and began changing lanes.

"I'll call the others."

"Jesus, could this guy be more of an asshole ... he almost hit that Celica!" he hollered.

I called Rabbit and he reminded me of my phone call.

Dixon took a right at the base of the off ramp and a left at the light, heading for the Mission district.

"The Mission house," I whispered.

"What?"

"When Dixon took John, I heard him say they were taking my weed to the Mission house ... he's heading into the Mission ... maybe he's leading us to John *and* my fuckin' weed."

Dixon stopped in front of a deli and, after double parking, jogged inside. I quickly called the others and told them where we were. Within seconds they were behind us, all of us inching along, looking for a place to park. Finally finding a spot a half a block beyond Dixon. I rolled down the window and adjusted the mirror until Dixon's pickup was in my sight. Skye rubbed his eyes, a black smudge appeared above and under them, and I asked him what it was.

"Eyeliner, bro."

"What?"

"Eyeliner ... didn't you get any?"

"No, no I didn't know we had that. No wonder you look prettier than me."

"Sheeiiit! Whup, there he goes." I turned around just in time to see Dixon climbing into his vehicle with a large grocery bag in hand.

I dialed Angus and Link picked up, "Linkolupulus."

"Hey Link, you're up. Call Beck whenever he takes a turn. We're dropping back and I gotta call Callihan in a few minutes ... I may not be able to answer the phone."

I called Beck and told Nerd to stay next to us. Suddenly, to my right, Young appeared and gave me a thumbs up, followed by a shaka sign.

Skye followed Young down a residential street, and quickly stopped when he spotted Dixon buzzing the doorbell outside of a rundown house.

Young continued past him, turning into an ally, while we backed up and parked in a red zone.

Dixon began pounding on the door until a man appeared at the door and took the bag from him.

Skye turned to me and smiled, "Well, this is something."

Chapter 21

JOHN'S STORY

This shit has got to stop. It hurts like a motherfucker. We haven't seen anyone for over a day, and I can't help but scream out for help. I'm not this tough. J.C. is doing his best to console me but he really doesn't have a whole lot to offer. He's been locked up in this room for a long time now, and he's scared shitless. I start pounding on the door and eventually a voice coming from the other side tells me to shut up. I would, but my rib is jamming into my fucking lungs, man! Shut up! At least get me some painkillers!

A few minutes later, Dixon opens the door and starts furiously grabbing for my arm. I ask him what he's doing and he tells me to shut my mouth. One of the other assholes comes in behind him and ties a belt around my arm. Are you trying to shoot me up? Shut up! Is that needle clean? I stop struggling when I realize they're determined to mainline a shot of H into me. If that's what I'm getting, I may as well let it do its thing. I've never shot dope but I've smoked Mexican tar before. I know the shit'll take the pain away. If I fight it, I'll just end up with a bunch of holes in my arm and more than likely some kind of fucked up abscess. Fine. Make sure that shit registers. Assholes.

It starts doing its thing. I become trapped in thought. I feel safe—everything better. J.C. is speaking but I can't tell what he's saying. Is he asking me something? I can't tell. And I don't care. I don't remember the heroin high feeling quite like this. This is psychedelic. Spiritual, even. Nice. My eyes are open but I'm somewhere else. My mom is here. She's smiling at me. What is this? Everything's okay, John. This is nice. Mmhm. Wow. She reaches out and touches my forehead. In an instant, it all comes back to me. Only much clearer—linear and structured, as if planned. The awful blur is separated and laid out chronologically and with meaning. Why hasn't it ever made sense like this? It doesn't for anybody. Really? Mmhm. That makes me happy. Yes. I am born. You were younger than me when you had me. Yes. I am so young but I can tell you and Dad really love each other. You have plans. We did. We are visiting grandpa in Minnesota, I've seen the photos but I've never remembered it until now. Of course not, you were a baby. Dad holds me. I am swimming. The water is cold. A day on a boat. A piggyback ride through a redwood grove. Naked on a sunny day. Black sand beaches. A yellow and black Huffy under the Christmas tree. Then a baby brother. Mike. Mike. Sweet Mike. You took good care of your brother—I am so proud of you. I had to. No ... you didn't. We got along really well for brothers, yeah? Yes. He did tell on me when I tried to steal a bud from the drying shed! Good for him. He threw a rock at my first surfboard! He was jealous. His came later. I am teaching him how to surf at Deadman's. We are fishing with Dad but we're jonesing to surf. Other days there's little swell. We learn to fish. Dad teaches us. He loved you boys very much. Have you forgiven him? There is nothing to forgive. Disneyland! I've always remembered that. I know you have. What's happening, Mom? It's ok. I am yelling across the visiting room in Bang Kwang prison. Mike can't stop crying. Everything changes. Things always do, John. But it's so hard now. You became a strong, kind man. But I am breaking a girl's heart. Rejecting her was very hard for you. I smoke my first joint. I help you with the patches. We haul soil together. An army green Toyota is given to me. I am on a warm water trip to Baja sleeping in the back of it. When I get home you tell us you're sick. We try to make sense of it. You couldn't. I understand that now. It's all okay. I can see that now, it's just life right, Mom? She keeps smiling at me. I have missed you very much. I know. I smile back at her. What's happening? It's okay, John. They gave me too much didn't they? It's okay, John.

Chapter 22

Young pulled up beside us and Skye pointed to me and signaled for them to wait until I was done.

Skye rolled down the window. Young leaned over and asked what we were supposed to do next.

"We wait ... see if he leads us anywhere else. This is surveillance, my man. It's boring," Skye answered. "You guys go get something to eat. We'll call the others and let them know. We'll take this shift. Keep your phone on, and don't go far. We'll call if he comes out."

Skye called the others and told them to do the same. Moments later, we saw their minivan pull out and continue down the street until it disappeared. I called Callihan and told him I was en route to Cabo and that I'd call when I got there. He didn't grill me at all. Skye and I continued our shift, using the same format to stave off the boredom as before, only instead of Volvos and Free Tibet bumper stickers, we counted Hondas and Spanish radio station stickers. A cholo-looking dude stepped to my window, hoping to sell us some coke or chiva, but quickly turned around when he saw our wigs and make up. I felt my ribs while moving back and forth. My palm and trapezius itched. Rather than outright scratching it, I opened and closed my hand a few times.

A few minutes later the phone rang. Skye answered it, and after a few words, hung up.

"Okay, you hungry?"

"Not really, but I could use a cup of coffee or something."

"Let's go. We'll call Angus when we get there."

We turned around and drove towards the restaurants and bars of 16th Street until we found a doughnut shop. After parking, while making our way up the street, very few people took notice of us. I glanced back and forth at all the people glancing back and forth. To the untrained eye, they blended in with the rest of the bustling bodies, but I could practically smell the coke and heroin coming out of their pores. Hipsters filled the taquerias and bars, old ladies hobbled out of the market with bags of veggies, working men jumped out of the buses, and in the middle of it all was a fully functioning, exceedingly dynamic drug bazaar. Within a half a block I saw at least five people who would have asked me, "what do you want?" or "coca ... chiva?" had I made eye contact. Skye and I knew that and so made sure we didn't.

After ordering a dozen doughnuts and five coffees, we found a table by the window. A minute later, team Angus appeared down the street, and I chuckled after seeing them.

"Did we *all* have to be in drag?"

Skye looked out the window and laughed, "I guess not! But it's a pretty good disguise when we're in the vans."

I noticed Rabbit's hair swinging walk looked completely natural with his long wig trailing behind him, but he still looked like a professional football player.

"We should tell Rabbit to try and look a little more feminine," I said.

"Yeah, he doesn't look right ... well, none of us really do."

Link came in first and hurried to the counter. With his powerful, compact frame stuffed in surf trunks, he looked utterly ridiculous in his big blonde wig. I had never before noticed that his calves were the size of a normal man's thighs and I pointed them out to Skye. He laughed and blew out a loud sexy whistle. Link looked over and gave us a big smile. With his watery brown eyes, and gentle looking features, he looked like he was on the verge of happy tears whenever he smiled. As genuine as a man can be, it was no wonder that he had so many friends. Rabbit and Jerry joined him as he scurried to the table.

"Right on, what do we have here?"

"Full assortment brother! Dig in!"

Rabbit kissed me on my head and whispered, "This is fuck-ing awesome, I bet John's in that house, Mike. I do, I do!"

"Maybe."

"Fuckin A, maybe! You told me Dixon called it the Mission house ... this is it, dude. Question is ... what do we do now ... Skye?" We all looked at him as the others scooted into the booth. He squinted his eyes and nodded his head. Looked out the window and mumbled something inaudible then rubbed his mouth, smearing more lipstick across his face, and scratched his wig.

Finally, Rabbit stood up. "Let's get him now. I'll do it. I'll ring the fucking buzzer right now!"

We silently studied his face, each of us trying to gauge his level of seriousness, when I asked, "And then what?"

"We rush him. He's off guard. We have an edge here. You guys do see that, right? We're not the sleazy pieces of shit they think we are, that they want us to be. We are good dudes, hon-est, we have balls, we have a pretty damn healthy disregard for their system ... shit, we've all spent our entire lives outside of it, outside of their authority, and we have ... loyalty. That's so powerful! Callihan thinks you guys are in this for the money, he can't conceive it any other way, and he never will. And this other motherfucker is a straight lunatic gone off the reservation. Their authority is false. As far as I'm concerned, they're no dif-ferent than the kings-men of old. Shakin' down the people. We won't be afraid of *them*. We won't. So what do you say? You guys down?"

"Hell, yeah."

"Definitely."

"You know it."

I looked at Rabbit and said, "Okay, let's call the others."

"That's what I'm talking 'bout!"

We quickly gathered ourselves and hurried back to our van. The phone rang as we began piling in.

I answered, "Yeah?"

Young was on the other line. "Looks like he's leaving. He and the other dude, they're loading a box, like a crate into his bed."

"Shit." I looked at Rabbit. "He may be leaving."

"Tell 'em to stay on him. May be time for plan D," he responded.

Skye told me to stay on the phone with them until we knew for certain.

"A crate huh," I mumbled. "You think it's my weed?"

"Not unless you grew a few hundred pounds. It looks heavy, Dixon's nuts are about to explode."

Rabbit asked for the phone and I handed it to him. "Anyway, you can get the drop on him ... I don't know, pull up and point your fucking guns at them ... We need to take Dixon, he'll tell us where John is ... huh? Okay, okay, well just tail 'em. We're on our way." He hung up the phone. "They took off, Dixon and the little dude. What do you say?"

"I think you should stay with Mike and me. Jerry and Link take the other van and call Young. Stay a block or two behind. Go," Skye ordered.

Link jumped out of the car, "What about you?"

"We're gonna try to get in there."

Looking worried, Link and Jerry stepped back from the vehicle. Skye started the van and leaned over Rabbit, extending his hand out the window. Link shook it and we all exchanged handshakes and "good lucks." Seconds later, we were parked down the street from the house, planning what to do next.

Without protest, Rabbit remained the man to lead the charge.

As my body began flooding with adrenaline, I asked Skye if he thought this was the best idea.

"Who knows, Mikey ... it'd be nice if we had a few days to get the layout of the building, find out who's in there, but decisions gotta be made kinda quick right now. This is what's happening, bro."

Rabbit handed me the same kind of—or possibly *the*—Beretta I had used at Rabbit's trailer. "May as well have this one. Get reacquainted, yeah?"

I laughed nervously, "Yeah."

Skye pulled the two vests out of his duffle. "You guys take these."

Rabbit refused. "No way, no way, no way ... hell no. Those are for you and Mike. C'mon Skye. I'm gonna have the human shield."

The phone rang.

"Hey."

"Mike?"

"Yeah."

"They're eastbound again," Young reported in a worried voice. "We're going over the bridge. Did I hear Link right? Are you guys really going in there?"

"It looks like it."

"Put Rabbit on the phone."

I handed the phone to Rabbit. "Hey. Why not? We'll be okay, Young. Probably nobody in there, anyway. Just make sure you stay on Dixon. Uh huh, thank you, here he is." He handed the phone back.

"Sounds like there's no stopping you guys, so good luck, man."

"Thanks, Young."

"Call us as soon as you can."

"We will."

"Bye, Mike."

"Yep." Skye handed me a vest and a sweatshirt to put over it. Rabbit fixed his wig and began stretching. He asked if I was alright.

"I am. I'm ready," I answered. Struggling to get the vest on.

We finished preparing and stepped onto the sidewalk. Grass grew through the cracks in the cement and the air smelled like piss. I was glad to see that the streetlights barely hit the house, which was built directly onto the adjacent homes in typical San Francisco style. Most of them had been converted into apartments, with four to six buzzers on each steel gate, but not ours; we were happy to discover only one buzzer when we reached it. Rabbit motioned for us to take our positions on either side of him. Skye and I moved to his right, bumped shoulders and together switched directions.

Skye whispered, "You stay on this side."

Another nervous laugh and I whispered back, "Not much of a start."

I leaned against the cold brick wall and closed my eyes. My heart was racing but, regardless, I felt far less terrified than when we had busted into Rabbit's trailer, which considering the circumstances, was completely irrational; we knew exactly what we were facing then. I took a deep breath and opened my eyes. Rabbit looked at me and nodded. After I returned the nod, he pressed the button and stepped back. Seconds later, a voice from above asked what he wanted.

With an over-the-top lisping Mexican accent Rabbit cried, "Oh dios mio, help me, call the police, please!" I thought he sounded just like the "Ju like dis Mexican poosy" girl from Cabo and, after quickly shaking the thought out of my head, I forced myself to focus.

"What's wrong, what happened?" the man asked, in such an annoyed voice I became certain our plan would fail.

Rabbit stepped it up. "Please help, he try to keel me, he coming," and then *really* stepping it up, taking hold of the gate and shaking it, shouting, "he coming! He coming!" I looked across the street to see if anyone was looking out to see what the disturbance was all about, but no one was; in that neighborhood, unless you were in the line of fire, other people's business was just that.

"Get the fuck outta here, you faggot!"

But Rabbit kept at it.

"I'll come down there and beat your ass right in the street, motherfucker!"

After a moment of silence, Rabbit stepped back and looked up. "He's coming down, get ready!" Then squinting through the gate, "I see him, here he comes."

"Please help!" The gate opened. With rocket-like force, Rabbit stepped forward and slammed the heel of his boot into the man's chest, throwing him onto his back, then pushed the barrel of his gun deep into the man's forehead. "Beat *my* ass!? Shit! On your stomach, motherfucker!"

I rushed up beside them, expecting a barrage of gunfire, and glanced down at the man. He had a dark brown mullet and an earring in his left ear. His beer belly was convulsing as he tried to breathe, and I wondered if Rabbit had just killed him with that ridiculous kick.

"How many others are there?" Rabbit asked as he cuffed the man's hands. The man tried to speak, but it was pretty clear that he'd be lucky if he ever spoke again.

We were in an empty room that under normal circumstances would be a dining room. The walls, molding, and floors were all painted a glossy white, giving the impression of being in a government facility, which, in a way, we were. Skye, after motioning me to cover directly in front of us, had moved to the staircase, squatted and leveled his aim on the top landing. I momentarily questioned the "run if shot at" part of the plan but stayed focused on the entry into the kitchen.

"Yeah, that's your solar plexus, asshole! Kinda scary, huh? Give me a nod—is there anyone else in the house?"

He shook his head. Rabbit pulled him to his feet by his hair. "This one's got some hair! Rock and Roller, huh? You must be under cover! Get to look cooooool!" He pressed the barrel into the man's skull. "Well, listen here, dipshit, anybody tries any-thing, I'll blow your fuckin' brains out."

He moved towards the kitchen, growling, and signaled me to follow. I came up beside him while Skye stayed at the base of the stairs. Looking back at him, I was impressed with the level of calm he seemed to be maintaining. Professional. I quickly turned on the light, jumped around a corner, and drew down on an empty breakfast nook.

"Mike, shut that and put the padlock on it," Rabbit said, pointing to the basement door. "We'll check upstairs first."

I scrambled to the door, slammed the massive hasp shut, and hung the padlock in the hook. "Should I lock it?"

"No. It's just in case someone's down there. I doubt it though ... lights are off. Open the back door, we may have to use it." He rag-dolled the heaving man towards the stairs while saying, "Okay, here we go, you better not be lying to us, man."

The man exhaled a whisper, "I'm not."

Rabbit stepped around Skye and hollered, "Anybody up there tries shit and I execute him!"

He began climbing. Skye followed, motioning for me to cover the rear. Rabbit stomped up the stairs as comfortable and casual as if he were in his own house. With total control of the man, he looked like an angry father taking his kid to his room. After reaching the top landing, Skye told me to stay there and shoot at the legs of anyone I saw. I squatted and aimed at the base of the stairs. I looked back as Rabbit kicked open a bedroom door. Seconds later, I heard them comment about the locks on another.

"What's in there?" Rabbit asked. The man tried to speak and Skye quickly told him to shut up.

"J.C.?!" he yelled. "J.C. is that you?"

I didn't hear an answer.

But Rabbit started laughing.

"Hang on, bro! We're getting you guys out!"

It took every bit of discipline I could muster to keep from running down the hall to them. Whether or not I had really expected to find John, nothing could have prepared me for the level of excitement that overtook me. I wanted to rush to the door and break it down myself. I wanted to stand up and cheer. I couldn't wait to hug him. I lost track of what the voices were saying. I barely heard Rabbit kick the door down or J.C. scream and attack the man. I wondered if angels existed. I smiled at the possibility and thanked God.

John had always looked after me. He always had my best interest in mind. My brother. My family.

Chapter 23

It wasn't until they were back in the hallway, Skye struggling to hold J.C. while he swung wildly at the man, that I turned and heard what he was yelling.

"They killed him! They fucking killed John!"

No. It can't end like this. It can't. Not John. My brother. Everything converged into a storm of rage and horror. I lost control. Throwing wild punches. Shouting. Kicking.

Rabbit grabbed me. Wrapping me into a full nelson until I stopped struggling. Then, slowly, carefully, he let me go. Extending his knife, handle first, as he lifted the man's head by his hair until his throat was exposed and vulnerable.

J.C., thin, beaten and traumatized, said I *needed* to.

Skye reasoned, said we would all be accessories ... this was *murder.*

Rabbit said, "If you do it, do it *quietly.*"

The man shook and pleaded. His voice had returned.

The handle was black and pointed. It looked like a lever to a terrible, evil machine.

Skye put his hand on my heaving chest, "Mike, you cannot do this ... Rabbit, please."

I looked at Rabbit's eyes. Silently, he agreed. Seeing that I understood he returned the knife to its sheath and let go of the man's hair. My rage subsided. I was glad that I hadn't killed him. Frightened that I almost had.

We locked him in the room and returned to the world. Two shadows cast eerily toward us from down the street. Strangely proportioned and alien in movement, they came from two hookers posing next to a streetlight. I turned to them and watched. I wondered if they were real. They looked like spirits, or demons.

"Mike c'mon. We gotta go," Rabbit said, gently taking my arm.

I looked back as we walked to the van, "Do you see them?"

"The hookers? Yeah, I see 'em."

"That's good."

In the van, J.C. told us everything. There were four agents, dirty fucking filthy, acting on their own, figuring out a plan to get a hold of the money. Dixon was the leader. A psycho. A moron. Scary combination. They called one of them Jones. Mullet man was Agent Cravelli. He'd only seen the other one once and didn't know his name.

"What happened to John," I cried. "How'd they kill him?"

"They beat the living shit out of us, man. Our bodies. Look at this shit!" he yelled, lifting his shirt, exposing dark blue bruises. "They wanted to know where the money was, or where any money was! They're fucking crazy! Oh God ... God, thank you guys! John was in serious pain and they wouldn't help him. His ribs or something, it was bad this morning, he was screaming. Dixon and that other piece of shit up there gave him a shot of H to shut him up. Fucking overdosed him! Sick fuckers!"

Everyone moaned, and he continued, "I watched him o.d. right in front of me. I yelled and yelled and they wouldn't do anything. They didn't do anything."

"It happened today?" Rabbit hollered. "Skye, give me the phone!"

I remembered the crate. I held my stomach. I told Rabbit to hurry.

He dialed and put the phone to his ear.

"Young, Young you have to get the crate! It's John. It's-"

I grabbed the phone from Rabbit and shouted into it, "Young, they killed John, he's dead! They have his body. You get him, Young! You get John's body."

"Mike, Mike calm down. How do you know? Are you guys okay?" he asked, his voice breaking.

"We have J.C. That's John in that crate, where are you."

"They ... oh Jesus, we were wondering."

"Where are you?"

"Mike we can't- "

"Where are they?"

"We're at the marina. They went out. It's too late."

"Fuck! Goddamnit! What marina, where?"

"Emeryville ... oh Jesus."

I handed the phone to Rabbit and told Skye to get us across the bridge.

Rabbit kept Young on the line while we drove.

J.C. began crying and mumbling, "We didn't know what they wanted to know. John held up. John was strong, man. He was trying to hold up. Thank you guys. Thank you so much. He really held up. I didn't. He did, though. Fuck. Jesus fucking Christ. Jesus Christ."

Skye's expression and movement was robotic as he drove us over the bay.

Rabbit sat shotgun, telling Young about all that had happened.

I sat silently, my head forward, eyes locked on the road, praying we reached them in time.

They were *dumping* his body. Dumping him like a random murder victim. I fantasized about the next few minutes. I prayed we reached them in time.

Beaten and murdered.

J.C. went on, his face turning apple red, "Anita didn't tell me. She didn't. I didn't know how heavy this shit was. I really didn't. I was so into her. I didn't think they'd take me seriously. You know about the money? You guys know about the money? Oh God, I ratted him out! I fucking got him ... it's my fault! This is my fault!"

J.C. sounded insane. Confessing. Whining. I could tell Rabbit was getting frustrated and angry but he let him go on.

I stared at the boats in the bay. Next to the still, black water, they looked like wandering ghosts. I wondered which one was Dixon. More than likely he'd be moving, probably heading at least couple of miles out, into the Pacific. I imagined they'd done this before, feeling no remorse—or at least pretending not to—as they motored under the bridge, past the concrete pylons and Fort Point, the only decent surf spot on the bay.

Powell Street was the only road that led in and out of the yacht harbor; it cut straight through the narrow peninsula like a broadsword. With rocky shallows to our left and condos and office buildings on our right, I felt like I was trapped between two dimensions as we drove. The buildings seemed entirely unnatural rooted in and towering over such a narrow piece of land.

The boys had met up in the Pier 2 parking lot after Dixon set out, and we found them all in the same van, wigs off and guns out. The area was barely lit and there were quite a few cars parked there, but I still felt we were sitting ducks as I stepped into the crowded van.

An explosion of confused, unintelligible arguments followed and continued while I sat watching. Listening to some of them panic, others trying for calm, and at least one calling for war, something happened to me; my confusion faded and I realized what had to be done.

"You guys shut up! Shut up! Shut up ... I'd love to kill them, I would." They quieted down. "But if we do-"

"Nobody's killing anybody!" Skye interrupted, and the others shushed him.

"If we do that here," I continued. "If we do that now, we are screwed. No question. All of us will go away. You guys have already risked enough for me, everything really ... I can't ask for this. John's gone. He's gone, and there's nothing left ..." I began to choke up and stopped myself, "If we had caught them before they went out then yeah, maybe, but it's too late for that. Now ... now we need to leave. We have to leave here right now."

It was as if I'd had an epiphany, the appearance of which was indistinct, and only a lingering hazy, memory of it remained, but it was a strong enough memory that I didn't care what the others thought. Not Rabbit, Young, or Skye. I'd never been more certain of what my next move should be and nothing was going to change that.

"We need to go to Cabo," I said. "We need to go there now."

And immediately, quietly, everyone agreed. Deciding we should stay out of SFO and, even though we'd lose some time, drive to L.A. We jumped in the vans and raced to the motel. Once there, we showered, packed our bags, and checked out.

In the parking lot we quickly mapped our drive to LAX—as if there were more than one option—and decided who should go and who should stay. Even though they all wanted in, we only needed six guys and so it was decided that Link and J.C. would return to Humboldt to let Gene know what was happening. We told them the name of the hotel where the boats were docked and to tell Gene to hang out in the bar if he decided to come.

We said goodbye to J.C. and Link and set out for L.A.

Rabbit took the first shift while the rest of us tried to sleep. Since we had no weapons in the van, he barreled down 101 at 90 miles per hour, stopping in Pismo for toilet, gas, and food. I looked at the clock as we filed slowly into the minimart.

Chapter 24

It was 12:02. The attendant watched us intently, not so much out of suspicion, but fear and curiosity. We were unquestionably men on a mission, angry and desperate, certainly not a bunch to be trifled with. He wouldn't even let us clean up after Rabbit accidentally spilled Slurpee all over the floor. Told us not to worry about it, that he'd get it later, but it was obvious he really wanted us as far away from the store as possible. Back in the van, Skye gave a quick pep talk that included a fairly extensive segment about controlling our emotions.

He said, "Just look at the counter guy in there. We had him all freaked out; we gotta try and mask that when we get to the airport. Can't be lookin' so crazy, you know."

Skye took over driving and quickly pressed on as we sat in silence. Rabbit and Nerd were actually sleeping, but the rest of us peered out the windows, waiting for Gaviota and the long stretch of beach before Santa Barbara, where on certain days, it feels like you're driving just a few feet from the ocean. I tried to preoccupy my mind so I wouldn't think about John. After seeing the sign to Lompoc, I thought about a friend's dad who'd done a long stretch in the penitentiary there and how he had come out very different than when he'd gone in. He always said he got out just in time, before the changes became permanent, but we all knew that was bullshit. He was never the same. I rested my head on the window and contemplated his situation. I figured some people were more resilient than others, not necessarily tougher, just less affected by certain kinds of trauma. My friend's dad was a 'Nam vet, but it wasn't until he spent three years in prison that he became a walking time bomb. He hated crowds and cities. I wondered if maybe that had something to do with it.

Looking at the midnight blue beach of Ventura County line I felt anxious to get back in the water, even if it was only by boat. I began trying to visualize what seeing Dixon would be like, what the sight of him would do to me, what it would make me become, and I whispered a question to myself, "I wonder what I'll do?"

"What's that?" Young whispered.

"I'm not sure why I'm so eager to do this," I answered quietly.

"You wondering if you're just after revenge? Well yeah, we all are."

"I know. But this is insane, what we're involved in is insane. We could all die."

"Why are you here, Young?"

Rabbit had woken up and without moving his resting head, whispered from the front seat, "Mike ... we are your bros, we have no choice."

When we reached the airport, I stepped into the harsh lights of the parking garage. Feeling the merciless effects of sleep deprivation, I shook my head, trying to shake it off. From behind, Rabbit told me not to worry, that my third wind would be kicking in soon enough.

"Man, I hope so."

Skye reminded me of a drill sergeant as he stepped back to get a look at all of us. Rabbit, black t-shirt, boots and old jeans, pure bikered up badass. Young, a carbon copy of Rabbit. Nerd and Jerry in ratty baseball caps and fishing tour t-shirts, fish mongering nutjobs. Me, in typical surf wear.

Skye, looking straight and narrow, said, "You know what, alone we all fit the profile for a spontaneous trip to Cabo, but we'd better not all go at once. Check the times of United, one at a time ... it'd be too weird if we all stormed up together. No talking once we get in. We go in alphabetical order, one every ten minutes or so. Depending on the time. Jerry. Mike. Nerd. Rabbit. Actually, you two look like the fish head twins, you stay together. Young. And me. Split up and hang out at a restaurant or bar."

We all agreed.

"Okay, everybody got everything? IDs"

Yep.

"Should we say something about John now?" Rabbit asked, looking at me.

Again, on the verge of crying, "No ... Let's do that later."

Rabbit gave me a head hug and took off in a light jog. The rest of us shook hands and separately, headed to the elevators and into the terminal. I made my way to the United Airlines information board. The next flight was at 7:46 a.m., more than four hours later. With that much time, I figured it really didn't matter when we got our tickets, so I headed to the counter. Of course, when I got there, Jerry and Nerd, looking cool and casual, were in the middle of buying theirs. I passed them and continued to a small doughnut shop, where I ordered a Coke. Seconds later, Rabbit walked in. A couple of minutes after that, Young, and then Jerry and Nerd—so much for splitting up; real stealthy.

We sat alone, doing our best not to make eye contact, Jerry and Nerd struggling to keep the conversation low, while the cashier, like a short-timing prisoner, stared solemnly out the window. He had a tattooed tear under his eye and looked like he was ready to murder something.

Young pretended to read a newspaper while running his hands through his hair, obviously a man in turmoil. Jerry and Nerd stopped talking. I finished my Coke and stood. When I passed Rabbit, his chin resting on his hand, I noticed he was crying. His face, like a stone, still and hard, had no expression as tears ran from his eyes. I walked out, glanced back and realized I'd just been witness to something very rare. Stopping for a moment, I wondered if he'd noticed me. It didn't matter, I decided. Continued to the bathroom, where I took solace in the isolation of a stall, and did some mourning of my own. I emerged red-eyed and exhausted. After splashing cold water on my face, I decided to buy my ticket and try to sleep.

The woman at the counter couldn't have been less interested and I felt relieved by her rudeness; glad that she barely looked me in the face. I sauntered to the gate and collapsed in a chair.

Someone kicked my foot and I jumped awake.

"Oh, excuse me," a voice said as I opened my eyes. I recognized the back of Nerd's t-shirt. It had an airbrushed tarpon jumping out of aqua blue water; a souvenir from his trip to Boca Grande, Florida last year. The L.A. sun blasted through the window and into my eyes. I squinted at the line of tourists that had formed along the divider as the rest of the boys casually blended themselves into it. Rabbit was standing in front of three middle-aged housewives, facing them, practicing his game, while the others stood silently. I dug my shades out of my bag and walked to the line. Slowly, I made my way into the plane and sat down. I said hello to the yuppie couple sitting next to me, buckled up, and shut my eyes.

"Did you want something to drink?" I awoke to the stewardess leaning over me talking to the yuppie woman.

"Coffee, please."

"And you?"

"The same."

"How about you?"

"Nothing, thank you."

"Would you like a pillow?"

"No thanks. I'm fine."

Again, awakened by the rustling of a plastic bag as the stewardess collected trash, followed by the captain on the intercom and the beep of the seatbelt sign.

The yuppie couple was still together in the bathroom, and I wondered if they were getting busy.

Finally, the sound of impatient stirring as the captain announced our approach. The whole thing seemed to last twenty minutes. Knowing how badly I needed it, I was pleased to have slept. I sat up and wiped the drool from my chin. Rubbed my head and cleaned my shades. I thought of John and checked my resolve. It was all still there.

After breezing through customs we met up outside, where the cabs parked in waiting.

Nerd was the first to speak, "Whoo, Cabo! Are we really not drinking tonight? I mean is that ... that's really the plan?"

Rabbit, who'd been leaning on a palm tree, walked toward him, "Nerd shut up."

"I guess it is, then," Nerd whispered.

Rabbit asked me if I wanted to stay at the same hotel and maybe see our vicious little waitress one more time. I said sure. After a bit of catch up chatter we piled into two cabs and headed for the hotel. Checked in and went to see our child waitress. She still hated us. We discussed the weather, Colombian drug lords, and sailing. It occurred to me that, although Rabbit, Nerd, and Jerry knew plenty about sailing, they were a little rusty in the navigation department. I reminded them that we'd have a transponder.

"Probably more than one," Rabbit said. "The Joses got some beacon on those things, for sure. We got radar, as long as we follow the coast, it ain't like we're sailing to Hawaii."

"So we're going to meet the Joses after this?" I asked.

"Well ..." he started.

"Why not? Let's get it started," I insisted. "We got a bit of planning to do. Jose wants to go out with the rest of the guys, check out their skills, we gotta get supplies."

"Ok, yeah ... the rest of you ready to meet the Colombians?" Rabbit asked.

"Let's do it."

"Sure thing."

"Let's go."

We headed to our rooms, changed clothes, and met outside of the hotel. The temperature was nearing eighty, so we all showed up in shorts and t-shirts. Walking across the mall, I noticed that a lot of the vendors seemed to be selling the same shit and I wondered how the hell they competed with each other. Nerd stopped and bought us each a puka shell necklace. That's how.

"You don't all have to put it on ... I just figured it'd be cool to have a souvenir, you know?"

"Thanks Nerd." We put them on.

Rabbit led the way to the back of the hotel near the marina and asked the others if they wanted to chill on the beach or in the bar.

"If we're not drinking, I don't want to go in there," Nerd grumbled, while peering into the open door. "Wow, I guess it's got like ... an iguana theme."

"Yeah, pretty funny, huh." I told him about big Jose and his big plastic iguana cup and he laughed.

Skye had already begun crossing the hacienda toward a group of sunbathing beauties. Young and Jerry began walking towards him.

"I guess it's the beach then," Nerd sighed, while turning to follow them.

Rabbit looked at me and asked how I was doing.

"Fine."

"I mean about John."

"Trying not to think about it."

"I'm sorry."

"Thanks."

He looked out at the ocean, "You know, last night, I was thinking, I was really fucking sad, and angry that we didn't get his body, but I was also thinking that if we had, we'd have put him in the ocean. But that's where he ended up ... at least they dropped him in the ocean."

"Yeah."

"You thinking of ratting out Dixon?" he asked.

I looked out with him so that neither of us was facing the other. The warm breeze was calming. I could have stood there for a long time. "No. Fuck him. Let's just go. See how it plays out."

"I like that. But you do know we're in for surprises ... this won't be smooth."

"You think I don't know that ... or that I even give a shit?"

He looked at me, "You ready, brother?"

"After you." I held my hand out and, after a nod, he began to walk to the palm tree Jose had pointed out to us. Once there, we turned and waved to the man in the window.

"Hello Colombian sniper man, don't shoot us please," Rabbit hummed, barely moving his mouth. The man waved back and disappeared from the window. Walking back to the crew, I asked Rabbit what it was like going through life fearless and he told me he wouldn't know.

Skye had struck up a conversation with the giggling sunbathers and was sitting on their blanket while they giggled. Young lay awkwardly in the sand. With his thick, very hairy legs and arms splayed in conflicting directions, he looked like a freshly slain Sasquatch. Nerd and Jerry sat gape-mouthed, watching Skye show them how it was done. They had taken off their shirts, exposing their lean, butt-white torsos. With their tanned arms and faces, from a distance it looked like they were wearing white t-shirts. Rabbit and I sat down next to them and began watching the horizon. Jerry asked us if they were coming.

"We don't know," I answered. "We did what he told us. We gotta wait in the iguana bar."

I told Rabbit I wanted to get my feet wet first and he told me to take my time. Cabo water gets a little colder in the winter but it still felt like bath water compared to the frigid temperatures of Northern California surf, where, even in the rare summer south swell, a 4/3 mm wetsuit is necessary. I shuffled around in the water for a few minutes, studying the horizon, thinking. Skye called my name as I shuffled past him, on my way back to Rabbit and the bar. I turned around. The girls were pretty. Real, normal, and intelligent looking; nothing like the super-toned perfectly tanned spring break brats I thought they were. Score Skye.

"Hey, bro."

"Mike, come meet my new friends."

And in a historical act of coolness, I ignored him and kept on walking.

I retrieved Rabbit and we walked across the hacienda to the bar, where we ordered two cokes, and waited.

Forty long minutes later, just as I was beginning to worry about my Callihan call, the Joses lumbered through the doorway, wearing white shorts and polo shorts. Their smiles and casual dress quickly put me at ease as they approached our table.

"Amigos! I have to say I'm surprised to see you! But here you are."

"Here we are!" I laughed nervously.

"And you are ready?"

"Absolutely," Rabbit answered, as we all shook hands. Little Jose seemed, and smelled, drunk.

"Where are the others?" Big Jose asked.

"Across the hacienda, at the beach. We've got a great crew, Jose. Seriously. Looks like we're in for good weather for a bit. I saw your boat had a nice VHF so we can keep on it ... we'll be fine and if we don't get weather, shit ... we'll get up there in under two weeks," Rabbit rambled.

"Let's not waste time. Come!" Jose shouted happily as he walked out the door.

We followed him to the beach where we discovered a merger had occurred. Skye had convinced the girls to let the rest of the crew join them. They were talking and laughing loudly as we approached. Big Jose asked if they were our crew and I answered yes, a bit embarrassed until he hollered, "I like them already!"

The boys fell silent when they saw us, as if the reason for our being there had been forgotten. I wanted to tell them to stop looking so shocked, that they looked like assholes, as I introduced them to the Joses. I noticed at least one girl giggle after I said, "This is Jose and ... Jose," but I imagine they all did. Jerry tapped Young, who still looked like a dead man-ape. He snorted and sat up, quickly realizing what was happening. After the introductions were finished, Jose wasted no time, asking us if we wanted to go for a sail.

I needed to make my Callihan call in ten minutes. I whispered this to Rabbit, and he told me to think of a reason to go back to the hotel. I feigned a headache and told them I'd need to sit it out, that I was also just a first mate, no captaining for me. With that, I was sent on my way.

Worried that I'd be late, I tried to jog to our hotel, but my injured rib kept sending jolts of pain through me. I stopped and wondered what the big deal was. Fuck Callihan and his TV show. Coach. Coach could fuck Callihan in his ass with a giant football. I stopped and had a cup of coffee. After I was finished, I sauntered the rest of the way to the hotel and moseyed up to my room, where the clock said 6:32. I picked up the phone and dialed his number.

"Mike, what did I tell you about being late?" he answered.

"I'm here."

"In Cabo?"

"I'm in Cabo. We're all here. The boys are meeting with the Colombians right now."

"Well what have you been doing all this time?" I realized he knew nothing of Dixon and his shenanigans.

"I'm doing what you wanted me to. So what's the problem? You just tell me what's next."

He sighed, "Okay, fine, okay, do you remember the coordinates?"

"Yeah, although I'm not really sure we'll be on the spot. I believe we're a little rough in the navigation department."

"Doesn't matter. Just get them to San Diego, we need to get you a set of transponders ... we're going to give you a total of six. Two for each boat, we'll know where you are at all times. Where are you staying?"

I paused.

He repeated, "Where are you staying? C'mon, Mike, what are you worried about? It's a go, but you cannot leave without the transponders."

"We're in a hotel. Listen, why don't I meet your man somewhere, get them that way. Imagine what would happen if I got made by the Medellin boys."

"Fine. Where?"

"There's a little pastry shop in the mall. It's the only one. When do you want me there?"

"Good. I gotta make a call. Call me back in five minutes."

I hung up the phone and stepped out into the veranda where I sat with my head in my hands. After a few minutes, I called him back.

"Twenty minutes."

"No problem. Is that it ... see ya in San Diego?"

"Yep. One thing though ..."

"What?"

"You sound different. Why?"

"What do you mean? My voice, the connection?"

"No, no not like that ... you sound ... never mind. That's it. Good luck, Mike."

I laughed nervously and answered, "Yep."

I rinsed my face and left for the pastry shop. Still jittery from the last cup, I stayed away from the coffee and opted for a glass of milk. I sat down across from a freakishly good-looking honeymooning couple. Judging from their language, height, and blonde hair I marked them as some form of Scandinavian. I watched them make out over pan dulce until I realized they were giving each other hand under the table. I looked away and began daydreaming about the day I'd finally be getting action like that.

I snapped out of it and my thoughts quickly drifted to John. The shock still fresh, I couldn't believe that he was gone. He had always taken care of me, and I began imagining what life would be like without him. It was nearly impossible. And if my dad were to kill himself, I felt like that would be it. Unless I got myself a girlfriend right quick I would be left with very little reason to be on the fucking planet. A deep voice interrupted my wallowing.

"Mike?" A tall, bald American with a Pancho Villa mustache stood beside me.

"That's me," I answered.

"Here you go. Got extra batteries in there as well."

I took the bag, set it next to me, and turned toward my white wall. The man didn't move and I told him he'd be there awhile if he was waiting for a thank you. He called me a smartass and walked away.

Assuming they'd be along soon enough, I figured I'd wait for the crew, but I scrapped the idea after twenty minutes. I walked back to the hotel and did a Christ pose in the bed until I heard them clamoring to open their doors. I peeked out the door and caught Jerry's crazed eye.

"Holy shit, Mike!"

"Hey, Jer ... how'd it go, man?" I asked as I stepped into the hall.

"Smooth," Rabbit whispered, moving into my room. "Joses were impressed. It's on, Mike. We could leave tonight. Now. They're waiting. We just need groceries really. Everything else is set. Dude, they got everything on board ... dive suits, fishing rods, AK-47s. No shit! What'd Callihan have to say?"

The rest of them began to file into my room as I told them about the transponders.

"Yeah," I finished. "We're ready on that end, too."

Skye flopped into a chair and said, "Well shit, guess that's it then. Can't say that I'm entirely thrilled to be doing this, but we're in it now. Hopefully we can exact a little revenge on that Dixon fuck by the time we're done ... but really, we just need to worry about staying alive now. Rabbit tell him what Jose said."

"When?"

"After you asked him what would happen if we got busted ..."

"Oh, yeah, he said, 'not to worry about it, that it will be ok,' and that was it. It sounded like he's got the harbor masters and Mexican police taken care of ... maybe they got some coast guard pay-rolled, I don't know. They're trying to avoid the DEA ... so we'll just have to see how it all plays out. Callihan told you it'll look official, like a real bust ... course we can't trust that cocksucker for a second. But maybe we'll be ok."

We went on discussing the odds and possibilities, the route and plan, what sort of food to pack, and so on. Our confidence grew. They were the best friends anyone could have but what made them invaluable, in this case, was that they all really were just a little bit crazy. We talked about John, told stories about him, brought him into our minds until the anger fully dug in and we were ready.

We packed our bags and charged to the marina, where we found the Joses in the bar, getting proper shitfaced with a bottle of tequila. Rabbit and Skye followed a driver Big Jose had summoned to the parking lot. They were off to the groceria for supplies. Jerry reminded them to get some bait. We pulled up chairs and positioned ourselves around the table. Nerd looked at the bottle longingly. Jose ordered another and more glasses. Only Jerry and Nerd partook. I noticed an old man with a shock of white hair walk in. Young turned around when he saw my expression.

Old Gene Pistelli, looking alert and energized, was standing at the doorway smiling.

"Oh, my God!" I said, jumping up to hug him.

Gino told me he was saddened to hear about John. I told I was happy as hell to see him, as I stepped back and let Young, Jerry, and Nerd greet him. Having old Gino join us, after he'd heard about all that had happened, somehow fortified our mission and left me feeling somehow blessed. I patted him on the back as he walked to the table. Upon meeting him, the Joses accepted him immediately, doing away with any worries regarding their attitude toward having such an old man involved. He impressed them with his knowledge of sailing and they loved him right off. Young asked him how he got there so quickly and he told us he'd called a pilot buddy of his who picked him up in Shelter Cove and brought him the whole way.

"That's awesome."

"Isn't it, though?"

Big Jose joked that we should catch the pilot before he leaves and fill his plane with cocaine, why waste a trip? We gave him nervous courtesy laughs. I was amazed by his nonchalance.

I thanked Gene for coming.

"What, are you kidding? I wouldn't miss this for the world," he answered enthusiastically.

Young returned from the bar, a scotch for Gene in hand. A second later we were interrupted by a jumping, hooting Rabbit.

"Gino! Yes, this is trout! So trout! Gene made it!" He hollered, "As fucked up as this is, Gene's here! Skye, it's Gene. Gene Pistelli."

Skye followed him to Gene, smiled and shook his hand. After a few minutes of revelry, we decided it was time to go. With a cart full of supplies, we shuffled passed the drunken, happy partygoers of Cabo towards the docks. As we approached, I noticed the lights were on in the cabin of the boat that Rabbit had taken out. The cozy glow helped temper the anxiety that had been growing since learning of John's fate. On the plane, it had been decided that Rabbit and I would sail her. Young and Nerd would be on the other boat, while Skye and Jerry took the third. Rabbit jumped on first and ordered us to start handing him boxes. Canned chili, cereal, dried meat, a cooler full of bait and various other goods made their way through the fire line, below deck. The money had been relocated to the sleeping quarters and other storage areas, leaving us a little more room than expected, and we stacked the goods in the galley and dining area. We quickly finished, walked down the dock, and stocked the others. We tested our equipment, using our rock God code names on the radio, bid adios to the Joses, and just like that, we were off. Rabbit backed out of the slip and followed Nerd and Jerry out to the open sea and into unbearable vulnerability, as Rabbit said, smiling, "Like ducks in a motherfucking pond!"

Chapter 25

We motored until the lights of Cabo looked like small stars, and then Rabbit's inner-Bligh took over. He ordered me back and forth until we had the mainsail full and tight. After he was satisfied, he had me take the wheel. I was supposed to be watching little ribbons on the sail to know when to steer, but I kept fucking up and pissing him off.

"Mike, you gotta watch 'em! Keep that trim. See look, starboard, starboard!" he hollered.

He explained the problem with sailing to California in a northwesterly, like I was a kook who'd never seen the ocean before.

"Dude, I know what tacking is!" I yelled back, as he jumped below to call Teams Angus and Beck.

After he returned, he punched my shoulder. "Let me have the wheel. We're gonna have to come about pretty soon here. Nerd and Jerry are actually a lot better at this than I am, you know. We'll just follow them the whole way. It's possible to do this alone, but you gotta be fast, make sure you got enough speed or ye get stuck in the irons *aaarrggh!*"

We saw the lights of Nerd's ship switch directions. I imagined Gino was having the time of his life, as long as he wasn't getting seasick; we had encountered seas of some size while motoring around the cape. After a few minutes, I ducked the boom as Rabbit, working alone, cranked the winch, and came about.

"I can do that," I said. "But what's our course? How do I keep track of where-"

"We're following them," he interrupted, pointing to the others. "Don't worry, I'll take tonight. You can sleep when you're tired. We'll get you good and trained tomorrow."

"I'm not tired, bro. I'll stay up with you for a couple more hours."

The night turned cold and we put on sweaters and jackets. Heated up chili and hot cocoa. We talked about the last two weeks. Talked about John and everything that had happened to us. I told him that I hoped everything would be okay, that I'd rather all of us get through this and be left alone than exact some form of revenge on Dixon and get fucked in the end.

"Yeah, well ... it'd be nice to get a bit of vengeance *and* stay alive. That's not asking too much considering everything that's happened."

"I guess not," I agreed. I took a sip of cocoa and asked him if he'd kill Dixon if he had the chance.

"You're Goddamn right! Would that even be a question for you?"

"I don't know. I think about the dude ... in your trailer."

"Yeah, except his thing was killin' people! Mike, that motherfucker would've cut your Goddamn tongue out if he thought he could make some money from it! I'm telling ya, only the most ruthless are sent for shit like that. Stop trippin'! They killed John, man! That's where your head should be! In fact, I wish I'd have let you smoke that shitbag in the Mission house ... or done it myself. John, man! That's where your head should be!"

I nodded and told him it was. "I'd love to kill that psycho piece of shit, I would, but I've always felt like no one has the right to take another's life, you know. So, yeah, I'd do it, but just to satisfy myself ... one way or another, he'll get his."

"That's not true. You know how many Nazis lived out their days in Argentina without so much as a 'shame on you'? How many scumbags die peacefully in their bed while five-year-old kids die in house fires? It's all-"

"I know, I know, I think Karma's bullshit," I interrupted. "Just chill, man! John was my brother! I want to avenge him. But I don't see things as black and white as you, Rabbit. I wish I could, but I don't."

"I know, bro. I'm sorry. I don't want you to change that. I love that about you."

"I will say this," I grunted, while tossing the contents of my cup overboard, "I'm not really afraid."

"Nothing to lose," he said quietly.

"Exactly." I stood and stretched. "You sure you'll be okay alone?"

"Hell, yeah! I slept on the plane. But I'm gonna wake your ass up in about four hours."

I told him he was an awesome friend as I climbed into the cabin, where I was quickly lulled to sleep by the sound of waves lightly splashing against the hull.

Chapter 26

The sound of voices woke me and I jumped to the companion-way to listen. Jerry was telling a fishing story in a way that had Rabbit and Skye rolling with laughter. While emerging into the morning sun, I noticed the sails were down and all the boats were tied together. On their boat, Jerry and Ron were busy rigging fishing lines while Gene poured coffee.

"Uh, what happened to getting there as quickly as possible?" I asked sarcastically.

"Dead calm, Mikey," Rabbit said, throwing his arms up. "What are the fucking odds?" The air and sea were almost completely still.

"Why don't we motor for a while then?"

"Because we're going fishing, Goddamnit!" Jerry hollered joyously.

"Just in time, Mike," Gene happily announced. "I got oatmeal and coffee comin' over in a couple of minutes."

"You the man, Gino!"

Young stepped onto our boat and told me a thousand dollars goes to the first tuna.

"Shit," Rabbit bellowed, "let's call it ten thousand at least ... I'm sittin' on a few mil right now! Any of you snuck a looksie at the scrilla?"

"The what?" Gene asked as he climbed into the cockpit.

"Any of you guys looked at the money? Like unwrapped any of it?" Rabbit repeated.

"Hell, no."

"Good."

As the sun warmed the air, we changed into shorts and t-shirts, and spread out among the boats. Ron and Jerry rigged our rods with #2 hooks and 20-pound floura-carbon leaders while we dumped live and dead sardines into the ocean for chum. The first hour brought nothing. Jerry lamented that we weren't in a great area, but what the fuck could we do? When we'd almost lost hope, we started getting bites and the day turned happy. First two durados, one for Nerd and one for Gene, who'd never caught a fish in his life, and then the yellowtail came for it. Other than the three-hour siesta, we spent the entire day catching and releasing, saving only one, Rabbit's twenty-pounder, for dinner. It became the thing to call out, "This one's for you, John," as we reeled them in, and I found myself crying under the cover of my sunglasses.

That night, Gene made one of the best dinners I'd ever had. We grunted and complimented him throughout the meal. Discussed what might happen, what we wanted to happen, and what probably *would* happen. Afterward the wind picked up and we decided to pull anchor and try to make some headway. Shook hands and said, "Goodbyes for now." Again, Nerd, Young, and Gene made sail first, Jerry and Skye second, and Rabbit and I followed.

I sat up with Rabbit as we slowly cut through the water, talking very little, both of us watching the light of the other boats, until I couldn't lift my head anymore.

"Go ahead, Mike. You're still healing. If we don't end up dead in the water again, I'll wake you in a few of hours and let you take over."

"You sure?"

"You can't even keep your eyes open."

As I climbed down the stair ladder, I called, "Hey Rabbit?"

"Yeah."

"Thanks, man."

Rabbit woke me from what felt like a coma. Yelling for me to get on deck as he rushed past me to the cubby, pulling out an AK-47.

"A chopper, man. Coming from the east. Fuck we only have one of these! Shit! Shit!"

I followed him up the ladder. A chopper was heading toward us. Rabbit squatted and positioned himself for a shootout. I looked ahead and noticed that we'd gotten fairly close to Jerry. Something shimmered a few yards from their boat and I saw that they were motoring off in their dinghy.

"Rabbit! The dinghy! Get in the dinghy!" I yelled, as I rushed to untie the rope. He pulled a knife from his boot and told me to get it started first. I began pulling the cord.

"SHIT! SHIT! FUCK!" I screamed, when it failed to kick over. I pulled it three more times and nothing.

"Try priming it!"

"Where's the fucking thing?"

The chopper had almost reached us.

"Just pull it!"

I pulled four more times and still nothing. I looked up at the chopper closing in. Jumped back onto the yacht and hollered for Rabbit to follow. He handed me the gun, and it slipped into the water before I could get a grip on it.

"Go, get below! Hide!"

We jumped into the cabin just as a spotlight lit up the deck. Rabbit tore open the piano-hinged seat of the steel reinforced dining bench and threw the plastic wrapped stacks of cash out of it. Pushed me in and climbed in after me. He struggled to shut the hatch with the two of us packed inside and slammed the seat down on his body. I tried to shift and stifled a groan as his elbow dug into my ribs. A machine gun roared above us. I closed my eyes and clenched my fists, figuring we'd be ripped to shreds. Within a few seconds, except for the distant hum of the chopper, everything was silent. A few seconds after that, we heard it happening again, further away, but still very loud. The sound of a chopper, one long deafening stream of machinegun fire, the chopper again. And then, further away still, one last time.

After a long stretch of quiet and stillness, Rabbit climbed out of the bench.

"What the fuck was that?" he said, wide eyed. I noticed holes torn throughout the ceiling, walls, and floor, as I climbed out. If not for the pieces of steel attached to the bench-top, we would have been cut to fucking pieces. Water shot through some of them like a high-pressure washer.

"Jesus Christ. Jesus. I hope the others got away," I said. Then gripping the wet slippery railing I slowly climbed the stair ladder towards the deck. Up top, I saw only the dim flicker of our cabin light. Everything else was dark as Rabbit came up behind me.

"How's the dinghy?" he asked.

I could just make out the small boat's silhouette against the night, bobbing up and down in the black water.

"Looks okay," I answered. "I think this baby's sinking though."

"Yeah," he looked into the cabin. "Pretty fast too."

I glanced at the horizon. "I hope those guys are okay! That must've been Dixon and friends, otherwise how'd they find us like that? They must have known about the transponders, there's no way they could have reckoned us to this point, is there?"

"Nope, we better get off this sinker. They'll be coming back."

"Let's grab something to paddle with in case we can't get her started."

"I'd say that's our only option," he answered, as we rushed below to find something. "We're probably only a couple of miles from shore."

The cabin had already taken in over a foot of water and our boots filled as we tore into the hold. Yanking a cabinet door off, I heard the sound of a speedboat approach, and began scrambling to the companionway.

Chapter 27

Rabbit spit, "Fuck, that was fast!"

A moment later, we heard a thud on the deck, and a voice call out, "Nothing left alive on this fucka! Go ahead and get to the far one before it fuckin' sinks ... this one's got some time before it goes down! I'll start bringing it up."

And the speedboat roared away.

Rabbit stooped to pull a knife from his boot. "Come behind me, Mike," he whispered. "Get his gun."

As I processed what he was doing, none other than special agent Dixon began climbing down the stairs.

As he descended, his right hand appeared at his waist holding a pistol.

Rabbit launched himself across the galley.

The right hand rose and a shot fired.

Rabbit's knee buckled as he fell into the pool of water along with the pistol as Dixon dropped to his knees clutching the shoulder above the knife wound, frantically searching for his weapon. I dove, hands first, latching onto his neck. He tried gouging my eyes, but my reach was much longer. He seemed incredibly weak to me as I controlled him, digging my thumbs into his throat, until he panicked himself to exhaustion. I let go and stood up. Rabbit was struggling, but his knee was gone. He told me to kill the motherfucker.

Dixon, wheezing and coughing, began searching for his gun again. Feeling as though I had almost superhuman strength, I stepped in front of him, grabbed him by the jacket and threw him across the cabin where he landed on his back. I leapt on top of him, slamming my knee into his chest, and he let out a high-pitched cry. Again I took hold of his neck, this time holding him under water. His eyes looked into mine as he weakly flailed his arms and legs, and although I hated him more than I'd ever hated anything in my life, I let go.

"Mike, what are you doing?" Rabbit grunted, trying to hide his pain. "Will you kill that piece of shit!?"

I stood up and kicked Dixon in the head. He squealed and brought his hands up defensively. I told Rabbit that I couldn't do it and that we should keep him alive.

"What the fuck? Why?"

"In case that chopper comes back! We gotta get that dinghy going! Can you walk?"

After trying to stand, again in vain he answered, "No, shit, my knee is fucking jacked. Completely."

By the look of it I figured even the mighty Rabbit would be going into shock soon. Dixon told us he'd give the order to let us go if we left him there. I ignored him as I pulled his gun out of the pool of water and handed it to Rabbit.

"Watch him," he said, releasing the magazine and blowing into the barrel. Handing it back to me, handle first, "Careful, it's ready to fire. Now have him help get me into the dinghy."

Rabbit dropped into the small boat with a loud a string of "fucks," while Dixon, whose right side was covered in blood, jumped in after him. "Take it easy, tubby," Rabbit groaned, while awkwardly positioning himself into a seat.

After grabbing my bag and a wrapped stack of cash, I pushed us off, pulled the cord and started the motor.

Chapter 28

Although they were still a distance away I didn't want to take any chances, so I idled the motor until I couldn't see their spotlight anymore. At the bow, Dixon, held his head down, like a shamed child. I tried to take a bearing but couldn't find the big dipper, the only set I knew, among the fading stars. I asked Rabbit to help but he was becoming disoriented. So I sped for ten minutes towards what I thought was east and killed the engine. I told him we were going to wait for the sky to lighten, that I didn't want to waste gas. Setting the gun down while keeping an eye on Dixon, I tied a towel around Rabbit's knee and told Dixon to fuck himself when he asked for something for his own wound. Together, the three of us silently shivered in the darkness.

I watched Dixon. Wondered what I was going to do with him. How had he become such a crazy asshole? I eventually settled on blaming Hollywood, imagining little boy Dixon, watching Dirty Harry righteously blow away the bad guy over and over and over, losing touch with reality and any ability to empathize with the rest of humanity. Or maybe he was just a natural born asshole. Either way, I knew I wouldn't kill him.

The Eastern sky began to lighten and I realized I'd made the right call; I was completely turned around. I started the motor and headed towards the dawn. Dixon asked me what I was going to do with him and I didn't answer.

Just as I caught sight of land, the sun shot into my eyes; I slowed the boat to a stop. About to ask Rabbit where we were, when there was an explosion in the distance. Two more followed. Dixon told me they'd be looking for him and I lied, telling him it didn't matter—that I'd blow his head off before they were within shooting distance.

Rabbit was going steadily into shock and I realized it was up to me figure out which part of shore I should aim for. Close enough to see one section was sandy beach, easy enough to catch a shore break, and another, farther South was rocky coast—our best bet for staying out of sight, but trickier to put in.

I looked down at Rabbit, realizing there was no way I'd be able to get anywhere with him unless I got to a town; I decided to dump Dixon.

"Rabbit, Rabbit!" I hollered.

He looked at me glassy eyed.

"I'm gonna let him go, dump him by those rocks!"

He shook his head.

"I'm not gonna kill him, Rabbit."

He suddenly sat up, "Give me the fuckin' gun ... I'll do it."

Dixon's eyes, red and tearful, opened wide as he began shuffling toward the edge of the bow. His right arm hung to his side like a broken branch. I wondered what ligaments had been severed.

"No Rabbit," I answered. "We'll dump him, he'll be stuck here a while. And then we'll get you somewhere to fix you up."

To which he answered, "Are you fucking kidding me? My leg is destroyed, Mike!"

"Just hang on."

I motored to the rocks, killed the engine less than a hundred feet away, and told Dixon to jump out. Without any argument, he was in the water, breathing loudly as he swam sidestroke toward the calmest section of coast.

Rabbit looked up at me, "Mike ... he'll come after us. Last chance."

"I know," I answered, starting the motor as I turned the boat southeast.

As I did, it occurred to me I had no idea where the fuck we were and I asked Rabbit.

In a weak voice, he answered, "Dude, we barely made it ten miles out of Cabo. Follow the coast. We'll be seeing fishing boats in no time."

I quickly discovered he was right and, relieved, aimed for the closest boat. As I approached, I dropped the pistol into the water and began calling for help. They killed their engine and waved for me to come to their starboard.

The captain of the charter, a burly, grey bearded Mexican, asked me what happened as we pulled up.

"Spear gun," I answered. "Went off accidentally."

"In that?" he asked, while he and a deck hand helped me get Rabbit out of the dinghy.

"We were sailing."

He ordered the deck hand to full speed us back to the marina and apologized to his fishing group, five wealthy looking Germans, who turned out to be much more interested in beer drinking than fishing. The most fluent English speaker, who called himself Fabio, even though his real name was Hans, offered us a "breakfast beer" and I refused. Rabbit took one. The captain called ahead and an ambulance greeted us when we pulled into the marina.

I helped the captain get Rabbit out of the boat and then stood back while the two ambulance drivers positioned him in the stretcher. In the bright sunlight, people stood watching as they wheeled him away. I wondered if and when we'd be getting a visit from Dixon and friends. I knew I had to get to a phone as soon as possible and so did Rabbit. He told me to get going and we shook hands. I asked what the address of the hospital was and the driver gave me a card. I changed into a clean shirt, shouldered my bag, and began to jog to the iguana bar.

"Mike," Rabbit called out. I stopped. "Come here."

The driver stepped back as I leaned over him. "Yeah, man?"

"If you don't get Callihan on the phone, if you can't find anyone, just leave. Get a car and drive or something. They'll be looking at the hospital and airport, Mike. Don't worry about me. Take that cash, and bail."

I knew there was no way in hell I'd ever leave him and I told him that.

He looked at me and knew not to argue. "Right on, Mike. It's all you now, brother."

"I'll see you soon, Rabbit."

"Okay, okay, but be careful ... be careful."

I turned and continued my run to the restaurant. Standing outside for a minute, collecting my breath and thoughts, before stepping through the doors.

A gentle looking elderly woman greeted me straight away and, in bad Spanish, I asked if I could use the phone, that I had an emergency. She told me she spoke English as she led me into an office. I quickly dialed Callihan's number. Repressing the urge to panic, sweat dripped from my brow as I listened to the unanswered ringing. I tried the other two numbers he'd given me; still no luck. I hung up and threw my bag on the desk. Noticed blood smeared all over it, and feeling bad for that, moved it to the floor, where I tore out the stack of cellophane wrapped bills. After struggling a few seconds, I reached into my pocket and pulled out a key. Using it as a knife, I cut into the plastic and dug my fingers into the hole. It tore in half in one explosive instant, sending money all over the floor.

It was fake.

Not counterfeit fake. Kiddy-money fake. All of it. Totally fake.

I dropped to my knees, laughing like a maniac, and began bunching the bills up in my fists.

"What the fuck?"

Chapter 29

I tried calling Callihan a few more times, still no answer. Tried to make sense of what I'd just discovered—to figure out who was fucking who and why—got nowhere. Eventually I ran outside, and five minutes later I was sitting in the back of a cab, approaching the hospital, completely unsure of what I'd do next. I wasn't entirely surprised to see Dixon, the earring mullet asshole, and two other men piling out of a Land Rover as we drove towards the main entry. Dixon's right arm was already in a sling, and he looked absolutely intent on murdering something. It was hard to believe he was the same man who, an hour earlier, had been sobbing and begging for his life. Two of the men carried pistols. It was clear they were looking for us. With little time to react, hoping they'd all come after me, I ordered the cabbie to drive past the door. As he did, I hollered obscenities and flipped them off. Dixon's expression turned to a combination of shock and joy. He yelled for his crew to get in the Land Rover. The cabbie stopped the car and began ranting at me in Spanish. I jumped out, opened the driver's door and grabbed him by the hair, dropping him in the street. Jumped into the seat and floored the gas-pedal, almost slamming into a parked ambulance in the process, regaining control just in time to slide around the corner. With no idea where I was going, my only hope was to find the police station and run inside with my hands up. Maybe the federales would protect me for a little while. I cursed myself for not going there with Rabbit straight off. What the hell did we have to lose now?

With the Land Rover on my ass, I scanned the streets as I barreled along. Turned onto a heavily populated street and instinctively slowed down. Dixon and his team could easily have shot or rammed me, but instead they stayed directly behind me. They knew I was as hopeless as I felt. I looked in my rearview and saw Dixon grinning in the passenger seat.

"Damn, I should've killed you, you piece of shit," I whispered to myself. "You fucking scumbag."

Seeing that I had vehicles blocking my way ahead, I took another turn. A woman and two children were crossing fifty feet in front of me and I slammed to a stop. Jumping out to run, I saw that the street was full of school children and paused just long enough to be surrounded by Dixon and his men.

"Get in the vehicle, fucka!"

"Shit," I hissed. "I let you live, man. Just leave us alone."

Women and children scattered as I was led to the Land Rover at gunpoint. Ready for the bullet, I bolted for the entry into what looked like a candy shop, and felt a crushing blow to my head. I fell to the ground wondering if I'd just been shot. Two men grabbed each of my arms, while a third took my legs and threw me in the back of the Land Rover. I noticed mullet man had a small club in his hand as he slammed the door. Dizzy, I touched my head and felt warm blood pour between my fingers.

"Where's the fucking money, Mike?" Dixon demanded from the front seat as mullet cuffed my hands behind my back. The dizziness wore off just as the second cuff was secured and I brought my legs up, but Mullet punched me hard in the nose before I could kick him. I groaned as more blood began to pour.

"Fuckhead! You tell us what you did with the money and I'll give you a bullet in the head, you don't and we go on like this until you do. Either way, this ends with you dead," Dixon said.

I tried to tell him to fuck himself, but the blood in my throat choked me.

The driver grabbed the radio, spoke into it, and waited for a response. The voice on the other end said that they had captured the other one and were waiting in the chopper.

As we drove out of town, Dixon bitched about his shoulder and went on about what he was going to do to the fucka' that stuck him with the knife.

Clearly exhausted and ready for death, Rabbit smiled at me as I was boosted up and shoved inside the helicopter. Dixon rushed in behind me and began punching Rabbit, who turned his head so that Dixon's fist landed right on top of it. Causing the prick to yelp while shaking his hand like a cat with a wet paw, all the while screaming for Mullet to give him his club. Before that could happen the pilot told everyone to sit down and buckle up, which probably saved Rabbit a bad beating.

As we took off, I began scheming a way to grab Rabbit and jump to our death—turn Dixon's latest plan to shit—but there were too many men in the way. Dixon tried staring me down, but quickly looked away when I stared back. He knew the only reason I was on that chopper was because I'd let him go and I wondered how that knowledge was affecting him, and whether he was less, or more, inclined to torture us because of it. Probably more.

After following the beach for a minute, the pilot took us down. I peered outside of the door as we landed. A twenty-five foot powerboat rested just beyond the shore break while a smaller, faster looking version lay half beached. A man left the bow and walked toward us, stopping just beyond the whirling windstorm of the chopper. I watched him as the pilot killed the engine and we were dragged into the crisp beach air. He turned out to be no one of consequence, none that I recognized anyway, and I stopped paying attention to him. With the chopper down, the sound of the surf was clear and bright. I squinted into the sun and wind as I was ordered to my knees. Rabbit, with his destroyed knee and wearing only a hospital gown, could do nothing but lie down, while Dixon's boys prepared for the interrogation. Although badly hurt, Dixon seemed upbeat, joyful even, as he gloved his hand and began twirling a club.

He was the first to approach, his right arm dead in a sling, wielding a police baton in the other, "Tell us where the money is, and we don't have to do this, Mike!"

"We didn't touch shit," I gurgled through the blood. "Somebody set it up. We didn't …"

As he swung at my head, I ducked, rolling backwards away from him. He lunged at me and I snapped my right heel into his groin, sending him to the ground. He curled up, took a deep breath and whimpered.

"Wow, Dixon," Rabbit noted calmly. "That's oh for three. You may want to stop fucking with Mike, there."

The rest of Dixon's crew seemed indifferent to his suffering as he crawled towards mullet man and demanded his weapon. As he reached for it, all of our heads turned east, toward the dunes and the sound of another chopper. Dixon snatched the gun while the rest of the men drew theirs and began nervously searching for cover. Whatever was happening was obviously not in the plan. I pulled my cuffed hands under my ass, to the front of me, and scrambled back to Rabbit. Within seconds the chopper—black, armed, and military—flew low and fast over us, two men kneeling in the opening, one with an automatic rifle, while the other manned a massive, 50 caliber Browning. A loudspeaker voice demanded we drop our weapons, but Dixon fired before the voice finished. Instantly, the Browning exploded into action, and in the time it took for me to kiss my ass goodbye for the tenth time that week, Dixon was no more. The echoing voice above then demanded that everyone get down face first. There was no argument.

Chapter 30

As the helicopter swept towards a flat area to land, I glanced at what was left of Agent Dixon. Wondering why he was so foolish as to shoot at the chopper. Had he just panicked or was he so consumed with pain that he had lost all control? He died badly, but I took no pleasure in it. In fact I felt nothing. No comfort or joy. Nothing.

Rabbit crawled to me as the engine shut down.

"You okay, Mikey?" he breathed.

"Yeah. You?"

"For now. Can you believe this? I mean, is this shit really happening?"

Three men were running toward us.

"Who the fuck are these guys?" I groaned.

Three sets of legs, all combat boots and black fatigues, stopped in front of me.

"Congratulations, Mike, you made it," Callihan said kneeling down, offering his hand.

I took it, pulled myself up and stared at him dumbly.

"I'm not sure why you're so shocked, considering all you've been through," he smiled. "You boys look like shit. Is this Clifford?"

I nodded.

"Glad to meet you! The Rabbit!"

Rabbit struggled to an elbow, "Glad to meet you, too—and it's just Rabbit, if you don't mind."

Callihan laughed, "Get him a stretcher. Goddamn, I am happy to find you boys alive, I really am! The rest of your crew make it?"

"I don't know."

"Well, we'll find out soon enough. Sorry we didn't get to you earlier. We didn't think they'd work so quickly. Let's get you cleaned up and back to the States. We got a plane waiting. C'mon."

I asked him what the fuck was going on.

"I'll explain later. Let's go."

As two men loaded Rabbit on a stretcher, I heard one lamenting, "You know, I expected Dixon to go through with it, but Cravelli ... I figured he'd wise up."

Callihan answered, "Yeah, he should have known better. He'll have plenty time to think about it."

We loaded in and flew directly to the airport. I kept my head in my hands, trying to work things through and figure out what was happening while Callihan assured me the rest of my friends would not be harmed. That is, if I agreed to fly home with him.

On our private flight to San Diego, Rabbit's wound was temporarily dressed as he was pumped with morphine. After I was cleaned up and my busted nose set, Callihan motioned for me to sit next to him.

"You did a great job, Mike."

"I need answers," I said.

"I'm sure you do ... First, I want you to know, none of this is personal. You could have been anybody. In fact, I like you guys, you all look after each other, I respect that, but the way things happened, you became an important player." He lowered his voice. "I'm sorry about your brother, I never thought he'd be killed."

"You knew Dixon had him?"

"I am who I say I am. I do what I say I do, but this particular investigation was internal."

"What do you mean?"

"I mean, we were going after a few of our own … some rotten eggs."

I looked back at Rabbit who was sound asleep on his stretcher, and rubbed my head.

"Are you for real? My brother died for some ... fucking entrapment scheme?"

He squinted. "Hey c'mon, Mike, your brother got involved in some serious shit. I'm not saying he deserved what happened to him at all, just that …"

"This whole thing was a set up? The Joses? The money."

"Yes. Yes it was. But not like you might think. We planted the bait. We had no idea how it would play out. No clue as to who might be involved."

"The fucking Joses work for you."

"Not directly. They set this up for us and we turn a blind eye on a shipment or two."

"What about the Cali guy? Rabbit's dead Colombian?"

He nodded, "Yeah, that shouldn't have happened. They believed the money was real and that, for helping us, they'd get a chunk. We're working very closely with the Cali cartel right now. That is true. It's all very fluid. But no, no those men really were supposed to just bring in whoever might have showed up at the Rabbit's property. I never expected you guys to actually go there. That's why I didn't waste any of our agents on it."

"Rabbit, just Rabbit. How'd you find us? They blew the boats up."

"That wasn't supposed to happen either. But we had transponders in some of the money stacks."

"The *fake* money stacks," I noted. "Wow, so the fucking Joses … are they Medellin?"

"The Joses are real, they work for Medellin, but they're sort of like double agents, you could say. Like I said, it's fluid; we plant the seed and sow the setting, and from there the scenario grows. As far as the Joses knew, we just needed a diversion. They don't know any details, and they don't want to. They're happy to be clueless as long as they get a pass or two."

I looked out the window and took a sip of orange juice, "But what about the man Dixon took out in the city, Jose's buddy ..."

"Mike, it evolves all on its own. Obviously, that's how you came in. We certainly didn't plan on a bunch of Humboldt pot growers becoming so integral to the operation. The point is we knew Dixon was dirty and we started to get the word out; we faked some bank statements, filled up some boats, stepped back, and waited. You really think the cartel would have trusted you guys with tens of millions of dollars? That's what worried me more than anything, the thought that Dixon and his crew would figure out something wasn't right. It's completely implausible, but hey, like I said, if the players believe it, like you and your crew, it takes on a life of its own."

I couldn't believe what I was hearing.

He took a deep breath and continued. "Right now we are very close to taking down Pablo Escobar. He'll be dead or appre-hended within the year, mark my words. And I don't care who wins the presidency, they're gonna be pumping a lot more money into Colombia within months. It's a very complicated business. Huge amounts of money involved. When our own agents are corrupted, like Dixon, it becomes impossibly complicated."

"How did you know about him? I mean, why did you set up a trap?"

"We were informed of his involvement in a drug money rob-bery a year ago but we had no concrete proof ... so we couldn't do anything about it. Like I said, we set the bait. Could have been that nobody went after that money and you guys would have had an all-expense-paid sailing trip up the Baja coast."

"So what now?" I asked.

"Well, when we get home we'll debrief you. I'll write a report and we'll move on."

I sighed, "I can't believe this shit. Can't believe John's dead."

"I'm sorry."

"And then there's my dad."

"Don't worry about David," he interrupted. Then, after a long pause he continued, "This may be hard for you to believe, but when I was in 'Nam I was in charge of a rescue team."

And then it struck me. Dad's photo. No fucking wonder. Like an explosion, the image of the man standing next to my dad tore into my mind. John Callihan. A young, smooth faced, shorthaired John Fucking Callihan was the man from my dad's picture. This was my Dad's rescuer. My brother's namesake. The shock of the revelation drove the last couple of weeks deep into my consciousness and I broke down.

"I recognize you-"

He put his hand on my shoulder, "Don't worry about your dad. I got a lot of contacts in Bangkok. He's going to be okay."

"Did you do something?"

"Yes. Twice his rescuer, you could say."

"Un-fucking-believable. This is unbelievable. I recognize you from a picture of my dad's! Jesus! Fucking crazy. Is he getting a transfer? Did you get him a transfer or what? He was ready to kill himself, and Ron–"

"What?" he interrupted. "How do you know that?"

"His last letter to me."

"Shit." His smile disappeared. "My friend from the embassy is due to pay him a visit … well, today, so I hope he hasn't done anything yet."

"My friend Ron flew to Thailand a couple of days ago. He may have reached him in time." I couldn't help but believe that. I had to. The thought of anything else was intolerable. I told him that and he agreed.

Distracting ourselves, we talked about Vietnam. I asked him what it was like finding my dad.

"Mike, any successful mission is joyous but pulling off a rescue, you can't even imagine. He was tough, your dad. He took a big risk taking care of his buddy. He could have left him, marked the position and gotten the hell out of there, you know, but he stayed with him. He also stayed relatively close to the wreckage while managing to evade the enemy. Expert soldiering."

"You know, he renounced the war after he got back. Threw away his medals and everything."

He nodded, "That doesn't surprise me a bit. I understand. There's no black and white in this world, Mike."

We spent the remainder of the flight in silence.

After landing, Rabbit was taken to a hospital and I was taken to an office building where I spent less than an hour telling Callihan all that had happened to us. Before I did, he told me he'd put a call in to his friend at the embassy and that he would get word to me once he knew anything. He gave me the official story of what happened, and handed me a folder.

"What's this?"

"Instructions. You'll be compensated. Not much, I'm sorry to say, but it's something."

I stood up and he followed me outside. People and cars snaked through the shadows of the buildings, in and out of the sunlight. He told me Rabbit's surgery would be taken care of, compliments of the United States government.

"Wow, I guess it was all worth it now," I said sarcastically.

"Mike, you're lucky to be alive."

"Yeah, I feel like I won the lottery!" I sounded like a cartoon character with my busted nose. "You know what, I think I'm going to enroll in College of the Redwoods this spring."

"Good. Good, I'm glad to hear that. So what are you thinking of majoring in?"

"Law."

"Well, you'd certainly bring an extraordinary level of experience along."

"Thanks."

He held out his hand, "I'm sorry, Mike. Whatever happens … you're young. You can still make a nice life for yourself."

I shook his hand, unsure of what to say. I had a feeling that this wouldn't be the last time I'd see Special Agent John Callihan of the Drug Enforcement Administration.

Rabbit was still in surgery when I arrived. I called Ken and told him everything; it was over.

"Over?" he asked. "Is everyone okay?"

"Rabbit and I are. I don't know about anyone else."

"Oh Jesus."

"Yeah. They're probably alright—I just don't know yet. Have you heard from Ron?"

"No, why? When will you be back?"

"Nothing. Tomorrow night I suppose, depends on how Rabbit is, the doctor said he'll be in a wheelchair for a while."

"Wheelchair? I thought you said he was okay."

"He is, Ken. He's hurt, but he's ok. Look, I'll see you soon."

"You come by here, you hear me, Mike."

"Of course. I'll call when I know more."

"Mike?"

"Yeah."

"I'm glad you made it."

"Thanks, Ken."

I hung up the phone and waited six more hours for Rabbit to regain consciousness. When he woke, the first thing he did, after greeting me, was call the nurse.

"Is she hot?" he asked, while pressing the button.

"Dude, you're amazing, really," I sat down on the bed. "You should be studied. No, she's not, really."

"Oh well, she's got Morphiiiiiiiiiine," he sang, studying his I.V. drip, clearly plenty high already.

He charmed the nurse into giving him another blast and me a high strength Ibuprofen. He'd tried to get me Morphine and I told him to cut it out, while smiling nervously at her. After she left, I talked and Rabbit drooled, until he eventually fell asleep.

Chapter 31

Four days later

Driving down the hill, I began tapping my hand on the dash in time with the music. This would be my first time back in the water since the whole thing began and I was actually feeling a little nervous about it, almost certain that I would start crying out in the lineup. Oh well, the boys would understand.

Ten minutes later, changing into my wetsuit on the beach, I noticed a pleasure boat anchored near the jetty, taking shelter from the ten- foot seas. My rib began to hurt as I walked toward the channel. I wondered if I should wait a few more days before surfing, but after watching Skye shred his way to shore, even tucking into a small barrel, I knew I needed to try.

He ran towards me, asking if I'd seen him. Barrels were a rare thing at Deadman's.

"That was killer, bro. Hooo! How long's it been pumping like this?"

"All morning, man," he hollered, breathing heavily. "Everyone's out, man. They're all stoked you're here, dude! Get out there and paddle right fucking past everybody!"

"How long has that boat been there?"

"Huh? I don't know. Since I've been here. Let's go!"

"Do you have a set of binos in your pack?"

"Yeah, why? Waves are right there, Mike!" he laughed.

"I just want to check that boat out," I said, as if talking to myself. "I'm sure I'm tripping but it ... it looks like ... grab your binos."

He dug the binoculars from his backpack and handed them to me. I looked into them and nearly fell over upon seeing the stern. Written there, in the same blue cursive, with two stars on either side, was El Dispuesto.

"Holy shit!"

"What?"

"Holy shit!"

"Mike, what?"

"It's them! It's the fucking Joses! Skye, that's their boat, I remember, I know, shit, what the hell are they doing here?"

"Are you sure? There's no way, man. Really?" He took the binoculars.

I rubbed my head. Everything came back, and without taking off my wetsuit, I took off running down the beach.

Skye dropped his surfboard and followed hollering, "Mike, wait up! What are you doing?"

"We gotta check on Ron and Rabbit, find out what they want! Skye!" I stopped and looked at him, "That's the same fucking boat!"

I mumbled, "fuck" over and over as we ran to the landing and struggled to climb the ramp. I had finally begun to feel like everything was over, like we were safe. We'd had a small ceremony for John and had agreed never to speak of our experience. We were getting through and we were letting go.

Jogging in the direction of Torrio's, I noticed two men hunched over bread bowls and beer. The Joses. Having lunch. Drinking beer. There, in our small local deli, sat the fucking Joses, laughing and getting drunk. We moved toward them, cautiously. If I hadn't seen the boat, I would not have recognized them in their big wool sweaters. Big Jose was the first to see us.

"Mike! My friend. We were about to come looking for you!"

"Hey Jose," I nodded. And nodded again, "Jose."

Little Jose laughed drunkenly as Big Jose stood and bear hugged me. Skye chuckled and waved nervously.

"What are you guys doing here?" I asked as cheerily as I could.

"We made our delivery in Santa Cruz and we thought, since we have the time, we'd come see the Sheltered Cove!"

"Delivery? Santa Cruz?" I stumbled, getting over my shock.

"Santa Cruz," Little Jose giggled, "I liking Santa Cruz. *Pero hay muchas brujas!*"

Big Jose laughed, "The kids in Santa Cruz, with the white faces and black clothing! Jose thought they were witches! Mike, we're here also because you did a good job for us ... what a fantastic, how do you say ... diversion. Every eye was on you and those sailboats, you did a good job and you must be compensated. Here ... for you." He reached under the bench and pulled out a large Adidas duffel bag. "You can divide this however you wish, but I think you and Rabbit should get a larger percent."

"Are you serious?" I swallowed. "Does Callihan know about this?"

"Not entirely. He knows things go both ways. We have proven our worth and he understands our value. Our ability to freely do as we like is our payment. You take this, please, it is nothing like what we had previously arranged but, as you now know, that arrangement was untrue." He stood and gestured for Little Jose to do the same. "I hope this will at least ... I hope this helps you."

"Uh, well of course, we didn't expect you to, wow ... thank you," I stammered.

"Yeah, thank you," Skye laughed.

"I'm glad we didn't have to sit here too long," Jose said, extending his hand, "I see why you wear those suits. It's fucking cold here!"

We shook their hands and let them go. Skye waited until they were picked up and on their way back to El Dispuesto before heading back to gather our packs and Nerd and Jerry. I headed straight to Ron's, where I found him sitting on his deck arguing with his travel agent about when he should book his trip to Costa Rica. He looked at me and told her he'd call her back.

"You ok, Mike? Why are you in your wetsuit?"

I told him what had just happened and, after calling Rabbit, we sat staring at the bag, waiting for the others to show up. When they did, we set it on the table and before opening it, agreed on giving Rabbit half and splitting the rest between everyone else. Since he would never be able to properly walk again, we figured he deserved a bigger share. After opening the bag, Ron pulled out a stack and cut it open. He placed the pile of hundred dollar bills in his "bitchin" electronic money counter that he'd never once used and let it go, a few seconds later the digital readout read $25,000.00.

Ron asked Nerd, who'd been counting the stacks, how many there were.

"Forty. That's what ... a hundred grand," he said excitedly.

"That's a million, Nerd," I said softly.

Just then, with Young in tow, Rabbit barreled through the door and crutched his way to the table, "What's wrong? Why'd we have to get here so quick?"

I put my arm around him and pointed to the pile, "Rabbit, my good man, I give you one million reasons."

We celebrated for a few minutes. Unable to get entirely excited after losing John, we all in our own way, felt justified enough in accepting it. The last few weeks had taken something from all of us, we would never be the same, and if we could delude ourselves into thinking a chunk of cash could make things just a little better, then so be it. Besides, within seconds, I'd decided I was going to buy a new pickup and use the rest for school.

Rabbit pulled up a chair next to me and grabbed a stack of cash. After a few seconds of studying it he asked, in a perfect English accent, "Mike, my dear lad?"

"Yes, Rabbit, good sir," I answered in a terrible English accent.

"Yesterday I was thinking ..."

"Yes."

"Once you've finished law school, you'll be needing a dashing, daring, dangerous private eye ..."

"Indeed I will."

"Well then," he looked at me with his classic grin, "let's get to it."

And Rabbit, using cash to pay for his tuition, enrolled in the College of the Redwoods the very next day.

Epilogue

I thought I'd be nervous but I wasn't. Not in the slightest. I was pure happy. Ron had reached Bang Kwang in time. Standing next to him and about thirty other Humboldt folks outside the bustling international terminal of SFO, I felt joy. Nothing else. This was no transfer. There would be no more prisons. Dad had received a full governor's pardon. Callihan. Ron pointed down the corridor. Rabbit nudged me. I saw him and began to run. He was limping and his hands and arms were bandaged. Still, when he saw me he began walking very quickly. He looked as I had always imagined him. Just like John. By the time he reached me, he was weeping. We began hugging and he said my name.

I answered back, "Welcome home, Dad."

About the Author

Cory Marchese was born on the Gulf Coast of Florida where he spent what he's pretty sure was the good half of his childhood. After his parents' divorce, he moved to Minnesota with his mom and sister where he spent the other half, and many cold winters dreaming of the sun and sand he'd left behind.

There he became an avid (but discerning) reader, heavy (but happy) drinker, regular (though not too regular) pot-smoker, courageous (but cautious) skateboarder, reluctant (though proficient) fighter, confirmed (but moderate) delinquent, and average (but severely un-enterprising) student, athlete, dancer, and employee.

So, after graduating high school in 1991, it only made sense to move to Humboldt County, California, to grow pot and learn to surf. Having been raised solo by a progressive mother in a not-so-progressive place—a cold, hard, bleak, God forsaken place—Cory felt an immediate affinity to Humboldt's people and culture. The next years were a time of surfing, growing, and generally enjoying life until the DEA, like an angry drunken father, put the leather belt beat down on it.

In 1998, Cory finished a two-and-a-half year prison term in which he made many friends and spent hours listening to the completely outrageous—but often true—stories that would eventually inspire him to write. A means of catharsis in the beginning, his writing has developed into a full-on passion.

Newly married in 1999, he established a construction company in the San Francisco Bay Area. A couple of years later, his daughter was born. In 2009, his marriage ended.

Cory remarried in 2011, and is now living in the San Francisco East Bay with his lovely wife, daughter, and stepsons. He recently finished remodeling their dream home. It was the first time during his twelve years as a general contractor that he was able to renovate his own home.

Working long days and living far from the beach, he traded his surfboard for 16-ounce gloves and headgear and began training in Krav Maga, Grappling, and boxing—experiencing the same Zen-like sensation while sparring that surfing once afforded him. Other than that, and the occasional hike, bike ride, book, or movie, he spends his free time cherishing the company of his family and putting words to paper.

He is crime free, drives like a granny, and has a perfectly healthy fear of authority. Along with his four longtime, loyal employees, he maintains his business—diligently laboring at his vocation in the greater Bay Area—and, at thirty-nine years old, eagerly looks forward to the next half of adulthood.

Deadman's Bust is Cory Marchese's first novel; inspired by his former life of crime and the time he spent paying for it.